Micah Seven Five

Howard Robinson

Inspired Quill Publishing

Published by Inspired Quill: June 2014

First Edition

Chief Editor: Sara-Jayne Slack
Typeset in Garamond / Fira Sans

Paperback ISBN: 978-1-908600-28-8
eBook ISBN: 978-1-908600-29-5
Print Edition

Printed in the United Kingdom
1 2 3 4 5 6 7 8 9 10

Inspired Quill Publishing, UK
Business Reg. No. 7592847
http://www.inspired-quill.com

Dedication

For Melanie, Ella & Noah… and for *real* friends.

Acknowledgements

First a big thank you to everyone who has encouraged me to write and to keep writing, whether from nearby or far away. I hope this book justifies your faith. Second, thank you to the team at Inspired Quill for seeing something and taking a punt on it, for their faith and their expertise in sharpening up my ragged little manuscript. I'm a big believer in independent businesses and hope this book can play its part in taking you further. And finally a big thank you to all of the people who turned this book down as it merely made me even more determined to get back up again.

Micah Seven Five

"Trust ye not in a friend,
put ye not confidence in a guide."
Micah, Chapter 7, Verse 5

Chapter One

THERE ARE FEW better feelings in this world than the gradual realisation, somewhere between sleep and waking up, that you've got the day off.

Take that Tuesday, for example. For the previous few weeks I had worked myself into the ground and on that particular morning, the euphoria felt better than sex: the same climatic high but with none of the mess. Not that I'm an authority on that these days. Not since one, unplanned moment of madness provoked the end of my marriage. In the four months since, I had wrapped work around me like a comfort blanket; avoiding the truth, according to my friends, and suffering the consequences my mother warned me about: not eating properly, drinking too much, not getting enough sleep. Not exactly textbook traits for a policeman.

As for me, I didn't read quite so much into it. I was run off my feet; more nose to the grindstone than head in the sand, like it must be high season for homicide. And as for sex? Probably best to gloss over it. Let's just say I've been ploughing a lone furrow these past few months. I think you catch my drift.

That Tuesday, though, was going to be different. One of

those stand-out days in your memory. A Kodak moment. An extra day on the end of the August Bank Holiday, quality time with my son Connor, rather than with my mobile, a bottle of Becks, and a take-away Chicken Jalfrezi for one.

I woke around eight, just long enough to drift for five more minutes before I'd have to yield to the shower and some coffee. I stretched myself out to the tip of every finger and the end of every toe and laid my head back on the cheap polyester pillow, pulling it up on either side of my face to cover my ears as the mobile started to ring. I urged it to stop, reminded it of my day off and threatened it with solitary confinement in the bedside table drawer or replacement with a 'pay as you go'. But it continued relentlessly. I had to answer.

"Munday."

As I spoke, I recognised for the first time the forty-a-day throat my mother had mentioned when we argued the previous evening. The voice on the other end carried the familiar Welsh lilt of Harry Duggan; my friend, colleague, and sergeant.

"Jack, I know it's your day off, but I've something I know you'll want to see."

I propped myself up against the pillows to offset the shock of the cold, painted wall against my back, running my hand up to shake my tousled hair into life and feeling around in the half-light for my glasses.

"Uniform has a body," Harry continued without waiting for instruction, "dumped outside a charity shop. Apparently he was found in one of the black bags left by a do-gooder over the weekend. It was only rung in a half-hour ago. I overheard the call."

I glanced down at my watch. Ten past eight. There's

something about seeing a body where it was left, the whole look and smell of the scene that has always influenced my approach to the rest of an investigation. If I didn't see it for myself, it was like reading a novel without starting at the first chapter. But if I went with Harry, I would be stuffed for a ten o'clock start with Connor. I'm ashamed to admit I didn't wrestle with my conscience long enough for it to be considered a fair fight.

"Pick me up in ten. I'll call Connor from the car."

Harry arrived as I ran a black leather belt through the last loop on my Gap chinos. I pulled the leather through the elegant gold buckle and fastened the belt tight. It had been a present from Elaine. She probably hoped I'd hang myself with it now. Harry looked contemptuously around the bedsit, using his fingertips to pick up one of a stack of many empty foil boxes. This one held the congealed remains of a Lamb Pasanda and a stubbed out Marlboro Light. He pushed an overflowing ashtray to one side and moved some empty lager cans off a worn armchair.

"I see you're settling in," he commented, "you know, making it nice."

Harry, like the others, felt I had given in too meekly to Elaine and had been left in undeserved squalor. They thought she was a bitch and weren't afraid to tell me so. But then he, like the others, didn't know the real reason for the break-up. He held up both hands in mock apology.

"Just making conversation."

"Well don't," I replied curtly, pulling on a leather jacket. "Just take me to see the stiff."

Chapter Two

I LOWERED MYSELF into the passenger seat of the unmarked black Mondeo, ignoring the plastic 'no smoking' signs stuck crudely onto the leatherette fascia to light up another cigarette. I drew the first slug of nicotine deep into my lungs, and then coughed most of it back up again. The blue smoke that expelled from my nose and mouth met Harry full in the face as he positioned himself in the driver's seat alongside me. There's no-one so irritating as a reformed smoker. He coughed his disapproval. I ignored him.

"So who found the body?"

"One of the blue-rinsers that works in the charity shop."

"What the hell was she doing there at eight o'clock in the morning?"

"Not everyone lives the way you do," Harry commented.

"Even so, don't you think it's a bit early to be opening a charity shop? She must be very committed."

"I know as much as you do." Harry looked away to guide us into the flow of traffic on a busy morning roundabout. "I guess there are three types of volunteers; keen, very keen, and insomniacs. She probably comes somewhere between two and three."

5

"Do we know anything about the deceased?"

"Nothing at all this early, only that it's male. Uniform are already there and are holding onto everything pending our arrival. SOCO should be there by now and the pathologist said he'd pop by."

I pulled my mobile from my inside jacket pocket and punched in Elaine's number; our number until just a few weeks ago. Jason answered.

"Can I speak to my wife?"

I didn't feel compelled to say who it was or to share with him the reason for my call. He picked up on my reticence immediately and quickly passed the handset over. Perhaps he wasn't as stupid as I'd given him credit for. Elaine's reaction was as I had become used to: selfish, irrational, and straight for the jugular.

"Jack, I don't care what today's excuse is, but if this means I'm going to have to cancel my shopping trip, I swear I'll swing for you."

I refused to rise to the bait and this seemed to take the wind from her sails. She calmed down, and even hinted at an apology.

"Anyway," I continued, "I'm particularly pleased to see that the possibility of Connor missing out is your first concern."

"So you *are* letting us down," she replied, "again."

"Calm down. I've never deliberately let either of you down and you know it." I tried to speak evenly and rationally, which isn't always easy on an unreliable mobile with a colleague sitting inches away. "I was always there for both of you. I still would be given half a chance."

"Jack, I'm not taking a lecture from you on selfishness.

6

You're the past master at it. How can you ever hope to be there for us while you're so wrapped up in yourself?"

"Is this where you give me all the clichéd crap about the job and policemen not being suited to marriage?"

"It's nothing to do with the job," snapped Elaine. "It would be easier for you if it was; to have something else to blame it all on. No, this is about you, Jack. It's you and relationships that aren't compatible."

I reeled a little from the attack. My defence just seemed petty and half-hearted in comparison.

"Now that's not fair. It might have been easier to make things work if you had ever stayed at home rather than swanning around with your mates as if you were still on the pull."

"It might have been easier to make things work if you'd have kept your hands to yourself that night."

The bitterness in her voice was palpable. I turned towards the car window and spoke quietly in an effort to prevent Harry from hearing.

"It happened once Elaine, only once. I've lost count of the number of times I've apologised for it. It won't ever happen again."

"Too right it won't, because I won't give you the chance. You let all of us down that night and now you're doing it again."

"Who said anything about letting you down today?"

"Well why else would you call?"

"I'm just going to be a bit later than I thought."

"This is how it starts, Jack. Every bloody time, this is how it starts. I'm going to be a bit late, and then we wait and we wait, and you never show. Well, I'm sick of waiting. So how late are we talking today; an hour, two hours, Christmas?"

She sounded defeated. I found myself worrying for her as well as for Connor. I even started to feel sorry for Jason, the flat pack lover she let move in within weeks. After all, I'd felt that low myself enough times. I didn't only have the tee-shirt and the board game, I owned the whole bloody toy shop.

"Calm down," I tried to reason. "I've got to stop off at a crime scene and then Harry will bring me straight over. I promise. I should still be with you by ten-thirty. You'll still get your shopping trip and Connor will still get his day out. No dramas, no crises, no no-shows. Do you think you can pass that onto Connor without telling him what a bastard you think I am?"

The phone clicked.

I wound down the window further, threw out the cigarette butt that had burnt down to the filter, and slipped two pieces of nicotine gum into my mouth and chewed as hard as I could to release my frustration.

"You know you're not supposed to smoke the cigarettes *and* chew the gum," Harry mentioned, breaking the silence.

"Nobody likes a smart arse," I snapped. "Just drive."

Chapter Three

I WOULDN'T WANT you to think that it was love at first sight. I'm not a great believer in eyes meeting across a crowded room being powerful enough to melt hearts. Like most people, I expect, we started out as mates. Things must have developed faster than I remember; almost as fast, on reflection, as they deteriorated.

At the time, I was still a raw recruit at Hendon, impatient to get out on the streets and make a living from what I'd been taught. I was nineteen years old and utterly invincible in my own mind. I'll admit that lust may well have been on my agenda, but long-term commitment was certainly not. I only had eyes for my career. Elaine would tell you that I've suffered from similar tunnel vision ever since.

I wish I could recount an elaborately dramatic story about the circumstances in which we met, but I'd only be lying. And there's been enough of that going on to produce another book. We first met on a warm Friday night early in June 1983. Elaine and two of her friends had positioned themselves strategically in the doorway of the back bar of the Doctor Johnson, a tired old pub close to the training college. They quietly watched three young cadets desperately trying to impress with their prowess around the pool table. The reality, of course, was that we were as far removed as you can get from Paul Newman in *The Hustler*. As the evening wore on and their rum and cokes went down, the girls' silence began to be punctuated by occasional comments, which tended to produce either a knowing nod or a shared laugh from within the group.

It was some days later that I learned that we hadn't all been completely unknown to each other. One of Elaine's friends, Tina, and one of my mates, Mark, had previously encountered each other late on the previous Thursday when drunken fumbling after closing time had led to Tina giving Mark an impromptu blow job in an alley round the back of Hendon Central station. As I recall, they left together again that night. Like us, they also embarked on a relationship, but theirs was even more torrid than ours and certainly more short-lived. They met briefly again for what proved to be the last time when Elaine and I were married. Soon after, Mark was killed by a hit and run driver as he ran for a bus across the Finchley Road. We told Tina but she decided not to attend his funeral. Neither of us had contact with her after that.

Of the three girls, Tina was the dominant personality. Big and brassy with more jewellery than H Samuel, she did the best she could to accentuate her assets. Her fleshy body was squeezed into (and spilling out of) a deep pink vest top that was similar in colour to the uneven flashes of red across her chest and shoulders where the sun had left its mark on the previous hot, early summer days. She chewed gum with the dedication of an Olympic sportsman and periodically ran a steel afro-comb through her wiry, bleached hair. Her equally fleshy legs ran down from the bottom of a tight, white denim skirt to black patent high-heeled shoes, topped with a delicately hung gold ankle chain.

Elaine and her other friend Linda stood very much in Tina's shadow. At that time, Tina set the tone not only for their evenings but for much of their lives as well. She dictated the where and the when, took care of all the arrangements and they, in turn, looked to her for almost every instruction. Elaine later admitted she had been taken by surprise by my interest, which, as it developed from flirtation and friendship into a relationship, seemed to anger Tina, who detected a lessening in her influence. The start of our relationship gave Elaine the opportunity that she had needed to detach herself from Tina. I watched with no little pride as she grew in confidence, began to establish her own personality, and then stand firmly on her own two feet. She was certainly making up for lost time and I enjoyed being the catalyst for it.

That particular night, though, was all about pairing off and which of us would end up with which of them. Tina clearly had the taste for Mark. She would wait until he went down on a shot before sidling up alongside him at the table, suggestively stroking the end of his cue. At first he found it off-putting, but by the second or third time, he realised there was more on offer than the game and the chance to get one over on the lads. That left my other friend, Matt, a tall, blonde-haired rugby-playing type. He had long lost interest in the game and was leaning against the doorframe where Linda stood, draining the dregs from another pint of lager. He would later make his intentions clear to everyone by returning from the gents brandishing a vending machine pack of condoms with a sly nod and a wink in Linda's general direction. Everyone, it seemed, understood the rules. By now,

Elaine stood with her back to the game, carefully studying the options open to her on the jukebox. I walked up behind her and held out a handful of coins.

"Play me something," I suggested.

She smiled and took three pieces of silver from my palm.

"What do you like?"

"Your call. Surprise me."

As someone who was usually swayed by The Smiths, The Jam, and Echo & The Bunnymen, "Take That Situation" by Nick Heyward probably – well, certainly – wasn't the song I would have chosen. And it was hard to disguise the fact.

"You don't like Haircut 100?"

"I've never looked good in a chunky-knit sweater."

"So I suppose Nik Kershaw's out of the question too?"

"And Howard Jones, and The Thompson Twins, and Wham."

She laughed; I did too. And at that point the connection was made.

We were the last to leave the bar that night. And while Mark and Tina got it on again in an alley somewhere and Matt and Linda road-tested the vending machine condoms in the back of his Ford Cortina, Elaine and I just walked and talked. I tried to argue that "Bring On The Dancing Horses" knocked "Wake Me Up Before You Go-Go" into a corner, but she was having none of it. We kissed as I walked her home, but nothing more.

The rest followed in its own good time. We started to see more of each other and soon found ourselves looking for ways of meeting away from the rest of the group, during the day as well as in the evenings. Elaine showed genuine interest in what I was doing and I was only too happy to regale her with tales of life inside Hendon and paint her fanciful pictures of the glittering police career that I believed lay ahead of me. She always indulged me, not once displaying the cynicism that, on reflection, she must have been feeling. We seemed emotionally, sexually, and socially compatible and, though I had always promised myself I wouldn't, I found myself seeing her as inextricably linked with my future.

It came as no surprise to anyone when we moved in together as soon as I graduated from Hendon. She was there to see me pass out alongside my parents and hers was the first face I looked for as I scanned the watching crowd. She told me she was proud to be there and I was equally proud to have her there.

I have asked myself since whether we then slipped inevitably but unnecessarily towards marriage and whether things would have been different if we had chosen to just continue cohabiting. I have asked myself whether the formality of marriage, the whole, serious grown-upness of it all, put us under a pressure that we could have done without. Connor's birth was certainly a source of great excitement. I remember vividly, though, as I left the hospital in the early hours afterwards, that in some way it had changed everything. No matter how hard we might try to convince ourselves, neither of us could possibly expect to be the same people, unchanged by the experience or the expectations of parenthood. Our responsibility for this new little life simply confirmed our move into a different league.

I can't pinpoint a precise moment when it all started to go wrong. Believe me, I've thought long and hard about it, expecting one particular event to hit me like a bright light as the defining moment in our relationship. It hasn't. Maybe things don't work like that. Certainly that night may have brought things to a head, but it was a symptom rather than the cause in the breakdown of our relationship. But *when* compatibility became incompatibility is still an unknown for me.

Chapter Four

BLUE AND WHITE police incident tape ran from one street lamp around two others and back across the front of the St. Margaret's Hospice 'Nearly New' shop, "all paperbacks only 50p". It fluttered gently in the late summer breeze, the sun bouncing harshly off the white panels, projecting back a light that made it difficult to focus on the scene at hand. The early morning mist had already burned off. It was going to be another scorching day.

A white screen, which had been hastily erected around the front of the shop, protected the scene from prying eyes, although a small group of mainly middle-aged women continued to huddle outside the taped area and speculate eagerly among each other in hushed undertones. A uniformed constable I vaguely recognised nodded as we reached the edge of the cordon and then waved us through. Harry parked the car haphazardly at an angle out from the curb. I pulled a pair of Ray Bans out of my inside pocket, slipped them on and focused through the polarised lenses as I climbed out.

The pathologist, Dr Andrew Cook, was already at work as we manoeuvred ourselves into the confined space behind the white screens. He was balanced on his haunches, his back to us, huddled over a stack of black plastic bags, his gloved hands cradling a human head that was slumped almost lazily out of the bag nearest to him. I have known him for years and yet know nothing about him at all. He's just one of those people that never allows you to get close. I watched in morbid fascination as he first inspected every inch of the corpse's head, running his fingers through the hair, staring into the forced-open eyes, laying the head to one side and then the next before gently rolling the bag down to reveal the neck and the top of the naked torso. He carried out his responsibilities not only professionally and methodically but also with a relish that on occasions drove right up to the boundaries of taste and sometimes beyond. He always put it down to little more than an enthusiastic and professional pride in his work. I decided long ago to give him the benefit of the doubt, not only because I couldn't ever muster the enthusiasm to do what he has to do in order to earn a living, but also because he's the best in the business.

He sighed a little as he stood up and removed his cream linen jacket, reflecting the fact that he had been locked in an unnatural and uncomfortable position for too long. A large oval sweat patch cast his light blue, double-cuffed shirt into a much deeper shade across the back. He shook each leg in turn and then stretched each shoulder, when there hardly looked the room to do either. He brushed the jacket down, folded it neatly and then hung it from one of the poles that supported the white screen, before climbing awkwardly into the standard-issue white overalls to be used at a crime scene like this. It was then that he noticed me for the first time.

"Terrible business, Jack." He took a white handkerchief from his pocket and dabbed multiplying beads of sweat away from his increasingly reddening brow.

"Aren't they all?"

"It'll be a while before I can tell you anything for sure."

"Usual pack-drill," I replied. "We'll wait until the PM's finished if we have to, but anything you could send us on our way with would be gratefully received."

He nodded and smiled again. "I understand."

The smell of heat and death didn't mix well and as Andy Cook returned to his haunches for a closer examination of the cadaver, I saw little point in merely watching over his shoulder. I had never rated pathology as a spectator sport. I pushed the flap of the white screen aside, my eyes readjusting again to the brilliance of the sunshine. If anything it was hotter outside than under the screen, but a different kind of heat. Inside it had been moist and humid, outside it was an airless, claustrophobic heat that latched on to any part of exposed flesh and began to sear it.

I looked around. It was a pretty, quiet spot. The charity shop sat in the middle of a traditional parade: a newsagent, a small convenience store, a florist, and a sub-branch of a High Street bank. To the right, more shops followed the road as it meandered up a gentle hill; to the left it led towards leafy, affluent housing. And in front was The Green, neat and tidy, with benches beside flowerbeds for people to while the hours away by watching the world go by. I looked around and tried to lock the image away, visualising how, on a beautiful, warm, late summer's day, someone chose a spot like this to unceremoniously dump a man's body and leave it for others to find.

Spotting the growing huddle of onlookers, an enterprising ice cream van had stopped and opened for business on the edge of The Green, a luminous poster in the rear window advertising "ice-cold drinks" at some vastly inflated price. A young uniformed constable, barely old enough to shave, seemed about to quash the man's entrepreneurial spirit when I pulled some coins out of my pocket to exchange for a Diet Coke. I don't know if the constable was intimidated by my rank or just had a sudden change of heart, but seeing me hand over the money stopped him short of moving the van on and resorted instead to issuing a slightly conceited warning. I smiled and winked at the van driver as the constable turned away. He just shrugged his shoulders.

"Kids," he said, "they think they know everything."

"You weren't down here yesterday were you?"

"Sorry, mate, no." He sounded almost disappointed. "Is it a bad do?"

"It's never a good one when we're around."

He pulled the cold can out of a rusting refrigerator before wiping it dry with a dirty white and orange towel.

"Rumour says there's a body in there."

The ice cream man filtered out change from a battered biscuit tin and laid the coins in the upturned lid to check the amount.

"Rumour's right," I smiled, sliding the coins into my pocket without confirming that the change was correct. "Do you do this pitch often?"

"Not as much as I used to. I try and hover around the bigger shopping areas mainly. Funny thing is, though, I did think of coming down here yesterday."

Hilarious, I thought. But it had been worth a shot. I turned and walked back towards the crime scene, glancing to my left at the huddle behind the tape. I raised my can in a mock toast and asked if they were "enjoying the show". Instantly, the huddle turned in on itself, like a small animal in some act of self-preservation against the threat from an external predator. Harry Duggan came up alongside me. I offered him the Diet Coke and he took a swig.

"Looks like you're in there," he laughed, gesturing towards the women.

"Trust me, that's the very last thing I need." I took the can back and gestured down towards the pavement and curb. At first I don't think Harry really knew what I was pointing at. "You know, the body had to have been moved here by at least two people, maybe more."

He waited for further explanation. I let another mouthful of Diet Coke travel south before continuing.

"I mean, even if he's not a big guy, he's still a dead weight. That makes him hard to get rid of anyway. Plus, think about it, I stick three things in my bin bags at home and they tear or split and I'm left picking crap up off the floor in my dressing gown. They just couldn't have pulled a bag with a thirteen stone man in it from the curb to the shop, not without tearing the bottom of the bin bag on the pavement. And that would mean risking having the body splayed out on the pavement for everyone to see."

"So he must have been carried?"

"Absolutely. Now, what sort of things do people donate in these bags?"

Harry warmed to the task. "Clothes, shirts, old records, paperbacks, that kind of thing."

"Right, so all stuff that you can just throw into a bag, chuck into your car and then just drop off as you're passing."

"Guess so."

"So, it's not going to be often that someone would donate something so heavy that it needs at least two of them to carry it from the car. Agreed?"

"Agreed."

"So when you get uniform to do their house-to-house and street interviews, let's get them asking if anyone saw people struggling with what they thought was just an extremely generous donation."

Harry wrote it down in his notebook, as if it were too difficult to remember without assistance.

"Another thing. Check to see if anyone along here has got security cameras and get the films for yesterday, and see if there are any speed cameras nearby and let's have a look at the images from those."

He nodded.

My last few words were obliterated by the over-polite coughing of the young police officer with the ice-cream vendetta.

"Sorry to disturb you, Inspector, but the pathologist has asked to have a word."

Cook had stripped off the overalls and was rolling his shirtsleeves back down when Harry and I re-entered the screened-off area. The sweat patch on his back had expanded round to the front of his shirt, along either side of his neck and in two large swathes under each arm. He seemed oblivious to the fact. The body was still in position, its head, neck, left shoulder, and left arm exposed.

"Look, like I said earlier, there's not too much that I can tell you until I get him back to the mortuary..."

"But?"

Cook crouched again and gestured for us to join him

down by the body. The surgical gloves gave his fingers an unnaturally pale pallor. He gently moved the head away from us to expose uneven bruising around the neck.

"Well he's naked and he's certainly been strangled, but what with I have no idea. The marks are unusual and there's particularly uneven bruising at the back of the neck, almost as if someone had been tying a knot."

"How long's he been dead?"

"Provisionally, I would say at least 24, maybe up to 48 hours, but I'll know more later."

"Is there any chance that he wasn't dead when he was put in the bag, just badly beaten and left to suffocate?"

"Unlikely, but I can look into it during the post-mortem. But look at this," he continued with excitement in his voice, holding the inside of the forearm up to the light.

"Needle marks?"

"Your man was a drug user."

"Was he drugged before he was killed?"

Andy Cook smiled.

"You see, that's why you're the celebrated detective. A question that goes like a laser to the heart of the issue." He shrugged his shoulders. "The post-mortem will tell us. I'll call you as soon as I know."

Chapter Five

INSIDE THE CHARITY shop, Marjorie Bentham was a shaking bag of nerves. Perched on the seat of an old wooden chair, the arm of a female police constable around her shoulder, she clutched tightly onto the screwed-up white tissue that she had been using to dry her eyes. She sipped carefully from a china tea-cup, biting occasionally into a solitary digestive biscuit that huddled in the saucer. From time to time, the WPC squeezed her shoulder and spoke quietly and sympathetically into her ear. She nodded silently in response to whatever was being said to her, looking up from her tea cup as she heard me approach. I leant down a little, introduced Duggan and myself, and then offered my hand, which she took into her own. She reminded me of my grandmother. Her hand trembled as I shook it and I could feel the bones standing out beneath her mottled white skin. Although at this particular moment she looked vulnerable, you could also tell that she had retained much of the beauty of her youth, her sapphire-blue eyes couched in soft, sympathetic features, her snow-white hair enhancing rather than detracting from her looks. She was just a nice old lady.

"I'm sorry Mr Munday," she said falteringly, in apology

for her distress. "I'm seventy-nine and I've never been in trouble with the police before."

"And you're not in trouble now, Mrs Bentham. Not unless you were responsible for the man's death and I find that very hard to believe."

The preposterousness of what I was saying was enough to secure the hint of a smile. I pulled up another wooden chair and sat myself down next to a table of neatly folded knitwear, sneaking a look at my watch as I did so, conscious of my commitment to Elaine to collect Connor by ten-thirty. It was nine-forty. I glanced around among the shelves stacked full of brass and china ornaments, down at boxes of dog-eared paperbacks and dated records and tapes, and across rails of gaudy ladies' clothes and dummies dressed in gents clothing never intended to be worn together. It was easy to dismiss it as little more than a jumble sale, but it was more ordered and organised than that; the detected commitment and passion by the people responsible was hard not to admire. The shop clearly did good business, demonstrated by photographs and letters of thanks from the hospice that had been put into frames and left on the counter for customers to read.

The WPC introduced Norman Smith, the co-volunteer that had discovered the body with Marjorie. He nodded, shook hands, and offered me tea. He seemed calm and collected, less traumatised by the morning's experience than his friend, though I put it down more to his generation's belief that men shouldn't display such signs of weakness than to anything else. He seemed urbane, serious and spoke with a quiet authority that had me put him down as probably a retired headmaster or bank manager. Even on this sultry summer morning, he was still kitted out in a navy blue blazer with a white shirt and tie, but showed none of the signs of discomfort from the heat that had characterised Andy Cook. He glanced disapprovingly at the can of Diet Coke and repeated the offer of tea. I was happy to accept.

I spoke quietly and squeezed Marjorie's hand reassuringly. "We will need to take a proper statement from you, but in the meantime, is it okay if I just ask you some questions?"

She sniffed and nodded.

"They told me that you and Norman called the police just after eight. Is that right?"

She nodded again.

"That's very early to be in the shop. Are you normally here that early?"

She sipped more tea and then turned her reddened eyes towards mine.

"Of course not," she whispered. "But it was a Bank Holiday weekend. We always get more bags over a Bank Holiday weekend than at any other time. I wanted to get all the bags in and out the back before we opened the shop at nine, and Norman kindly offered to help."

"It's not as if we have too many other things taking up our time, Mr Munday," called Norman Smith, walking back towards us with a cup and saucer for me and one also for Duggan. I got the sense that he would have strongly disapproved of my preference for a mug.

I placed the cup and saucer on the edge of a donated sideboard and turned back to Marjorie.

"Tell me exactly what you found when you got here this morning."

She sipped more tea for sustenance and played nervously with the gold wedding band that now hung quite loose on her slender but bony ring finger.

"We arrived at more or less the same time and were amazed by just how many bags had been left. It was more than we would normally expect, even on a Bank Holiday. Norman said that the whole of the area must have been clearing out its wardrobes this weekend. We were actually quite excited about it. You see, these days, charity shops like ours seem to lose out to boot sales and garage sales far more than we used to. We don't often get bags stacked up the way they were. Well, I mean, you've seen the pile for yourself."

I nodded.

"But that's a heck of a lot of bags for Norman and yourself to sort through on your own."

Marjorie smiled, as if to say, 'I may be old, but I'm not completely stupid'.

"Of course," she replied. "We weren't going to sort them out on our own, I just wanted to move them into the back of the shop.

Welcome though they are, they do make the front of the shop look a little untidy and uninviting just left where they're put. You know, like the bin men forgot to call. We may only be a charity shop, but it's still important for the presentation to be right."

"And then?"

"Well, I opened up and Norman went straight through the back to put the kettle on. But we had already decided that we would get the bags in before we stopped for tea. The first two or three bags were easy, light enough for us to take one each. They've probably only got a few sweaters in them. Then, I went to pull down…"

She stopped for a moment, sniffed and wiped her eye. I

squeezed her hand again to give her further encouragement, and when she restarted, her voice carried renewed strength and greater conviction.

"So I went to pull down *the* bag but I could only shift it a few inches. I called out for Norman and told him that I thought we had a bag of hardback books. That's the only thing I could think of that would weigh so much."

"I shouldn't really have done it," interjected Norman Smith, perhaps feeling a little left out of the conversation. "I've got a hernia."

I looked at him and smiled, and then returned to Marjorie.

"Well, we both reached across to the top of the bag to try and bring it a little bit closer. There were a couple of other bags in the way lower down, so it was a bit of a stretch but we managed to reach it and together we gave one large pull. The bag tumbled down on top of the other two bags. I told Norman that curiosity had got the better of me and that I had to see what was in the bag. If it was something really spectacular, you see, we would have made room for it in the window and put it on display today."

"So you opened the bag?"

She nodded, seemingly trying to go over all of the recollections in her mind before saying them out loud.

"The top of the bag was quite well tied up with some string which, I remember thinking, was unusual. Most people just tie a knot in the top of the bag. So, I fetched a pair of scissors from behind the counter and cut through the string. That's when I first saw the…"

She dissolved into tears. The WPC returned her arm around the old lady's shoulder and shook her very gently, in the way that you would comfort a baby. I didn't want to push her much further, especially as she would have to recount the whole incident again when providing her formal statement. I looked up to Norman Smith, who seemed to know instinctively that I wanted him to take over where Marjorie left off.

"Without the string at the top, the bag just slumped down and the top fell open. At first all we could see was his hair, but once we opened the bag just a little, there was no doubt what was inside."

"And that's when you phoned the police?"

"Marjorie did. I didn't want her standing outside looking at him. She was obviously very distressed. So I waited by the bag while she went in and made the call."

"Okay," I said, rising from my chair, "The WPC is going to stay with you and either DS Duggan here or one of my other colleagues will be along to take a written statement from you a little later. Obviously you won't be able to open the shop until we tell you."

She nodded her understanding.

"I know that it must have been a horrible shock, but there's nothing you could have done for him."

I didn't know whether this would make her feel any better or not. But I felt it ought to be said. I gestured for Duggan to follow me out and we met just inside the door of the shop, when I remembered something else I needed to ask.

"Marjorie," I called. She looked up again, looking greyer and frailer than I thought was probably normal. "Where exactly on the pile was the bag when you first saw it?"

"Just up from where it is now," she replied, "on top of most of the others."

Duggan waited by the door, notepad open, waiting for

28

instructions. This was where I thought I was at my best, seeing clearly through the melee at what really needed to be done first. I glanced down at my watch. Ten past ten. I had to be quick.

"Once you've dropped me off, come back here and get statements taken. Then get her home and find somebody to take him home, too. I don't want them left unattended; get the officers to make them some tea, phone their families, even their GPs if they need something for the shock. You know the type of thing, Harry, caring policemen and all that.

"Then liaise with SOCO on anything they pick up and keep tabs on how Andy Cook's getting on with the PM. Anything at all, you call me on my mobile. Got it?"

"Loud and clear."

"Also, when you do get back to the station, go and see the Chief Super and fill him in. Tell him I'll go into more detail when I see him tomorrow."

Harry closed his notebook and dug deep into his pocket for his car keys.

"One final thing," I asked, "have you got fifty pence?"

He looked at me as if the request was completely insane, but after surveying an array of silverware in the palm of his hand, passed the coin over nonetheless. I took it with a smile, bent down, picked up a dog-eared Ed McBain novel from a cardboard box on the floor and left the silver coin on the counter-top. Harry looked at me again, though this time with a hint of disgust.

"Right," I said breezily, "take me to get Connor now."

Chapter Six

B Y THE TIME the train pulled into Westminster underground station, the stifling heat had left my hair sodden with sweat. I must have resembled a straggler in the London Marathon as we disembarked, all arms and legs as I reached for the finishing line, looking as if I was only fit to take my final breath. I comforted myself with a quick glance around the carriage to see others dissolving in a similar state of discomfort. It was just an occupational hazard of being in London during the humidity of a particularly high summer. Connor, on the other hand, looked cool and unphased in his reversed Nike baseball cap and his Adidas tee-shirt: a walking, talking dream for marketing men around the world.

I had made it to Elaine's by ten-thirty, albeit with only a minute or two to spare, but by ten-thirty nonetheless. So I had kept my side of the bargain, something which I took pleasure in forcing my now-estranged wife to grudgingly acknowledge. We spent an uncomfortable few minutes in the hall waiting for Connor to collect his things, me feeling like the stranger I had become in my own home, and Elaine curiously conscious of it. The new man in her life was Jason, a mid-twenties, bleached blonde fitness machine. He nodded civilly towards me as he helped himself to a drink from my fridge and a clutch of biscuits from my cupboard before retreating to the sanctuary of my dining room, leaving Elaine and me to circle each other in the hall like wounded animals.

I'll hold my hands up now and admit that my next comment wasn't perhaps the most tactful in the circumstances. As Connor slid his baseball cap on top of his spiked, gelled hair, he asked Elaine where Jason had gone. The fact he was interested at all made me seethe quietly with suppressed anger. When Elaine replied that he was probably playing on his Playstation, I couldn't resist observing that this was how most kids seemed to spend their time these days. My inner sense of satisfaction at having landed the blow was quickly tempered by the venomous stare that it produced. I don't know for sure what was stored in her mind, but if she could have spat it in my direction, she would surely have tried. It was time to go.

The journey was fine. We spent the first few stops strap-hanging until a couple of seats became available. Connor couldn't reach the straps, of course, but held onto the rail by the doors and allowed himself to be thrown around in an exaggerated way by the movement of the train. As the carriage steadily emptied we got the chance to talk.

"How's life?" I asked.

He looked at me, the hint of a glint in his eye, and shrugged his shoulders. The comment was as flippant as you might expect from a lad of his age.

"Still breathing, as you can see."

"Glad to hear it. School going well?"

He nodded without looking up. I had come to realise that I was not only separated from Elaine, I was also separated from Connor. And that had made our relationship awkward in a way that it hadn't been before.

"So what are you doing best at? Maths? Science?"

"I'm still on summer holiday, Dad. I don't want to talk about school."

Silence reigned for a few minutes.

"I like history," he said a few moments later, "particularly the gruesome stuff."

I was anxious to keep the dialogue going.

"History's good. I also used to enjoy the gruesome stuff. It's probably why I do what I do now."

He nodded.

"And what about girlfriends? Any of those? Anyone special on the scene?"

Even with hindsight, I still can't be sure whether this was a crude attempt at paternal bonding or if I genuinely thought it would bring us closer together. In the end, it just sounded crass. I don't remember when I went from being cool Dad to embarrassing Dad, but Connor's glance confirmed the transition. It was the same glance I remember giving to my own father twenty-five years ago. It was also a cue to change the subject.

"So, are you happy at home?"

He shrugged again. I hoped that not every answer would be as non-committal as this.

"You know what Mum's like." But I wasn't sure that I did any more.

"You could always come and stay with me, if you like….?"

Connor looked up quickly but I couldn't tell whether it was in despair or excitement. He knew instinctively, as I did, that it was a statement that hadn't been properly thought through. It had merely seemed the right thing to say.

"…you know, you could stay for a bit?"

"Thanks Dad, but I don't think Mum would be too keen."

I felt slighted, even angry. I didn't want to get the day off on the wrong foot, but I felt it was important to set a few facts straight.

"You know it's not only up to your Mum. You have a say in this too."

"Mum says I should be wary of you trying to use me as a bargaining chip between you." It sounded as if he'd learnt the line by rote and then been rehearsed on it a hundred times.

"And is that what you think I'm trying to do?"

He shrugged again. I turned his face gently to look at mine and then leant down to get close to him. I kissed him once on the forehead. He wiped it away with his wrist and looked at me in disgust for kissing him in public.

"If you want to come and spend some time at my place, you can do. Just leave your mother to me."

"Do you mind if I pass?" he said a few moments' later. "Besides, you can hardly take care of yourself, let alone look after me."

His honesty was shocking but right. If Connor came to live with me, he'd probably end up doing more for me than I would for him. I knew that, and I also knew it wouldn't be fair. I put my arm around his shoulder and pulled him into me, enjoying the closeness that I had missed these past few months. I'd settle for more of the same. I wondered whether he had missed it too.

We sat in silence as the train trundled along the Jubilee

Line, through the shiny new stations at Canary Wharf and Canada Water. I studied Connor's reflection in the carriage window and realised how little I actually knew him; his likes, his dislikes, how he spent his time.

"What about Mum's new friend?"

I knew immediately that it was an unfair question to put to a ten-year old and wished I hadn't asked.

"Jason? What about him?"

"Well, do you like him?"

Connor thought for a moment. He shrugged his shoulders again and then reluctantly offered an observation.

"He's better than me at Tomb Raider."

"Enough said," I thought to myself, not feeling the need to express my satisfaction aloud.

"But he's not my Dad," Connor added a second or two later, "you are."

So I felt a better about life as we joined the snake of commuters out of the train at Westminster and made our way through the refurbished station. It was a bleak transformation, all dark grey steel work and imposing rivets that gave you the feeling of being alone beneath a bridge or deep in the bowels of a factory or a boiler room. It was with some relief that we walked across the slightly more inviting station concourse and followed the exit signs to Westminster Pier, stepping out beside the Embankment, and standing for a few moments at the foot of the stone steps that led up to the pavement across Westminster Bridge. We climbed the steps and then rested beneath the imposing statue of Boadicea, taking in the surfeit of different languages that thronged between the 'authentic' pancake stand and the souvenir stall peddling overpriced, poor-quality gifts.

For a split second we caught the hint of a breeze and enjoyed the temporary respite offered by the shadow cast across the road by the Houses of Parliament opposite. I glanced from the gothic splendour of Parliament across to the gleaming pods of the London Eye, which, shimmering in a mid-morning heat haze, seemed hardly to be moving at all. The Eye, for all the wonder of its engineering, looked strikingly out of place against this historic backdrop. What would all the great figures of history that had crossed Westminster Bridge in their time have made of the giant metallic Ferris wheel that now dominated the South Bank skyline?

As London moved around us, we stood rooted to the spot on the north side of Westminster Bridge. It brought back memories of all the trips I had taken as a child with my grandparents to places of interest and sites of importance. I wanted Connor to know something of those memories. I pointed Connor towards Parliament Square, where the statue of Churchill stared disapprovingly down on the modernisation of the city, and then along the Victoria Embankment towards Old Scotland Yard, the Savoy Hotel, and the skyline of the City away in the distance.

The sun bounced back off every car roof and bonnet, the noise from the traffic, as loud and intrusive as ever, simply melding together into one, long, unbroken hubbub. London doesn't seem comfortable in the sunshine. It's as if the heat gives it pretensions of being a European city, a role that it seems unable to carry off with the style of Paris, Bordeaux or Cannes. London – and Londoners – gives the impression of being altogether more at ease with itself in the rain and the gloom. I suppose it's what you're used to that counts. But in the here and now you could smell the heat. Office workers slouched on the sides of Westminster Bridge. The ties around the necks of their double-cuffed city shirts already loosened, they listened to music on iPods or glanced upwards to take in the sun through Armani or Versace sunglasses, periodically rehydrating their bodies from plastic bottles of chilled Evian or cans of Red Bull.

Connor and I walked purposefully across the Bridge towards what used to be County Hall, the one-time seat of London's government, now half hotel, half aquarium. Hoards of visitors thronged the southern embankment, causing the queues for the Eye and the Aquarium to become intertwined, much to the obvious frustration of the staff sent to sort out the confusion. The marvel of the engineering, admired from a distance, was even more impressive up close as the perpetual motion of the giant steel wheel lent it a kind of grace that I hadn't really expected. As we went through the turnstile and onto the landing platform I allowed myself a sideways glance to take in the boyish excitement that was written right across Connor's face. What made it feel good was that it was me and not Elaine who had put it there. I guess if Connor had realised just how eager he looked, he would surely have dismissed it as uncool and stifled the excitement.

We shuffled along together in the queue, sipping from extortionately-priced cans of Diet Coke, getting ever closer to the platform from which you boarded the Eye's oval glass pods.

"So why were you late this morning?"

"Just some work to attend to."

"Was it a murder?"

He said the word 'murder' with such undisguised relish

that it caused an elderly couple in front and a scout mistress behind to turn and stare with a mix of shock and disdain. I wanted to tell them I was the investigator and not the perpetrator but I'm not sure they would have believed me. Instead I gave a weak, embarrassed smile and ruffled Connor's hair playfully. He urged me to stop.

"Yes," I whispered, "it was a murder."

"Cool. Was there much blood? Had he been cut up?"

To answer would have not only spurred on the macabre interest of a ten-year old, but I am sure it would have further incurred the wrath of our neighbours in the queue; not something I wanted to do as we were about to share a pod 300 feet above the streets of London.

"We're not having this conversation now."

"Later then."

Connor spoke more confidently than I thought was proper in a young boy.

We skipped aboard the gently moving module, sat briefly on the brown wooden bench that ran down the centre, and listened as the young hostess gave out safety instructions and brief details about the structure and the 'flight'. I caught the part about it being the biggest observation wheel in the world and the bit about the design being modelled on something similar in Chicago when Connor called me to join him at the far end of the pod. We stood together, father and son, and watched as we rose serenely over the Thames, looking down on the green roofs of the Ministry of Defence, and across to the candy-striped awnings on the terrace of the Houses of Parliament. As we continued to rise close to the top of the elevation, I pointed Connor in the direction of Downing

Street and Buckingham Palace and away to the left to the Earl's Court exhibition centre. Cameras clicked relentlessly around us and the scouts with the disapproving leader swarmed from one side of the pod to another like marauding bees, calling their friends to point out one new building and then the next.

By the time we reached the height of the wheel's revolution, the heat gain from the sun had made the whole experience more uncomfortable. I wiped my brow on the sleeve of my jacket and contemplated what life must be like in a greenhouse. I tried to position myself close enough to the air vents to get a blast of passing air, but each time I got close, either Connor called me away or a scout got there first. I sipped the remainder of the Diet Coke, but it didn't taste good warm.

As the pod moved away from the twelve o'clock position to begin its return to Earth, the yellow masts of the Millennium Dome came into view way off to the east. And as it did so, my mobile began to ring. It was tough to make out exactly what Duggan was saying, being surrounded by twenty boy scouts and Connor, seemingly eager to point out every lamppost in the capital. I jammed one finger into my ear and pulled the phone closer to the other side of my head. Hearing was still a struggle.

"Where the hell are you?" asked Duggan.

"Half way down on the London Eye, slowly roasting in the heat."

"What the hell's all that noise? Sounds like you're in a fish bowl."

"I am. And it's just cost me fifteen quid to climb in."

"How's Connor?"

"Having fun. Now, what's up?"

"I'm at the mortuary, they're about to start the PM."

"And?"

"We found something on the body."

"Go on."

The mobile line was cracking up but I only realised I was shouting when I turned back into the middle of the pod to find the Scout Mistress's gaze fixed on me.

"A bit of newspaper torn from the corner of a page. I've sent it off for forensic. But Jack, it was in his fists. He had clenched fists."

"So?"

"Well, think about it. If you've just had the life strangled out of you, wouldn't you expect at the point of death that your hands would fall open?"

"Possibly. What are you driving at?"

"In which case, the bit of newspaper would fall out next to the body. True?"

"Probably."

"Well it certainly wouldn't survive the body being moved, put into a bin bag and then driven around the area before being dumped."

"Unless?"

"Unless, and I'm just throwing this in as a suggestion, someone wants us to find the bit of paper, so they put it back into the hand and create fists before rigour has a chance to set in."

"I'll take any lead but let's also keep an open mind. It could be nothing. I don't want to end up with more red herrings than a fish counter. What does Cook say?"

"He won't commit himself to anything till he's got his carving knife out. But he's not arguing with me either."

"Typical."

"Something else," Duggan continued, "not only are there needle marks on his arm, there are nasty scratches running down his back."

"Rough sex?" I ventured, to the dismay of the scout mistress.

"Maybe he knew some of the same women you do."

Chapter Seven

I REMEMBER VIVIDLY how I felt after watching my first post-mortem. It was a cold, wet Wednesday in October or maybe November, and I was a month into my first CID posting; green behind the ears in one respect, and across my face as well by the time the post-mortem had finished.

I had refused offers to take my leave of proceedings, forcing myself to watch as the badly bruised body of a teenage prostitute that I had discovered was dissected in front of me in the most matter-of-fact kind of way. I think it was that which I found most shocking. Not that the procedure lacked dignity or respect, but just that it seemed so mundane, as much a part of the job as form filling or making phone calls. I later realised this was just the professional detachment that came with experience. As my stomach started to tighten and the sweat became more evident around the back of my neck, I had loosened the top button of my shirt in an effort to free up the passage of air around my body. It didn't work and soon the tightness grew more intense and I bolted hastily to the door, unloading myself into a drain down the side alley. I stood for some minutes with the rain pouring over my face, like you do when you're standing in a shower, taking large gulps of fresh air to try and sort myself out, before unloading down the drain again.

I found out later that my DCI at the time, a considered, softly-spoken Scot called Henry Raven, had calmly apologised to the pathologist for my performance before following me into the alley, where he rested his arm sympathetically on the back of my folded frame and waited for me to finish. As we walked back to the car together, he offered me a cigarette and brushed aside my obvious embarrassment. I never found out whether he was angry or not. Any officer who said he hadn't been sick in the line of duty was a liar and any detective unaffected by murder was simply not an effective officer: the gospel according to Henry Raven. It was the first of many valuable lessons. The biggest compliment I can pay him is to confess to you now that, more than once in my career, I have stopped to ask myself what he would have done next.

My watch had just passed six in the evening as I entered the mortuary. There was a coolness inside that was actually welcoming after the humidity of the day, though my hair still stood up on the back of my neck as it had on that first occasion. I don't think anyone ever gets used to death. The mortuary was a stark facility, bare and functional, annexed uncomfortably onto the back of the local general hospital. The air hung heavy with the smell of chemical cleaners. Fluorescent lighting overhead cast the abundance of polished metal in a curiously pale green hue. It was quiet, almost funereal, you might say. Harry Duggan sat in Andy Cook's half-glazed office, sipping brown liquid from a brown plastic cup, and reading that morning's Daily Mirror. He didn't see me approach.

"Quiet as a grave in here," I commented, taking Harry a

little by surprise.

He folded the paper and laid it down on the desk, swivelling round in Cook's chair to face me. He held out his brown plastic cup to offer me something to drink, but I held my hand up to say no.

"You can get one of your own, if you like," he added helpfully. "The machine's only through the swing doors and it's on free vend down here."

"Probably not much pilfering from the patients, eh? I think I'll pass."

Harry looked almost disappointed and gazed back into the top of the plastic cup.

"You know, it's not too bad once you've skimmed the top layer off."

"In that case, I'll definitely pass."

I took a Marlboro Light from the pack in my pocket and lit it with the London Eye disposable lighter that had been Connor's gift to me at the end of the 'flight'.

"How was your day?"

"Good. Yes, good. In the back of my mind I thought I might be losing Connor before today, but you know I think he's bright enough not to be sucked too far into his mother's selfish little world."

"I take it she wasn't that pleased to see you."

"That's an understatement. She'd be thrilled to know I was here now. It's just the walking, talking, breathing bit that would disappoint her."

Harry laughed.

"What are you going to do then?"

"About what?"

"About Elaine? Are you giving up all hope of winning her

back?"

"You know, I'm not sure deep down that I'd want her back," I lied, "and I'm even more certain that she wouldn't want me."

"So, what next, divorce?"

"You ask too many questions."

"I'm a detective."

"Where's Cook?"

I wanted to make it clear that my marriage was not a subject for public debate, at least not tonight.

"He's gone to the staff canteen for something to eat. I tell you, Jack, the man's not normal. He got halfway through the PM, up to his arms in blood and guts, his hands wrestling with the guy's vital organs, and suddenly he decided he needed something to eat. So he finished off, closed him up and disappeared off for…"

"Don't tell me," I smiled, "liver and bacon?"

"He's disgusting." Harry shook his head, his Welsh accent getting more pronounced the more animated he became. "He even asked me if I wanted to go with."

"And you declined?"

"Are you serious? Of course I declined. I mean, *he* might be like Hannibal fucking Lecter, but I can assure you *I'm* not. Do you really think I'm going to sit here and watch the contents of a man's stomach emptied out in front of me, only then to nip off five minutes later for an all-day breakfast as if I hadn't seen any of it? No thanks, mate. I'll have some toast when I get home."

I tried not to laugh. But the breakout of a smile was inevitable and, when he saw it, Harry just couldn't understand how neither of us shared his revulsion.

"So is he coming back?"

I drew deeply on the cigarette and blew the smoke away from Harry's general direction.

"Probably, you know, after dessert, coffee and liqueurs."

We split the newspaper in half and sat together for five or ten minutes reading until the double doors by the 'free vend' machine swung open and Andy Cook wandered back in, clad from head to toe in clean theatre greens, a white coat slung nonchalantly over his shoulder.

"Was the liver and bacon good?"

I knew how much it would irritate Harry to prolong the conversation. Cook looked at me with a hint of confusion as to how I could have guessed at his choice of main course.

"Exactly as I like it Inspector, pink in the middle and just a hint of blood trickling out."

I turned to find Harry's complexion matching the magnolia of the walls. He excused himself to get fresh air. By the time he re-joined us five or six minutes later, Cook had donned surgical gloves and a clean plastic apron. He beckoned for us to join him at the table where the unknown body lay, on its back, hairless torso exposed, a thin green sheet preserving what little remained of its dignity. He lay like a fallen mannequin, the same waxy texture beginning to overtake his skin. Lines resembling zippers illustrated where the body had been stitched back up after Cook's explorations. They ran around the man's collar, meeting at a point below the centre of his neck before running down his chest in a straight line, disappearing beneath the thin, green sheet. Duggan and I stood on one side of the table, Cook on the other, facing us. He turned on an overhead halogen light, which brought every hair and pore on the body into much sharper focus.

"Well, I don't have much doubt that your friend here died of strangulation, but I'm not too sure what with. You see, if it was a rope, you would most likely strangle someone by putting the rope around the front of your victim's neck like so…" He walked around the table to demonstrate on Duggan. "And pulling from behind, relying on that to make him unconscious and then to snap the neck."

"But?"

"If it was something thinner, like wire, you would expect the strength required to strangle a grown man might be enough to break the skin somewhere around the neck. But with our friend, the skin hasn't been broken."

"So?"

"So it looks like some kind of ligature. Look here." He released Duggan from his grip, reached across the cadaver's left shoulder, rolled the corpse towards him and pointed at the bruising on the back of the body's neck that he had first brought to our attention at the crime scene. "I think that's a knot. I think somebody has tried to apply sufficient pressure to close off his airway by tightening a knot around his throat. That would mean, I guess, something that's quick and easy to tie…"

"Which would rule out rope?"

"…exactly. It would also probably need to be something that would stretch; elastic of some kind."

Andy Cook breathed out dramatically, as if pleased with the way he had brought this to our attention.

"Of course, finding the murder weapon is your job, not mine."

"Can't you be any more specific than that?"

"You're supposed to be helping me."

"I am *supposed* to be giving you a cause and approximate time of death which, if you let me continue, I will try and do."

I held my hands up in apology, though I didn't feel much like saying sorry. Cook laid the body flat again and straightened out the green sheet across his stomach.

"If you were being strangled like that, wouldn't you fight like crazy to get away?" asked Harry. "He doesn't seem to have put up much of a struggle."

"I would agree with you, Mr Duggan." The pathologist raised the body's left arm for inspection. "Remember the needle marks, gentlemen. You can't put up too much of a struggle if you've been drugged."

"What did he have in him?"

"Heroin, Mr Duggan," replied Cook, theatrically, "not enough to kill him, but enough to not care what anyone was doing to him. There was also some evidence of cannabis in his system."

"But if he was drugged and then strangled, why not just give him an overdose and save yourself the hassle?"

Andy Cook smiled at me and shrugged his shoulders.

"You're the detective. That's your call."

Cook returned to his side of the table.

"Now all of this will all be in my report, of course, which should be available to you tomorrow morning. But I do have some other things to give you which could help, particularly with timing."

He turned behind him, bringing back an opaque, plastic jug, in which a reddish-brown liquid swilled from side to side with his movements.

"Gentlemen, the contents of the stomach."

As Harry turned magnolia again, I have to admit that even I began to feel queasy. Momentarily, I was back in time, with Henry Raven at my side, about to make a bolt for the side alley. Andy Cook knew that and was clearly playing on it.

"Just put the jug down and tell us about it."

"It's Chinese, Inspector. Chicken for sure, some rice and I think some prawns, but I can't be too certain of that. Either way, my guess is that it's what your fella here had for dinner on Sunday night. And that means, judging by the level of digestion and the fact that rigour had set in and then subsided, that he was probably alive up until eight or nine o'clock, maybe later."

"I know some take-aways can be bad," piped up Duggan, "but this is taking it to the extreme."

"There's also plenty of alcohol in his blood. It looks like he went out on something of a high."

I know it's dangerous to speculate, but it's usually out of wild supposition that the most realistic leads begin to emerge.

"When you say plenty of alcohol, are you saying he was an alcoholic?"

"Not necessarily. His blood alcohol level was certainly consistent with him being drunk and the liver was very slightly enlarged, but there was no evidence of cirrhosis or alcoholic hepatitis."

"So, what are we saying here? That he bought himself a take-away, injected enough heroin to knock himself senseless and then washed it all down with a nice bottle of red. And while he's three sheets to the wind, somebody comes in, strangles him to death, lifts his body into a bin bag and then dumps him outside the charity shop. It's still not making a great deal of sense."

"Maybe I can assist you even further," continued Cook, in a self-righteous kind of way. "You see, I don't think he spent the evening alone. Well, at least, not all of it."

"Don't tell me," interjected Harry, "now you can tell how many dishes he ordered from the take away?"

Andy Cook ignored the comment, even turning his shoulder away from Harry Duggan to address his comments directly to me. Harry smiled out of his view. I gestured for Cook to continue.

"Sex, Inspector Munday. Don't these things almost always come down to sex?"

"I'm not with you."

"Our friend here had had sex shortly before he died. There's evidence of dried semen at the top of his thigh and around the tip of his penis and similarly some evidence of vaginal fluid elsewhere on his genitals."

Andy Cook leant across to pull away the thin, green sheet as if to prove his findings. I leant across equally quickly to stop him.

"It's okay, Dr Cook. We don't need to see. We'll take your word for it."

"But that at least could be consistent with the scratch marks on his back," chipped in Harry.

"It's possible."

"What about the general condition of the body?" I asked. "Was he reasonably fit and healthy? Please tell me that he had some nasty or unusual disease that might help us trace him through the hospitals or the local GPs?"

"None. I've scraped under the fingernails to see if there's

anything there, and there was what looked like dried blood on the underside of his top front teeth. I've scraped that off and sent it away. It could be nothing. I'll keep you posted on the results. The body itself was a bit dirty, like he'd been living rough for a while, but his teeth have been well kept, so if that's the case, he probably hadn't been roughing it for long. I don't mean to teach you to suck eggs but dental records may be your best bet for an early ID though you'll need a hunch as to who it might be to get you started."

THE SUN WAS just dipping at the start of another balmy evening as Harry and I walked back to our cars. Around us, relatives and patients had come out of the hospital to take advantage of the late summer weather, and nurses leaving at the end of their shifts breathed in hard as if they had been denied light and oxygen for the previous twelve hours. Early evening visitors to the hospital's maternity block passed us as we walked, carrying balloons, balancing pink and blue teddy bears and clutching armfuls of flowers. As I caught snatches of their animated conversations, I looked back towards the mortuary and thought again about the unknown man. In that moment it seemed as if his death had made way for one of the babies being welcomed elsewhere in the same building.

"A drug pusher who sold a dodgy batch of heroin turned over by one of his clients?" offered Harry without warning.

"A bit far-fetched, don't you think? It's not clean enough to be a drug hit. More likely he shared a joint and something stronger with a prostitute and when the sex got a bit too rough, she killed him."

"So now who's speculating?"

"Look, first off we've got to find out who he is. Somebody must have noticed he's missing. He's not too mangled up, so get some photos done of his face that we can hawk around and then get the team together for an eight-thirty briefing in the morning."

Harry nodded. "Do you fancy a pint?" he asked as we reached the cars.

"No," I replied, "not tonight."

Chapter Eight

I T WAS ONE of those nights. No matter how hard I tried
or how tired I was, sleep was only ever going to be an
object of ambition. And believe me, though it may be a
poor choice of words, by the time I got home I was dead on
my feet. The harder I tried to allow myself to drift, the more
cluttered my mind became with theory and counter-theory.
Then, sometime after two in the morning, I gave up on the
idea completely. I threw on a tee-shirt and some jogging
bottoms and went to sit in what passed for my lounge,
grabbing a beer from the bare-shelved fridge on my way
through. I slunk into the low, uncomfortable armchair,
avoiding the springs that jutted out at a variety of angles,
rested my bare feet on top of the small, teak-veneer coffee
table and lifted the ring-pull on the Fosters can.

Something had been troubling me ever since I left the
mortuary. I saw pictures in my mind that I just couldn't file
away. They bothered me rather than horrified me. God knows
I've seen sights a thousand times worse in my career than the
one that morning, and expect to do so again. Yet now, as I sat
alone in the darkness all I felt was an empty sadness. I had
experienced it before, growing up. It washes over me in

waves, mixing a curious sense of grief with a gripping anxiety, which always leaves me feeling insecure.

I stood, as if the action would shake the images away. I caught sight of my reflection in the darkness of the bare, uncurtained window. Like all of us, I suppose, the greater part of me still thinks I look like I did when I was eighteen. And to be truthful, there are times, even now, when I still feel like that as well. But they get more and more rare, and it was certainly not an eighteen-year old that looked back at me from the window. Instinctively I thought it was my father; middle-aged, nursing a broken marriage, unfit, unfulfilled, unshaven and unhappy.

I wiped away the condensation on the window and stared out into the blackness of the night sky, using it as a canvas on which to lay the images that I couldn't shake from my mind. Against the darkness they seemed more vivid and detailed than before, drawing me in, closer and closer to Andy Cook's table until I sensed myself back in the mortuary. I felt myself growing cold, even shivery. The room was just as I had left it, but now I was there alone. The contours of a body were visible beneath a thin green sheet. By now, to my surprise, I was bathed in a cold, clammy sweat. As my imagination moved me closer, the thin green sheet that covered the body pulled back to reveal my own face, my eyes peacefully closed, my skin the colour and texture of marble. The shock snapped me out of the mortuary and back to me senses, spinning me round until, with my back to my window, I slid down the wall and sat cross-legged on the floor. I looked in towards the room. It was a mess, dishevelled, disorganised and cluttered: a metaphor for my life.

I could feel my heart racing. There was a battle taking

place inside my head for my soul and my sanity. The same that had been taking place every day for the last twenty years or more. I have a wife who hates me with a passion that we rarely shared during the last few years of our marriage, and a son who seems oblivious to the fact that I'm no longer around. But then, in truth, he's had years to get used to it. I tell myself he's happier for it. And yet still I want them back. I hang on to the hope that I can make it happen, even though the chance disappeared with the first blow I landed. Occasionally I can block these feelings out, but more often they suck me in, leaving me mentally spent. And despite the Seroxat for the depression and the Xanax for the panic, the dark side always seemed to prevail.

How quickly fortunes change. Taking a cigarette from a pack in my pocket and lighting it with a disposable lighter, I drew nicotine into my lungs as I sat quietly on the floor trying to work out whatever had happened to the young and enthusiastic Jack Munday, the one that was fresh-faced out of Hendon, full of dreams as he embarked on the career he'd always wanted. I glanced up at the wedding photograph that I still kept close by; the one that Elaine had smashed into a thousand pieces as we both sobbed the night I first begged her not to break us up, the night I first promised her I would change. Happiness was etched all over the faces in the photograph: happiness and hope. I tried to remember the last time I laughed, not out of politeness, but simply out of fun. And I couldn't. There was no fun anymore. I reached up and brought the photograph down to my level. Those were days when we could say so much to each other, and yet equally say nothing at all. They were days when we felt comfortable together, whole, like we belonged, days when we talked of growing old; days when we relished the peaks and troughs of life rather than the monotone of existence. I would give anything to have them back, if only they were still on offer.

But in the here and now, I sat among the wreckage of a once promising future. I felt like I occupied the periphery of life, observing rather than taking part. An existence, rather than a life. I spend my time going through the motions, committed to nothing, working towards the moment each night when I can put my head on my pillow and say, "I got through another day." They'll probably put that on my gravestone. "Here lies Jack Munday, he got through it." What scares me most is that I think I prefer my life this way.

They talk about me being career-minded, 'driven'. How little they understand. It's merely self-preservation. Each hour I put in at work is an hour I don't spend acknowledging what a fuck up I have made of my life. But now there was no avoiding it. Here I was, alone, with my failures, my inadequacies and my insecurities writ large all around me in the one place that I couldn't hide from them – my own mind. What did I have to show for my thirty-eight years? Where exactly are the achievements I'm supposed to be proud of?

"Your late thirties are the time when you're at the peak of your powers," Henry Raven once told me. "You don't get any cleverer after that, you just get more experienced."

Well, life sucked the ambition out of me long ago and left me spending every day since trying to keep a lid on the rage inside and manage the exhaustion it brought. If it weren't so fucking depressing, it would be funny. You start off wanting to make your mark on the world and end up content with just being able to make the mortgage on the house you used to live in. Some achievement.

I LOOKED AT my watch. After six. In my poorly equipped

kitchenette, which would fail any cursory health and safety inspection, the milk had long ago embarked on its transformation into yoghurt and the bread was spawning bacteria that even the toaster wouldn't kill. I settled for black tea, stirring in two heaped teaspoons of sugar and squeezing the tea bag tight against the chipped side of a blue and white Chelsea mug, before dropping it from a height into the large black bag that functioned as my bin.

Before we were married, Elaine and I visited Ireland and stayed in a comfortable, family-run hotel high on a hill overlooking the harbour at Cork. It was an idyllic spot. We promised ourselves we would return, though we never did. During the night I had woken with searing pains in my side, the worst I had ever experienced. I paced the room for hours as she slept and the pain got more and more intense, debating where in the room would be the most romantic place for her to find me dead in the morning. I wanted to be her James Dean or her Kurt Cobain. I settled for a chair in front of one of the large picture windows, the harbour and the rising sun behind me. As I looked again at the images now painted against a similar rising sun in my uncurtained window, I mulled over the difference between the unknown body and me. And if I had spent my last hours here as he had probably spent his, who would notice that I was missing, and even if someone did, who would give a damn?

It was my job, my responsibility and my right to be the one that gave a damn, and to make sure everyone else did too. I wiped a dishcloth from the sink across my face, dropped the cigarette stub into the mug of tepid tea, and looked down at my watch. It was time to get dressed. Two hours until the briefing at the station.

Chapter Nine

"**Y**OU LOOK LIKE shit."

That was Duggan's objective assessment as he marched into my office uninvited at just before eight-thirty. I'd been there less than fifteen minutes and felt as bad as I thought I probably looked. His comment merely confirmed my suspicion.

"Did you sleep in that suit?"

I lifted my eyes as far as they would go and looked as disapprovingly as I could towards him.

"Don't be ridiculous." I watched an aspirin dissolve like a snow scene in a glass of water in my hand. "It was just a bit of a bad night."

He passed no comment.

"The team are in the incident room, waiting, but you've still got time for this." He placed a polystyrene cup on the desktop. "Drink it. You need something to bring you back to life."

"Isn't that more likely to finish me off completely?"

I sipped from the cup. In the short walk from the canteen to my office, all warmth and flavour seemed to have deserted the tea. The tepid liquid sent something of a shiver down my spine. I was having one of those days where nothing tasted of anything, everything tasted of my tongue, and my tongue tasted of cardboard.

"You know, you can talk to me about it if you want to. You don't always have to look on me as a subordinate officer. You could start looking on me as a friend."

I have to admit, he took me a little by surprise. I've never been good with opening up to people. In fact, I don't ever recall confiding anything of importance in anyone. I've always viewed the type of friendship where one person regularly unburdens their heart to the other as in some way artificial, not born of real life or real problems; friendships created for television or movies. I know from experience that knowledge is power; the minute you show weakness, your problems begin to mount. Trust nobody and no-one can get at you. So I keep my feelings to myself, locked away from the parts of my life with which they are not connected. I only let the world see as much of me as it needs to. And that's why I keep the real me, whoever he is, behind the mask that I wear for others.

"Really, there's nothing to talk about."

Harry sat unmoved in his seat. I sipped again from the cup, our eyes not moving far from each other.

"And you expect me to believe that?"

I was taken aback as much by the fact that he had pursued the conversation at all as by the challenging, persistent tone in his voice. I tried to speak slowly and calmly, but inside a rage was building, not as I had expected towards Harry, but towards myself. No matter how much I might want to, I couldn't bring myself to open up and tell him the truth. It was just a step too far.

"To be honest, I don't really give a shit what you believe."

I felt terrible as soon as I said it. He was only being considerate and instead of being polite and just gently pushing him away, suddenly I sounded vindictive. But where I would have walked out on the conversation there and then, he sat resolutely in his seat, just watching me with an intensity that was starting to work its way under my skin.

"What's it all about, Jack? Elaine? Connor? Or you?"

I slumped down onto the corner of the desk and rested my heavy head in the upturned palms of my hands.

"Don't go there, Harry. Just leave well alone."

"You've got to speak to someone, Jack. If it's not me, then find someone else. You may think that nobody's noticed, but don't forget I've seen the way you've been living and what you've been living *on*. And you've got to do something about it, about *her*."

I stood away from the desk and looked out of the window onto the station car park. The morning sun was already glaring off the roofs of the cars beneath. I couldn't bring myself to face him. I sensed him stand up and begin walking towards me. He stopped after three or four paces and started the conversation over.

"Listen, I know things have been hard, but it's been four or five months now and you're getting to the time when you're going to have to face facts and move on. You're certainly not going to win her back by continuing to wallow in self-pity like this, if that's what you think. I know she did you over, treated you badly, but you've got to show her that you're bigger than all that."

How little Harry really knew. How different would his perception of me be if he knew the truth, the whole truth, and nothing but the truth? And you could multiply the damage if the truth got out even further. Like the proverbial Pandora's Box, once the lid's off, there would be no getting it back on again.

We stood in silence for a few seconds before I responded. I felt cold inside, completely dispassionate. And it frightened me.

"Tell me, is all this affecting my ability to do my job?"

"Not yet."

I swung round to face him. Suddenly I felt venom towards him. The same venom I had felt towards Elaine on the night it all went wrong. The red mist was descending.

"Well, then call me back when it is."

The look on Harry's face was the same look of disappointment that my father would use when I was younger. He turned to leave the room.

"Like I said, the team's waiting. And I'd splash some water on your face before you come in. The Chief Super will be there. I don't think you want him to see you looking like that."

He closed the grey painted door behind him.

MY ENTRANCE INTO the Incident Room went relatively unnoticed. I had taken Harry's advice and stopped off to smarten myself up. There was only so much I could do, though. The wash at least brought a healthier colour to my face, in spite of the darkening five o'clock shadow, but my shirt was creased to buggery and still grimy around the collar, and the tie had the remnant of some meal or another up near the knot. A nicotine patch on my arm was clearly visible through the sleeve. I brushed my hair, but it was lank, so any improvement was only going to be minimal. I just prayed that nobody came close enough to smell me.

There were six or eight people in the Incident Room, a couple reading through files, drinking the same disgusting tea that Harry had brought to me, the rest huddled around something more amusing in one of the morning tabloids. On the left hand wall, a pin board had been adorned with half a dozen eight by six inch colour photographs: three of the corpse in various positions, at the scene and in the mortuary, including one close-up of the face, three more showing different aspects of the scene at the charity shop.

"Listen up, boys and girls," bellowed Harry, in his gruff Welsh brogue. "The bell's gone and playtime's over. Gather round and we'll tell you a story."

I coughed, more out of habit than nerves, and squeezed my hands together in a vain effort to give me added strength. Yet it is in situations like this that I feel most comfortable, most in control. Having everyone looking to me for a lead still gives me a real rush and, what makes it better, is that it's the one thing that I know I'm good at. In fact, very good. It's just everything else I'm shit at.

I was making a start on the preliminaries when heads turned at the sound of the door at the back of the room being pushed forcefully open. The not insubstantial frame of Chief Superintendent Brian Morgan, resplendent in uniform, silver buttons gleaming like diamonds on a swathe of black satin, moved forward into the main body of the Incident Room, seemingly unaware or more likely unperturbed that he had interrupted proceedings before they had even got underway. He liked the fact that he was now the subject of everyone's attention. He sat on the desk furthest to the back of the room, nodded in the general direction of the team, lifted his heavy hand to check the gold watch on this left wrist and then, with one lofty wave of the same hand, gestured for me to continue. All bar one officer returned their attention to the front.

"The DI's this way," barked Harry in the general direction of Mike Sheridan, a likeable young DC, full of promise, most of which he was still to fulfil. Sheridan responded with a start, the embarrassment at being singled out prompting a nervous cough not dissimilar to my own, and a redness that graduated from his neck up and across his face.

I stepped forward.

"Good morning, everyone. Thanks for being here."

There were a few nods, a few grunts, and a couple that seemed unsure whether they needed to respond at all. I moved across the room towards the board that held the photographs. Nine pairs of eyes followed me.

"Ladies and gentlemen, as you know, yesterday morning we took possession of the body of a white male, aged probably in his late thirties, which had been kindly donated to the St Margaret's Hospice 'Nearly New' shop in Kingsmere Lane."

I took a transparent, plastic ruler from the closest desk and pointed to the photograph on the board that depicted the body still in the black plastic bag outside the shop, and then to a red sticker on the local street map which indicated the location of the shop.

"As of now, nobody appears to have reported him missing, and we have no tangible idea of who he is. It wouldn't take the sharpest brains in the force to recognise that first priority is to get a name for him."

I was surprised to find at least three of the team, DC Sheridan among them, taking copious notes. It was particularly odd, given that I hadn't yet told them anything that they didn't already know.

"The post-mortem has revealed a number of things that may or may not be relevant. First, the primary cause of death appears to be strangulation. I say primary because..." and I pointed my ruler at a close-up photograph of the victim's arm..."the pathologist found needle marks on the inside of the guy's forearm, along with evidence of heroin and cannabis in his blood stream. Now, we don't believe that this was enough to kill him."

"Do we know if he was a dealer or just a user?" asked Sheridan.

"Didn't you hear the DI, sonny?" interrupted Harry. "We know fuck all about him at the moment, not even his name."

I thought that the response was unnecessarily harsh, something which others seemed to pick up on from my stare in Duggan's direction. I didn't want him taking his frustration with me out on a young guy like Sheridan.

"DS Duggan's right. We have no idea."

Sheridan continued, oblivious to the risk of derision from his colleagues, ignoring the old adage that if you find yourself in a hole, stop digging. Enthusiasm and eagerness to please can be wonderful things, but if they get in the way of an investigation, they can also be a pain in the arse.

"It's just that I thought if he was a dealer," Sheridan swallowed hard as he realised he had become the sole focus of the room's attention, "this could have been a drug hit. I don't know, maybe he sold someone a bad batch or something."

I smiled inwardly. Harry Duggan could hardly criticise the lad now for coming up with the same scenario that he had done as we left the mortuary. I didn't want to cut Sheridan dead and kill off his fervour so early. If we had the same passion from every officer in the force, we'd probably solve most of our crimes in half the time. But the more I had thought about it during these past twenty four hours, the less it looked like a professional job, and I could see the others in the room had already disregarded it as a non-starter.

"We've thought about it but it doesn't bear the classical hallmarks of a drug hit. It's not clean enough. Why strangle him and drug him, when you could just blow him away from the back of a motorbike as he walked down the street?"

"Poetic justice? Kill him with the batch of heroin that he stitched you up with?"

"So why strangle him? And why then bag him up in a bin liner and dump him, why not just leave him where you've killed him? I'm not saying no, Mike, I'm just saying it doesn't quite hang together. But why don't you go visit the drop-in centres and the rough sleepers, see if anyone shared a joint or a syringe with him."

"Did forensic come back with anything on the bag?" asked Hilton, a smart, savvy young woman in her late twenties, who looked more like a successful City executive than a copper. She carried supreme self-confidence around with her as an extra weapon in her armoury.

"Not yet. We hope to have that back later today, but you can bet your life they were wearing gloves."

"Well, that would look odd in itself," she continued. "Someone wearing gloves on a baking hot Bank Holiday would stick out like a sore thumb."

"If anyone saw them. Which takes me neatly forward to my next point. There appear to be no closed circuit cameras close enough to get a good view of the scene, so we need to do another house-to-house today to see if we can find anybody who saw anything, and I mean *anything*. I want you to speak to anyone who left donations outside that charity shop this weekend, even if it was just a solitary paperback book. I want a clearer idea of what time the bag with our friend in was donated.

And another thing; I'll spare you the details, but it seems like our man enjoyed a Chinese take-away on Sunday evening a couple of hours before he met his maker…"

"I know some take-aways where the food alone would have been enough to kill him," interrupted Danny Thorne, a wide-boy DC with aspirations to make DS but probably without the application to succeed.

"Well, visit them. DS Duggan's got multiple copies of the corpse's face, enough for all of you. Hawk it around, find me someone who remembers him ordering a number sixty four with rice."

Danny Thorne nodded as if he felt the joke had backfired on him.

"One more thing; there is also evidence to suggest that he had sex shortly before he died."

"See, Sheridan," piped up Danny Thorne again, "even he can get laid."

I found it hard not to smile. Even the Chief Super seemed to have a hint of a smirk. Mike Sheridan ignored the comment, and I waited for a few seconds for the laughter to die down.

"All I am saying is that if he was having sex with his wife, girlfriend or mistress, you would have expected one of them to start getting concerned by now."

"Unless she did it?" offered Sheridan.

"It's a possibility, but so is the idea that he was getting his end away with a prostitute or somebody else's wife or girlfriend. Rob and Paul, you start talking to the local pros and see if any of them have given him the benefit of their service."

Rob Shaw and Paul Price, both good solid officers who worked well together, nodded in unison.

"Ladies and gentlemen, I don't know if we're dealing with a domestic, a business dispute, a jilted lover, the first victim of a serial killer or even Mike's drug hit. What I do know is that we can't pass first base until we put a name to this guy. So get out there now and do your worst, and get straight in touch with DS Duggan or me if you've got anything to report. And I want a name by the end of the day."

As I turned away the team thronged around Duggan to collect packs of photographs, maps, and a summary of the bare facts to take onto the streets with them. At the back of the room Brian Morgan had lifted himself up and was moving slowly towards me, like a wide load on its way down a motorway. We moved to one side, away from the departing officers.

"So what's your gut reaction?" he asked.

"I'm not sure I've got one yet. But if you pushed me, I'm halfway between the jilted lover or the jilted lover's husband and a bit of business that went wrong."

"Not the drugs?"

"Don't think so. I mean even the sex could be a red herring. Everything we know at the moment could be irrelevant. Why?"

"I had a reporter on this morning asking if it was a drug-related killing."

"I don't know where he got that idea from, because we

haven't said anything other than confirming that a body was found."

"He was probably just flying a kite."

"Well let's hope he won't fly any more."

"I've got to tell him something, you know."

"Why?"

"Because it's just the way it works. It's all you scratch my back and I'll scratch yours. If we block them out of something like this, they'll not keep quiet when we really need them to."

"Just tell them we're pursuing a number of lines of enquiry."

"And if they want more detail?"

"Tell them the first one we're pursuing is to find out who the hell he is. If they can help us do that, maybe we'll give them a bit more."

"Are you alright, Jack? You seem under more pressure than normal, not quite your usual self."

"A bad night thinking about an unnamed corpse, that's all."

"Are you sure that's all?"

"Positive."

"Good," said Morgan unconvinced. "Walk with me."

We left the Incident Room and set off at a slow pace through the rabbit warren of corridors and out into the brightness of the car park. Behind us the red brick 1970s architecture of the station closed off at least some of the sunshine. It was a functional building to which (it seemed) almost no design thought had been given. Save for the blue light outside, it could have passed for any anonymous office block, whilst inside it conveyed the same functionality and formality as any public building: a school, a hospital, or a council office. Everything about it was utilitarian in nature; the chairs, the tables, the painted walls, the noticeboards, even the light fittings were a triumph of the ordinary over the stylish. It may have only been nine-thirty in the morning, but already you could tell it was brewing up into another sultry, late-summer day. We stopped next to the Chief Superintendent's dark green Jaguar, a young uniformed constable waiting attentively on the far side ready to open the back door for Brian Morgan to climb in.

"I had a phone call yesterday afternoon from an old mate of mine at Scotland Yard. He just wanted to tip me off that your promotion to DCI has been approved."

I nodded.

"I thought you'd be more thrilled."

"Sorry, sir. I am, really. Thanks for telling me."

I just couldn't muster the excitement that he was looking for, because putting in for the promotion had been Elaine's idea, a way of building our future together. Now it hardly seemed to matter.

"We won't get formal notification for a couple of weeks. But I've got to tell you that because of budgetary constraints, I simply don't have a DCI's role here at the moment. I'm sorry."

I nodded again. It wasn't a surprise.

"You can wait, but it could be a long wait, and there's no absolute guarantee that the job would be yours when it came up. It would also mean staying as a DI for the time being. Or I can ask around for you, see if there are any other DCI posts going."

I think he could tell my mind was elsewhere.

"There's no rush to decide." He placed a paternal hand on my shoulder.

"Whatever," I smiled.

He smiled back reassuringly before climbing into the car and pulling the door firmly shut behind him.

Chapter Ten

TWO DAYS AFTER the discovery of the 'body in the bag', as the press had chosen to label it, we still had precious little to go on.

Nothing solid had emerged from the first round of house-to-house enquiries and, even after such a relatively short period, I had begun to detect the earliest signs of despondency among the team. We live in an age of instant results, a world where if you want something, you simply log on and buy it, and if you want someone, you can call them, text them, or email them and you know they will pretty much always be within reach. Solving a murder doesn't come quite so instantly, particularly when you have no idea who the victim is.

The press and, because of *them*, the public sometimes choose to overlook the painstaking work that goes into piecing together endless strands of disparate information, which may or may not be relevant to the case. Though in this instance, we barely had the strands. These days, it's all about results and how quickly you can get them.

Some people really do believe that we function like a TV cop show, where the crime is committed, investigated and solved all within an hour, with time left over at the end for a humorous comment and some jaunty theme music. Were that it was.

I sat in my office that Thursday morning like an expectant father, waiting for important news to be brought to me. But expectant fathers at least know there is an end in sight. We aren't afforded such a luxury. And so, we waited. Still nobody matching the corpse's description had been reported missing. Photographs of his face had been circulated among the team and had been hawked around the streets but so far to little effect. Now they were doing the rounds of known drug dealers, drug drop-in centres, prostitutes, and even the winos and the rough sleepers that were known around the area. But to date, the underclass had produced nothing of note. Of course, we didn't even know if our man was a local. After all, if you'd just despatched someone to meet his maker, how far away would you want to drive to dispose of the body?

"Coffee?"

Duggan switched on the electric kettle that I kept hidden in the filing cabinet in the corner of the room. Like the toaster I kept in the drawer below, the kettle had officially been outlawed since the introduction of mandatory portable appliance testing to ensure compliance with health and safety regulations. I refused to be condemned to canteen coffee on such spurious grounds.

"Go on, then," I tilted my dirty cup in his general direction and pulled a pack of Rich Tea out of my briefcase.

"How calculating do you need to be to dump a body the way this one was dumped?" The kettle threatened to give us both an impromptu sauna. "I mean, killing someone's one thing, but then having the wherewithal to get rid of them like this; that takes a bit of doing. It's almost something to admire."

"There's a difference between a person who kills out of unstoppable rage or because they feel suddenly threatened, and someone who kills having first sat back and thought it all through in his mind," I replied. "It takes a certain kind of person to be a murderer. And that's what makes me think that this couldn't be a spur of the moment thing."

"All planned in advance?"

"Maybe. If it was a rash, spontaneous reaction, wouldn't it have been more violent, more frenzied? You know, a stabbing, a shooting even. After all, if someone had pushed you so far that you were about to snap, wouldn't you just grab whatever was nearest and get rid of them that way? I can't put my finger on anything in particular but something about this just seems too damned calm."

"Maybe he knew the murderer?"

"Most victims do."

"Well that would mean there could be a history, a dispute, something that would be difficult to keep completely to yourself."

"Somebody else knows about it, because for sure it took two people to move that body." I bit into my biscuit, brushing crumbs away from my tie as they fell. "But I tell you something for nothing, it's all worth shite unless we find out who he is, and I'm getting sick of telling Morgan that we still don't know."

I looked out of the office window across the vivid blue sky, watching the heat haze rise, in search of inspiration. None came.

"Just supposing it's the lover theory," Duggan speculated.

"Our man's been getting his leg over with some lucky lady, whose husband or boyfriend finds out and isn't best pleased. So he does away with him."

"Why doesn't he just confront his wife and tell her to end it?"

We did this from time to time, almost in the style of a parlour game where one person starts a story and challenges the other to carry it on.

"Maybe he does and she refuses," continued Harry.

"So why hasn't she reported her boyfriend missing?"

"He did away with her as well?"

"It's possible I suppose, but then where's her body?"

"No-one's found it yet. Or like you said, maybe the body was driven here from somewhere else."

"And where's the evidence?"

Harry shrugged his shoulders.

"It's a bit farfetched. I've got a better idea for the time being, let's concentrate on the body that we've got – not the one we *may* get tomorrow."

A knock on the office door rattled a loose pane of glass in the frame. Before the handle turned I could make out the figure awaiting an instruction to come in. Mike Sheridan didn't enter automatically, but stood, hunched forward, ear to the glass, pending a response.

"For Christ's sake, Sheridan, come in."

The corroding brass handled turned and the apologetic young officer entered and leant sheepishly against the grey filing cabinet that held the kettle and the toaster.

"You've knocked once, Mike, you don't need to wait for a printed invitation."

"Sorry boss." He glanced down at the steam that was

rising from my prohibited tea and coffee making facility. Its presence seemed to distract him momentarily. "There's a couple of things I thought you'd like to know about."

I tried very hard to not give the impression of short temper or impatience, but sometimes waiting for Sheridan to deliver information bordered on the painful. He's a bright lad, likeable and more capable than he realises, but sometimes you just need him to cut to the chase without the preamble he so often feels obliged to provide.

"Forensic's come back on the snatch of newspaper that was found in the body's fist. It's too small to get much in the way of fingerprint assistance from it, but they *have* been able to trace it to a copy of *The Times* from a month or so ago."

Okay, I thought, it's not much, but it was still the first piece of information we'd had and, without knowing it if was useful or not, I was just happy to seize upon it as some kind of evidence of progress.

"We'll need a back copy so that we can decide if it's relevant or not."

"Already ordered." Sheridan's face displayed the hint of a satisfied grin.

"Well done, Mike, we'll make something of you yet."

I stood and pulled my jacket off the back of my chair and signalled for Harry to do the same.

"Are we going out?"

"I think it's time we visited our troops in the field," I replied, buoyed up by this chink of light in an otherwise underground tunnel of an investigation.

"There was just one other thing," interrupted Sheridan, coughing politely as we pushed past him towards the door.

"Uh huh," I called, turning back.

"Rob Shaw just called. They've drawn blanks with the hookers and the dealers, but he's found a homeless lad who thinks he recognises our man."

"Well where the fuck is he?" I snapped, letting my excitement get the better of me.

"In the park," he replied, slightly shaken. "At the kids' playground."

Chapter Eleven

I HADN'T BEEN in a kids' playground since, well, probably since I was a kid. I can't even recall going to one with Connor. But then, I can't remember doing much with Connor. That had been part of the problem all along. Duggan parked alongside some crudely cut flower beds bearing rose bushes in full bloom. The sun beat down on the petals, burnishing them to a high shine and giving a kind of unnatural depth to the colours: yellows edged with a deep peach, white trimmed with a delicate pink, and a deep crimson red. Ah, red roses. No, I shan't dwell on red roses.

We walked together along the tarmac path that cut a swathe between two vast areas of grass – one marked out in the shape of a cricket pitch – and down two steps that led into a concreted, sunken garden held beneath a dark wooden pergola. Climbing plants twisted and turned their way around the wooden structure and, overhead, created the sense of shade if not actual relief from the heat. We continued across, past green iron benches defaced with black marker pen graffiti, and up a further couple of steps on the other side. I glanced sideways at the last bench and caught sight of what was written. Apparently Tina loves Jamie. Good for them.

The playground was visible now, as were Rob Shaw and Paul Price, like twins or bookends in identical short-sleeved white shirts, their backs to us, clearly in conversation with a third person who, legs apart, was completely blocked from our view.

"My turn next on the swing," I called out as we moved within earshot. Both men turned as if pre-programmed to do so, Shaw walking to meet me halfway. Their movement revealed the rest of the third person. A young, dark-haired lad, probably in his late teens. He sat on the roundabout, each arm over one of the metal handrails, his clothes as dirty and as poorly maintained as the roundabout itself.

"I wasn't sure you'd got the message," Shaw commented, in a way that suggested he hadn't been entirely confident that Mike Sheridan would pass it on.

"Eventually." I nodded. He returned a knowing smile. "Well, don't keep me in suspense, Rob, introduce me."

Ben Hailey stared relentlessly down at his decaying trainers as we walked across to meet him. Even when Shaw explained who I was, his head remained bowed and no movement was made towards making eye contact.

"Hello, Ben."

Nothing was returned. I held my hand out but it went unshaken.

"My colleagues here say you think you might recognise the man in our photograph. Is that right?"

There was just the hint of a nod.

"Can you tell me his name?"

Nothing.

I turned and walked a few paces away with Rob Shaw.

"Has he been this talkative all morning?"

"I told Sheridan he recognised the stiff. I didn't say he was particularly thrilled to tell us about him."

"There's a difference between not being thrilled and being a mute."

"We could take him in for withholding information?"

"And you think that will make him speak?"

Shaw shook his head.

"You need to go on a psychology course. You have no…what do they call them…inter-personal skills. If ever I need a nut cracked, I'll remember that you're the guy with the sledgehammer."

Shaw smiled.

"Do me a favour; go for a walk a minute. Take Price and DS Duggan with you." I dug into my pocket and pulled out a five pound note. "Buy yourselves an ice cream or something. And get me one too, with a flake in it."

I returned to the roundabout and propped myself up against the section next to the one in which Ben Hailey sat.

"I haven't been on one of these for years," I muttered, more to myself than to him, pushing off with my right foot as I did so to give the roundabout momentum. "Not since Debra Marks, in fact. She was the year above me at school. Face like an angel and tits the size of footballs. I think all of us made a play for Debra. We used to meet in a park like this, sit on the roundabout, share a secret ciggie and then go for a quick fumble in the bushes."

Still there was little reaction from my companion as we spun faster and faster. The park was beginning to become something of a blur, noticeable features coming back into view more quickly with each spin. I don't know why, but the faster we turned, the louder my voice seemed to become.

"I need you to help me, Ben. You see, I've got this bloke lying in a mortuary that nobody seems to be missing. I can't do anything till I know who he is. Frankly, it's beginning to piss me off."

No response.

"DC Shaw and DC Price seem to think you might know him."

We turned faster still.

"If it's you you're worried about, don't be," I yelled. "I'm not interested in what you're up to. Trust me, I've got enough on my plate."

Still no comment from the youngster. I bent down as we completed another revolution, what wind there was rushing past us at a pace, and got as close as I could to Ben Hailey's ear.

"Terrible thing, to die and nobody notice, don't you think?"

He looked up at me, his complexion paler than I had imagined.

"I think I'm going to be sick."

"Will you talk to me?"

"I'm telling you, I'm going to throw up unless you stop this fucking thing."

"Yes, but will you talk?"

He nodded. I dragged my right foot along the ground, doing irreparable damage to my shoe in the process, until the roundabout came to rest again. Ben Hailey threw his eyes up to the heavens and gulped in air. After a couple of minutes of deep breathing, he turned to look at me.

"Anybody ever told you you're a wanker?"

"My wife, constantly."

He smiled. Connection made.

"So will you help me?"

"Like I told the others, I don't know much. I just know the face."

"Right now I'll take all the help I can get."

We sat quietly for a few minutes, just looking round, enjoying the tranquillity and the calm after the excitement of the roundabout ride. I reached into my inside pocket and took out my copy of the corpse's photograph. I held it out in front of Ben.

"So what can you tell me about him?"

"Not much. He's just a guy I used to see around and about. You know, when you're living rough, you get to know the regulars."

"And was he living rough?"

"Not sure. I never saw him in any of the usual places, and he always looked at bit too clean to be living on the streets. He may have had a hostel place, I guess."

"Is that where you sleep?"

"I didn't think this was about me."

"It's not. I'm just being polite."

"No, I prefer the open air."

"Do you mind if I ask why?"

He looked at me as he took a cigarette from his pocket and lit it. He was vulnerable, younger than I had first thought, but with an edge of independence that had probably been the key to his own survival.

"I use the soup kitchens from time to time but not the hostels." He coughed as he inhaled, not a smoker's cough but a real bronchial bark that suggested he needed medical help. "They say the hostels are manned all through the night, but that's bollocks. And if you're the only teenage boy in a dorm full of middle-aged men who haven't had their leg over in a while, well, use your imagination."

I nodded, but it seemed to be a point he was determined to make.

"So don't go labelling me a rent boy, Mr Jack Munday, because I'm not. I don't bend over backwards for anyone."

"Point taken." I tried not to smile at his indignation.

Ben sucked again on the cigarette in his hand, his dirty fingers wrapped tightly around it, as if someone was about to prise away the most precious thing in his world.

"What happened to him?" he asked, pointing at the photograph.

"We're not sure. All we know is that he turned up in a black plastic bag outside a charity shop last weekend. We're not even sure how he died."

"That's a bastard. And it's a shame, he seemed a good sort."

"So if you don't know him from a hostel or from sleeping rough, where did you come across him?"

"There's a café down near the library, a really greasy spoon. I spend as much time as I can in the library to keep warm and also because I like to read. But the women who work there, they just look down on me and try and make out that I'm causing a problem, until I leave. So then I wander down to the café and hover around there. Sometimes, when it's not too busy, the guy that owns it, Mario, he lets me in and gives me a mug of tea and some toast to keep me going."

"So?"

"So, your man was often in there when I was, and we'd pass the time of day, speak and that. He knew I liked to read and so he'd chat to me about books."

"Do you know his name?"

Ben shook his head.

"No. Names don't seem to be important any more. You sit on the street and wait for people to throw you some loose change. Occasionally, if you're lucky, they won't look on you like something they've trodden in or, even worse, that awful look of pity. But nobody ever asks your name. Who's interested? It's all part of being a statistic rather than a person, I suppose."

"Would you show me the café?"

Ben nodded.

"There had better be some food in it for me."

Duggan, Price and Shaw were approaching us with arms laden with ice cream cones. I stood up and off the roundabout as they came within earshot.

"Dump your ice creams, Harry," I called. "You, me, and Ben are going out for a late breakfast."

Harry stared in half surprise but chose not to seek further clarification at this stage. I despatched Shaw and Price to continue their enquiries elsewhere and, Ben Hailey alongside us, we started to walk back through the sunken garden to the car.

"Just one thing," Ben asked, as I held the back door open for him.

I nodded.

"How far did you get with Debra Marks?"

I laughed a little at his nerve.

"Not as far as I just got with you."

Chapter Twelve

STEAM FROM THE urns and the griddles contributed to the condensation which trickled like a stream down the inside of the windows of Chez Mario. I watched as it dripped from the white-painted beading around the base of the sill to form little puddles on the tiled flooring at the sides of the main door. A small rotary desk fan was ineffectual in its attempts to spread a cooling breeze across the eating area, but far more successful in conveying the aroma of frying bacon and fat. Fading, discoloured pictures of once appetising meals clung to the walls behind Mario's counter, sharing the space with bright coloured stars cut from fluorescent card, advertising particular 'meal deals' to the regulars. In the refrigerated cabinet, a succession of oval stainless steel dishes held a variety of sandwich fillings, from 'Mexican Tuna' to 'Egg Mayo and Crispy Bacon Mix', though I quickly formed the impression that all looked too healthy for Mario's regular clientele. I was in no doubt that this was the spiritual home of the fry-up. Mario, I suspected, probably got through more oil in a week than Shell.

Cheap net curtains were strung along the inside of the windows, though in many places they clung to the glass where departing eaters had inadvertently pushed them up against the condensation with their backs. Evidence of Mario's Italian roots was all around, from the outdated calendar displaying breath-taking scenes of the Italian lakes and the framed portrait of the Pope to the yellowing poster of the great Juventus side of the late 1980s: a little piece of Turin in this suburban part of London.

We settled ourselves down at a table just inside the door, pushing the condiments to one end to give ourselves more room. I could tell that Duggan was less than impressed. He played nervously with the sugar while I attempted small talk with Ben.

"So, tell me how long you've been living rough."

"I thought we agreed this wasn't about me."

"I'm just interested."

Predictably he moved to get up, but seeing as he was confined to the seat by the wall and would have had to push past me to get out, there was little room in which he could manoeuvre. Sensing defeat, he slid back into his seat.

"I left home nine months ago."

"Where's home?"

"Not a chance, I'm not playing that game. You must think I'm stupid. You don't think I'm going to let you bundle me back into a car and drive me back."

"You're dead right I'm not. I couldn't claim the mileage back on expenses."

"That's never stopped you before," muttered Duggan under his breath. The boy tried unsuccessfully to stifle a smile.

"I don't understand the secrecy. I already know your name. If your parents have reported you missing, your details will be on the central computer. I could get your address in one phone call if I wanted to." I confirmed the point by laying my mobile down on the melamine table top for extra effect.

"I'm sorry." He spoke softly, almost apologetically. "Most people see people like me as just another statistic that needs clearing up."

"As DS Duggan here will confirm, I'm not good with numbers. I get paid to solve crimes not clear up statistics. And one more thing: I'm not most people."

He looked straight at me and I could tell he was mentally sizing up whether he thought I could be trusted or not.

"Folkestone," he uttered, after a few seconds.

"So what did you think, the streets of London were paved with gold?"

"No. I just had to get away from home, so I started walking and this was where my legs brought me. I didn't look back because I couldn't take what was happening any more. Once I'd made up my mind to go, I wasn't going to lose my bottle. This was just the direction I happened to going. So I kept on going until I got here, and when I did, I didn't really know what to do next. It's all a bit of a blur now."

"How long ago was that?"

"Eight months, two weeks, three days and…" he glanced down at the grimy watch on his left wrist, "about an hour and a half."

"Not that you're counting."

We both smiled.

"So why not go home? Haven't you made your point?"

"I wasn't trying to make a point, I was trying to keep myself sane, and I haven't gone back because you've no idea how much it took for me to leave in the first place."

A robust middle-aged woman, with dyed red hair and of

Mediterranean appearance, rested her small order pad down on the table top in front of us. Grease stains had given the paper a transparent appearance. She smiled through yellowing teeth. Judging by the generous nature of her frame, I guessed that she had probably paid homage at this spiritual home of the fry-up more often than was strictly good for her. She recognised Ben and projected a warm and genuine smile in his general direction.

"I see you've got friends with you for a change," she smiled. "I hope you're making sure they pick up the tab."

"Don't you worry Maria," replied Ben, more confident than he had been in all the time that we had been together, "they're my meal ticket for today."

"So, what are you three boys going to have?"

Duggan sighed. He clearly took exception at being classed as one of Maria's boys. I was rather flattered. I glanced at the laminated menu, my eyes running up and down the list of poorly spelt choices. Little white stickers had been crudely stuck on top of the laminate where Mario had deemed that the time was right for a price rise, the new figure scribbled on untidily in pen. I took the initiative.

I started, pointing at my selection in the menu to confirm with Ben that it was what he wanted as well, "we'll both have The Full Mario, with extra toast and a couple of mugs of tea."

Maria scribbled furiously.

"Beans?"

"Of course beans."

"Mushrooms?"

"Naturally," I smiled playfully, "otherwise it would only be a half Mario. On the other hand, Mr Duggan here doesn't approve of proper food, so my guess is that he'll want something with leaves."

Duggan looked at me the way a disapproving parent stares at a child that's taken one biscuit more than they were allowed. He concentrated for a moment on the menu and then looked up at Maria.

"Tuna salad sandwich on granary with a cappuccino, please."

"What did I tell you," I said to Ben, "it has to have leaves. Sometimes I think he's a rabbit reincarnated."

At last Harry smiled. I turned back to Ben, who by now was playing nervously with the salt and pepper pots.

"So what were you running from?"

"I try not to think of it as running, more starting over somewhere else."

I laughed out loud. Ben looked offended and moved to leave, only to run into the same problems as before. I pulled him back down.

"I'm not talking to you if all you're going to do is take the piss."

"Who's taking the piss? But, really, listen to yourself; 'starting over somewhere else', couldn't you come up with anything better than that? It's bollocks and you know it is. What are you, seventeen-years old? Seventeen-year olds don't make life-changing decisions like that unless they really can't hack it any more."

Now he looked like a typical teenager, slumped in his chair, his head sullenly bowed.

"If you know all the answers, why ask in the first place?"

I leant forward until our heads were almost touching, putting my hand on the back of his to reassure him.

"I don't know all the answers but I'd like you to tell me.

Maybe I can help."

"What's this got to do with the dead man?"

"Nothing at all, but I can make time for this too. I'm talented like that."

Maria returned to the table with two white mugs of tea and a more delicate cup and saucer for Duggan. I watched as Ben tipped three spoons of sugar into his tea and stirred. We sat in silence for a few moments. I wanted him to realise that the onus was on him to speak next. He sipped from the tea and, despite the oppressive heat of the day, wrapped his hands around the outside of the mug for comfort if nothing else.

"I left because of my father," he said, a few minutes later. "He's an alcoholic, he has been ever since I was a kid."

"Did he hit you?"

He shook his head.

"Did he hit your mother?"

Another shake of the head was followed by another sip from the mug.

"No, nothing like that. He was never abusive; he just drank until he collapsed. Sometimes we would drag him up to bed, sometimes we would just leave him where he fell. But the thing that got to me in the end was that we never ever spoke about it. There was like this conspiracy of silence, as if stopping anyone finding out about him was more important than doing something about it."

"Does he know he has a problem?"

Ben shrugged his shoulders.

"I used to try and talk to him, but it's hard when you're thirteen or fourteen to be the one to bring it up. My mother was too weak to do anything about it. She just turned a blind eye and did her own thing. I guess she'd put up with it for so long, it hardly seemed an issue to her any more. They kind of lived their own lives."

"What about other family, his friends?"

"What about them? It was never talked about and certainly not to me. They may realise something's wrong, I don't know. Now, I don't give a shit. I thought really hard about telling them, you know, letting the cat out of the bag. I thought it might be easier to sort out if other people knew, but every time I wanted to, something inside told me I'd be letting him down, dropping him in it. You know, deep down I still love him. I always have. He's still my Dad."

Ben's emotions began to rise and he started to sob quietly. I put my arm round his shoulder and squeezed. He stopped, wiped his eyes and nose on his sleeve, and took another sip of tea. He apologised. I told him it was unnecessary.

"So this had been building up for years?"

"I grew up afraid to bring friends home. I used to try and avoid it at all costs, simply because I could never be sure what state he'd be in when they arrived. That's about the time that I really realised something was wrong and that this wasn't how it was in everyone's house. I hated not being able to tell anyone about it. I remember when I was younger, ten or eleven maybe, trying to get some kind of reaction out of him, just so that I knew that he knew that I knew. I was off school sick and he was out for the morning. While he was out I took all the empty Scotch bottles that he kept hidden in his study and lined them up in the hall, one on each stair. There must have been fifteen or twenty of them. I didn't care what he did to me just as long as it brought it out into the open at last. If he'd have kicked the shit out of me for doing it, it would have been something, and then we would have had to deal with it.

But no, he came in, stone cold sober, and saw immediately what I'd done. He just hung his coat up and then one by one, without saying anything to me, picked up each bottle in turn and put it back in his study. And that was it, nothing was said, it was never mentioned again."

"So why leave now if you've put up with it for this long? Why not wait until you can go away to college and start putting it behind you there?"

Ben rolled a pack of chewing gum between his fingers and thought carefully before answering.

"Things came to a head before Christmas. Outwardly my father's your regular pillar of the community, well respected and that. So they threw a party for neighbours, people from work, you know the sort of thing. I'd been out most of the day, got home about six-thirty, and there he was, rat-arsed, reeking of Scotch, slumped on the couch. I just felt so angry that he could allow himself to be in this state when they were having people round. I felt humiliated for him. My Mum just said that everybody has a drink around Christmas. But this had nothing to do with Christmas, this was somebody who had completely lost it. He just couldn't give a shit."

"So you left?"

"No, we fought. I tried to tell him how I felt but he just looked at me as if he didn't know who I was or why I was making a fuss. You know, like the lights are on but nobody's home. I just wanted to kill him and get it all over and done with. I've never felt anger like it. I thought I was going to explode, the pressure inside me was just so intense. I swear to God, if there had been a knife there, I'd have run him through."

"So why didn't you?"

"My sister. She pulled me off of him, had to prise my fingers off of his throat. We sat together in the garden for a while and that's when I decided I couldn't stay. I threw some things into a bag and left there and then, and that was the last time I saw them."

"Are you close to your sister?"

"Yep, I love her. I love all of them."

"How old is she?"

"Fourteen. And before you send me on a guilt trip, yes I do feel bad leaving her there, but I wouldn't have been any good to her staying."

"What's her name?"

"Chloe."

"Pretty name."

"Yeah, it is."

Ben reached into his wallet and pulled out a creased, passport sized photograph that showed an appealing young face framed by a golden, blonde bob.

"So now you're away, you can't go back without losing face."

"I don't know. I wouldn't want to go back unless things had changed and I doubt they have. I do know now that it's not as easy as just putting distance between me and them. I thought if I got away, then I could put it all behind me and start trying to be myself. But the longer I've been away, the more I've realised that I could have gone to the moon and I'd still have all the anger there."

"So go home and face them down. Destroy your demons."

"Nice thought, but I think the going home would be harder than leaving in the first place. It takes a braver person than me to do that."

Maria returned clutching two steaming plates of cholesterol, with cutlery wrapped in cheap, white paper napkins. Duggan's sandwich was on a smaller plate and came decorated with an unnecessary salad garnish. We ordered more drinks. The meal was hot and cooked fresh and, laced with generous helpings of ketchup, it tasted good. Duggan looked on disapprovingly as I engineered space in my mouth for some fried bread and a mushroom.

"So tell me about my corpse."

"Not much to tell, really," Ben struggled with a mouthful of sausage. "He just seemed a decent, ordinary bloke."

"What did you talk about?"

"This and that, books mainly. He used to quote literature every now and then, the classics, Shakespeare, Dickens, Hardy, that kind of thing. I mean I don't know if he was accurate, but he never gave me the impression he was bullshitting. I'm more of a Stephen King kind of bloke myself."

"Was he ever with somebody?"

"Not that I saw."

"Did he ever talk about himself?"

"None of us do, not to each other."

"Did he say where this love of literature had come from?"

"Don't think so. I think he mentioned once that he'd been to university."

"Did he say where?"

Ben paused from scooping beans on to his fork and shook his head.

"And you don't know his name?"

Another shake of the head.

"Mario might," he added, gesturing towards the café owner, who was walking in our direction.

Mario was a fleshy, corpulent man in his late fifties. He wore a cheap white shirt with the sleeves rolled back up his forearms, his large stomach encased in an ankle length apron, tied behind his back in a double knot. His jowls hung low a little like a bloodhound and his hair, which he wore greased back, had obviously been coloured. I flashed him my identity card as he came to our table, clasping Ben's hand in a genuinely warm greeting.

"The food was alright for you?" He pulled a seat across from a neighbouring table and reversed it so that when he sat down his chest rested against the vinyl chair back.

"Excellent," I replied, "just what I needed."

I went to explain the reason for our visit, but Ben, growing in confidence, beat me to it.

"Mario, these guys are investigating the death of one of the rough sleepers, you know, the one I sometimes meet in here." Ben took the photograph from Duggan and passed it across to the large Italian.

"Was it murder?"

"We're treating it as very suspicious. We don't know very much about him other than what Ben's been able to tell us. We wondered whether you could add anything?"

"I don't think so. He came in often, sometimes we would pass the time of day, but you know thankfully it's never too long before it gets busy so I don't always have the time to chat."

To my right Ben ran a piece of buttered toast around the rim of his plate to soak up the excess egg yolk and tomato sauce from the beans. Duggan stared at him as if it were the first time he'd seen such behaviour.

Ben folded the dripping slice into his mouth. "He may have been a bit fond of the drink, but he was just a regular guy."

"Was he an alcoholic?"

"I smelled it on his breath. It's not always the same thing."

"Did he do drugs?"

"I never saw him."

I turned back to Mario.

"It must have been two or three days ago. He was in here early, he had his usual tea and toast."

"Was there anything unusual about him?"

"I saw him that morning, as well," chipped in Ben, seeming a little aggrieved that he was no longer the sole object of my attention. "He was leaving as I was arriving. He seemed, I don't know, almost excited."

"Did he say why?"

Ben shook his head again.

"Wait a minute," continued Mario, "he said something about going up to the West End to visit one of those swanky Internet cafes. Something about friends in high places to keep tabs on. He was probably just fantasising to pass the time."

"And you didn't know his name either, Mario?"

"Not directly."

"What does that mean?"

"He was in here a week or so ago and he was talking to a priest. I overheard the priest call him Simon, I think. Yes, it was definitely Simon."

"Do you know who the priest was?"

"No."

"Did it look like they knew each other? Did they seem friendly? Had they arranged to meet, do you think?"

Mario was reeling beneath the weight of the questions. I apologised.

"I don't think they had arranged to meet. It looked as if the priest was taken a little by surprise. From what I remember, they spoke for a few minutes and then the priest went to leave. Your man called him back and that's when I heard the priest call him Simon."

Mario breathed a sigh of relief as if pleased to have finally got out his recollection.

"What do you remember about the priest?"

"Not much. He was young, probably in his thirties, and he had red hair. I definitely remember his red hair."

"Could you overhear their conversation?"

"I didn't try."

I thanked Mario warmly for his hospitality before letting Duggan pick up the tab for the breakfasts. We dropped Ben back at the gates of the park where we had first met. As the car slowed I warned him not to go far in case we needed him again and, as we shook hands, I felt him take the folded ten-pound note that I had placed in my palm. So much for my policy on not giving cash direct to the homeless. He smiled and nodded before firmly closing the door.

Chapter Thirteen

I RETURNED WITH Duggan to the station buoyed up by
the morning's work and with confidence restored that we
were, at last, making some progress. I was keen to see if
any of the others had picked up leads that either supported or
supplemented the assistance that Ben and Mario had given.
It's funny, though, how things can conspire so quickly to take
the wind from your sails. As I pushed the station door open
to walk through a reception area that was littered with more
waiting members of the public than was usual for a weekday
afternoon, our desk sergeant, Tom Grayson, called out for a
word, beckoning me closer to the reception desk.

"Two messages, Jack. Mr Morgan would like to see you
on your return and your wife is in Interview Room One."

"Why, what's she done?"

"Nothing," replied Tom, amused by the sudden alarm.
"She popped in to see you. I thought it would be best for her
to wait in there than out here with all and sundry."

"Thanks, Tom. I appreciate it. Would you let the Chief
Super know I'll be up in ten minutes?"

Tom Grayson had been the desk sergeant at our station
ever since I had been based there. He was a good profession-

al, a thoroughly decent man, happy and content with his lot in life. I suspected that all he ever wanted to be was a policeman and, whilst he seemed to have no ambition for further promotion, you still sensed that he derived enormous satisfaction from the job he did. And the rest of us respected him for it. He nodded and returned to his desk as I made my way through the public areas into the depths of the station and the varnished, but still Spartan, wooden door of Interview Room One. The sound of my entry caused Elaine to start. She turned and smiled. It was an odd reaction, one that conveyed neither love nor enmity.

"Not like you to venture into enemy territory."

"I've never said you were the enemy."

"But don't deny you've thought it."

"Could you blame me?"

I held my hands up in apology. I hated being put on the back foot. I pulled a chair out from the table and sat down. Elaine remained standing. I think looking down on me was the position that made her feel most comfortable.

"Is there a reason for the visit or is it purely social? Only I've a murderer to catch."

"Work still coming first, I see."

"What do you expect? I *am* at work. You came *here*, remember."

She smiled again, more benevolently this time.

"I've no doubt you'll win the rat race, Jack, but doing so still makes you a rat."

"Touché."

"We need to talk."

"Agreed, but it can't be here and it can't be now."

"The situation's beginning to affect Connor."

"No shit, Einstein."

It was a remark born out of the frustration of no longer being in control of the way events were panning out.

"If all you're going to do is sit there and be facetious, then I think I'm probably wasting my time. I didn't have to come here."

Elaine busied herself with the zip on her clutch bag. I glanced down at my watch. It was just past one o'clock. Despite the hearty breakfast at Mario's, perhaps it wasn't unreasonable to take half an hour for lunch.

"Okay, but not here. Let's go for a drive."

As we walked back through the entrance to the station, Tom Grayson caught sight of us as we were preparing to depart. He called after me.

"Jack, where are you going? Morgan's expecting you upstairs."

"Tell him I'm following an urgent lead. I'll be back in an hour. And if Duggan asks, you've not seen me."

Elaine had parked her Ford Focus – *our* Ford Focus – in a permit holders' parking bay down the narrow residential turning, edged by Victorian terraced housing that ran down the side of the station. As it turned out, we didn't drive anywhere, but sat in the car, me in the passenger seat and Elaine in the driving seat. The irony was not lost on me. At first there was just a tense and uncomfortable silence. It had to be broken by someone, I figured, otherwise what was the point of being there?

"So, talk to me. You've pulled me out of a murder enquiry and made me hide from a Chief Superintendent because you wanted to talk. So talk."

Staring straight ahead, she spoke slowly but with a tremor

of nerves in her voice.

"Connor's confused. His confidence has taken a knock, he's nervous about going back to school and…" she hesitated, "…I heard him crying himself to sleep the other night."

"You throw his father out of the house, move in a new guy barely twice his age, all he ever sees or hears is the two of us at each other's throats, and you're surprised it's affecting him?"

"I should have known that this wouldn't be a sensible move." She tried anxiously to fit the key into the ignition, but failed. I reached across and gently pulled the key away.

"Why didn't you tell me about him sooner?"

"I'm telling you now."

"Do you want me to speak to him?"

"No, I want *us* to speak to him. Together. I think we owe him that much."

"When?"

"Tomorrow evening."

"Okay, I'll come round at seven."

This should have been the end of the conversation. It was, on the face of it, the issue that Elaine had come to address. But neither of us moved. The fact that we were alone, together and this close for the first time since that night meant we couldn't leave things unspoken.

"You know, I never had you down as someone who was handy with their fists."

"What do you mean fists? I never punched you."

"No, you never punched me. True. So you just slapped me about a bit rather than punch me. It makes you so much more of a new man. Is it supposed to make me feel better? Because strangely, it doesn't."

"There are only so many ways I can apologise and I think I've just about tried them all. But you're not interested, are you? You don't want an apology, you want revenge."

"You're dead right I want revenge."

"So is that was this is? First step towards getting your own back? What do you want to do, slap me, punch me, kick me? Whatever it is, do it, but don't think it's going to make me feel any worse than I already do."

"And that's supposed to satisfy me?"

"I don't know any more what would satisfy you, and I don't think I've got the energy to carry on trying. I hate myself for what I did. You can choose to believe that or not. But it's the truth. It shouldn't have happened, but it did. I've lost count of how many times I've beaten *myself* up over it, but I know I can't change it now. Every time I close my eyes I relive that night, I go over it and over it in my mind, and if I could take myself back and stop myself from doing what I did, I would. But that's not going to happen. I want to apologise to you, I want to make it up to you, I want us to get along, God knows I want to get back with you and try and make things better than before, but none of that is up to me. And I want to stop having to beat myself up over it."

She watched me speak with a stare which, while intense, was also completely devoid of any emotion, as if the blood in her veins had been replaced with iced water.

"Do they know what you did?" She gestured behind her in the direction of the station. "Your precious colleagues. Do they know you're a wife beater? Maybe I should tell them what kind of guy their revered Inspector is when he's off duty?"

"Don't do that," I pleaded, realising that she was toying

with me, the way a cat paws at an injured bird and then carries it in its mouth. "You've taken away my marriage, you've taken away my son and my home, please leave me with my job. It's the only thing there is left. Do you really hate me that much that you'd tell them? How would it help Connor to see you completely destroy me?"

Her stare thawed a little. She rested her elbow on the steering wheel and her face against her hand. Now the stare betrayed sadness, even pity. She wiped what looked like a tear away from the corner of her eye.

"How did we come to end up like this?"

"If we knew that it probably would never have happened. We'd been together a long time. Maybe we took each other for granted. Maybe we both just took our eye off the ball."

"I don't just mean the splitting up, but all the hatred and the anger. Where did that all come from?"

"I don't hate you, Elaine. That's what makes it hurt so much. I've tried to hate you. I've tried to pretend you don't mean anything to me anymore. Christ knows, I've tried. Just can't do it. Trust me, it would be so much easier to walk away if I hated you. But seeing you with what's his name…"

"Jason."

"…Jason…seeing you with Jason, and Connor with Jason, I can't stand that. It makes me feel sick, worthless, like something you've trodden in. It's true what they say, you don't know what you've got till it's gone."

"Joni Mitchell?"

"Joni Mitchell."

For the first time in months, Elaine smiled at me.

"See, you can't even make your apology original."

We smiled at each other but said nothing.

"You're still beautiful when you smile."

I wanted to pull her towards me, touch her face, smell her scent again, and for her to lean forward and kiss me. Instead I gently placed my hand over hers and, almost instantly, she pulled hers away.

"What do you think you're doing? You don't think I've come to make up with you, do you? I haven't come to make up with you. I've come to talk about Connor."

"What about Connor? We've talked about Connor. We'll talk more tomorrow."

As I spoke I noticed her furiously twisting the white gold wedding ring that she had now moved from her left hand to her right.

"I think we need to make things more formal, you know, maintenance, access, that kind of thing. So we both know where we stand."

"Why? Isn't it working okay as it is? Am I not paying you enough? Or are you trying to drive the two of us even further apart?"

"I knew you'd react like this. It was stupid of me to come."

"It's what you want, isn't it? You want to take me for everything and then, once you've done it, you're even going to take him away from me."

"No, no, of course not. I'm not asking you for more money and I don't want to stop you seeing him. You're his father and I know how much you mean to him. After all, it's us that's splitting up, not the two of you."

I breathed a sigh of relief, which I tried not to let her hear, but it proved to be but a prelude to her coup de grace.

"I just thought it would be easier to do the formal stuff

now, talk like adults and agree it between ourselves, before we start getting lawyers involved."

"Who's getting lawyers involved? What are you saying, that we're getting divorced?"

"No, not yet, but it's a possibility, a probability, you've got to face that."

I shook my head and laughed in resignation. Her look showed me clearly how little she understood or wanted to understand.

"Why do I have to face it? I got in this car hoping…expecting even…that we were going to give ourselves another chance. For Connor's sake, if not our own. And now, you're telling me that it's a probability that we're getting divorced. Where was I when all this was decided?"

I didn't want to face it, because despite my brave speech about moving on and not beating myself up, I knew I still wanted her back. More than anything. But there was an inevitability about all of this, like a train rolling inexorably, gaining momentum towards divorce. I so desperately wanted to pull it back and start again towards a different station.

"What's prompted this? Is it Jason? Do you love him? Is that what you're saying? Do you want to marry him?"

"This has got nothing to do with Jason. Jason just fills a need at the moment. I don't know what the future holds with him. Shit, I don't even know if there is a future with him. And anyway my relationship with him is none of your business."

"It is when it impacts on my son."

"Oh don't get all moral on me. It doesn't suit you."

"And what about my needs, my rights?"

"I kind of lost interest in those when you landed your first punch…sorry, slap."

We sat in silence for two, maybe three minutes. I wanted to say something but fought inside with what I *could* say that wouldn't make the situation worse. What I produced was weak and self-indulgent.

"Duggan's worried about me. He thinks I've been neglecting myself; that I ought to face up to stuff and move on."

"He's right."

"But that's my whole point; I don't *want* to move on. I hate this situation. What happened to working problems out, marriage for life and all that? Why break up at the first sign of trouble?"

"Because it wasn't the first sign of trouble, Jack. Be honest with yourself if nobody else."

"We can work on those things."

"No, we can't." She was insistent to a point that showed how completely powerless I had become to change the situation.

"You hit me, Jack. Hit me. You didn't shout at me, yell at me, throw things at me; you walked up to me and hit me. Do you know how bad that feels? For the man you hoped you'd spend your life with to show you such little regard, such little respect. Why should I give you another chance? So you could do it again?"

"Since the moment it happened I have felt like I've been falling, like I'm not living any more, I'm just going on. I don't feel like I *want* to live at the moment."

"I don't have to listen to crap like that. You've got plenty to live for."

"But not you?"

"No, Jack, not me. Talk to Duggan, you could use a friend."

"Can I see Connor whenever I like?"

"Of course."

"How much does he know?"

"About what?"

"I mean, does he think we're getting a divorce?"

"We haven't agreed that we are, but he's not an idiot. I think he's worked it out for himself."

"Was it the job?"

"Not only the job."

"So where did it all go wrong?"

"You need to make room at the centre of your universe for people other than yourself. That would be a good place to start."

"I can make room now," I pleaded, "for you and for Connor."

"Now's a bit too late for us."

She turned the ignition. I got out of the car.

Chapter Fourteen

"Have you been avoiding me, Detective Inspector Munday?"

Brian Morgan sat full-square behind his substantial desk and looked straight at me with the confidence of a man who knew he was in charge. Despite the size of it, the desk seemed dwarfed, almost intimidated by the stature of the man behind it. Morgan had retained the good looks and athletic frame of his youth and had carried them forward successfully into his late forties. His large hands were interlocked and rested on the desktop in front of him and my eye was drawn to a small gold signet ring on the little finger of his left hand. Occasionally, when the pressure of the job was particularly bad, I had noticed him toy with the ring repeatedly as a way of working out his nerves. Today it went untouched. His tone was formal, laced with the kind of controlled anger that makes you realise you're being backed into a corner. Whether I chose to resist or opted to admit whatever offence I was about to be accused of, either choice was bound to make my situation worse. This was the proverbial spot between the rock and the hard place. I fixed my gaze on a point two or three feet above his eyes and concentrated on not letting my obvious discomfort manifest itself in my body language, an almost impossible task.

"Avoiding you sir? No, I don't think so."

"Maybe I'm mistaken then. It's just that Tom Grayson told me over an hour ago that you'd be up in ten minutes and then, when I decided I couldn't wait any longer, I'm told you've left the station. Surely that can't be true, Inspector?"

The conversation was proving to be something that I worked out for myself a long time ago. One of the people skills that you need to acquire in order to make it to the top of this particular profession is the ability to make subordinate officers squirm at will and then sit back and enjoy the show. It's a kind of psychological torture and Morgan must have passed the test with distinction. Here I was, a relatively senior officer, and felt a freshman out of Hendon.

"I did leave, sir. I had an urgent lead to follow up."

"That would be the urgent lead that looked exactly like your wife?"

So there it was, the killer blow. He knew all along and now he had me done up like a kipper with nowhere to turn. Time to come clean and throw myself on his mercy.

"Sorry, guv, I didn't mean to mislead you, it's just that she showed up unexpectedly and insisted on talking. I thought that the easiest thing in the circumstances would be to go along with her."

"Circumstances. What circumstances?"

"We've been having a few problems. She wanted to talk about our son."

"I know about your marriage problems, Inspector, but we're also trying to catch a killer."

I looked at him as if he had just landed from another

planet. How could he have known? Only Duggan knew and he wouldn't have said anything.

"With respect, sir, how do you know about my marriage?"

"Don't worry Inspector, nobody has breached a confidence. I know because it's my job to know. You've been short with your colleagues, careless with your appearance and working yourself into the ground trying to prove to yourself as much as anybody else that you still have a contribution to make somewhere. I've seen the signs before. I just put two and two together. Call it police work."

"I apologise. I didn't realise I was so…predictable."

For the first time in our meeting, Morgan's face broke into a sympathetic, even paternal smile. He gestured for me to sit down.

"Do you want to talk about it?"

Christ, I thought, *no I don't. Not to you. I don't want my personal problems pored over and dissected in front of me one by one by my Chief Superintendent. In fact, I'm not baring my soul to anyone in this station, Jack, let alone you.* I couldn't tell him that, of course. Not in so many words.

"Do you mind if we don't, sir? I don't feel up to talking."

"Of course not."

I breathed a sigh of relief.

"Do you need some time off to sort things out?"

"Thank you for the option but that won't be necessary. As you said, we have a killer to catch."

"As you wish, but try and not let it affect the way you work."

"Understood."

The intensity of his stare was broken by a brisk double knock on the office door. It was followed after only the most minimal delay by the uninvited entry of Morgan's long time secretary Freda Powell. Freda was small in frame, mature in appearance but was a pocket powerhouse of a woman who had acted for successive senior officers at the station since she first arrived as a newly married thirty year-old in 1975. From what I had heard, her husband had died suddenly on holiday in the early 1980s, though I don't think anyone knew the precise circumstances, and I don't think anyone had ever plucked up enough courage to ask. Since then her role with the force had apparently been one of the main things that had sustained her. What was not in doubt was the huge influence she exerted over the lay staff and others. Canteen speculation had it that she, rather than Morgan, made many of the station's more difficult operational decisions. It may not be as fanciful a notion as it first seems.

She laid a tray bearing a white china teapot, cup, saucer, sugar bowl, milk jug and small plate of mixed biscuits on the corner of Morgan's desk.

"I'm sorry," she said huskily, "I didn't realise the Inspector was in with you. Would you like me to fetch another cup? There's enough in the pot."

Morgan shifted uncomfortably in his seat. He knew of the speculation about their relationship and was keen to dispel it at almost every public opportunity.

"No thank you Freda. The Inspector won't be staying for tea."

She backed out of the office in exaggerated fashion like a courtier leaving the presence of a monarch. He poured himself a cup and offered me a biscuit.

"I thought I wasn't staying?"

"Yes, I'm sorry about that. I just can't take her incessant

fussing. Now, bring me up to speed; where are we with our body?"

For the next ten minutes I told Brian Morgan all that I knew about 'Simon'. He was placated by the lead on the priest and the snatch of newspaper found in Simon's hand, which seemed to give him enough to put out yet another non-committal press statement. Keeping the newshounds from his door at least for another couple of days was obviously his priority.

I LOOSENED MY tie and undid the top button of my shirt as I made my way back down the single flight of stairs between Morgan's office and my own, stopping briefly at the vending machine outside the toilets to buy something cold to drink. Throughout the station the windows were open but there was no hint of a breeze. In fact, not only did the station not have air conditioning, it almost felt as if the heating was on. It wouldn't have surprised me if it were.

I rolled the cold can of Dr Pepper across my forehead as I walked back into my office, enjoying the temporary relief that it gave, before running my forearm once across my brow to dry the sweat. The dampness was such that every hair on my arm was now clearly visible through the large wet patch on the translucent sleeve of my white shirt. I pulled the ring-top on the can and shivered slightly as the ice-cold liquid travelled down through my body.

"They say it could be thirty-two tomorrow." Duggan read aloud from the weather page of that morning's newspaper.

"It can't be far short of that today."

"That's in the shade."

"There is no fucking shade," I shouted, "that's half the

problem."

"You've always been the bloke that complains in the winter that it's too damn cold and says things like 'roll on the hot weather', and now we've got the hot weather, you're complaining about it."

"What's your point?"

"No point really. I heard Elaine was here."

I pulled the chair out from behind the desk and lowered myself unceremoniously into it. Elaine's comments about confiding in someone replayed in my head.

"She was."

"And?"

"And what?"

"Are you getting back together?"

I looked directly at him and then down at the can, which I was unconsciously swirling around between my hands.

"No, we're not. She came to talk about maintenance for Connor."

I don't know what unsettled Duggan more, that fact that it clearly wasn't the reply that he had been expecting or the fact that I hadn't told him to mind his own business. He folded his newspaper, uncrossed his legs and cupped his hands in front of his mouth.

"Shit, Jack. I'm sorry."

"Yep, me too."

I was about to go further – how far, I don't know – when Lesley Hilton tapped on the open door and leant casually against the door frame. I don't know whether it was my newfound status as a single man, but she looked attractive in a way that I hadn't previously noticed: delicate and feminine yet ultimately professional and very sure of herself. I found her confidence beguiling.

"It's about your priest. I've been on to the local diocese like you asked and the only guy that fits that description locally is…" she looked down to consult her notebook, "a Father Thomas O'Neill at a place called St Mary Immaculate. Do you want me to call on him?"

She ripped the page out of her notebook and passed the contact details across. It was less than half a mile from Mario's café.

"It's okay, Lesley, I think we'll take it. It's been a while since either of us has been to confession. It could take some time."

Chapter Fifteen

I STOOD BEFORE the gates of St Mary Immaculate Roman Catholic Church and it occurred to me that, likely as not, the only thing I would have in common with Father Thomas O'Neill would be celibacy. And, though mine was enforced by lack of opportunity, believing just half of what's often said about Catholic priests, I wondered how likely it was that the same might be true of his.

I'm not a deeply religious person. Faith by its nature has to be blind and the moment you try to rationalise it, you begin peeling away the layers like skin from an onion. That has been my mistake. I have simply had to recall the irrational constraints of my religious upbringing to reaffirm my commitment to the course I have taken. In any case, in my line of work, I have to ask too many questions to have blind faith.

The moment I enter any house of worship part of me feels like I have returned to the dark, dismal days of my childhood and all the hypocrisy, inconsistency, and unnecessary constraints that were part and parcel of my parents' religious observance. It's an uncomfortable feeling and even now I could do without it. My mother, who's still a fully paid-up, card carrying member of the good Lord's fan club, despairs of me, taking every opportunity to attribute the problems in my marriage directly to what she views as my 'lax and promiscuous lifestyle'. I am, apparently, reaping what I have sown and am consequently enjoying the rewards of the Devil's work. The difference between us is that I believe I have found more plausible explanations about life, love, and the pursuit of happiness outside of organised religion. I don't need a God in my life to make me happy. I just need my family back. So, two fingers up to Mum. Thank God I'm an atheist.

Looking at the building from the outside, St Mary Immaculate was anything but. Paintwork peeled away from the windowpanes and the rose bushes that huddled the paved pathway up to the front door looked in need of some of the good Lord's attention. Neither could it offer the imposing grandeur of some of the world's most inspiring churches. This was not Cologne Cathedral. There would have been no architectural awards for St Mary Immaculate. A bland hangover from the fifties, it was a small red-brick building positioned almost apologetically on the corner of two residential streets, bordered by typical suburban semi-detached properties each with two cars on the drive. As an area, it was comfortable rather than affluent, though still I suspected the neighbours had enough money in their bank accounts not to feel the need to pray regularly for more. Surely, I thought, if they cared enough for the church they would have mustered sufficient between them to paint Father O'Neill's windows and pay for a gardener to prune his roses.

"As much as I hate places like this, I do feel a certain power entering a church knowing that I've got the law on my side," I commented as Duggan came round from the driver's door of the Mondeo to join me on the pavement.

"That's as may be," he shot back with just a hint of Welsh Presbyterian indignation, "but don't you think the good Father might be able to cite an even higher authority?"

Thomas O'Neill did not fit the stereotype of a Roman Catholic priest. He was young, handsome, a touch over six feet tall and with the form of someone who kept himself fit. His striking red hair was pulled back into a tight ponytail that fell easily over the back collar of his modern, three-button black suit. His white Converse trainers, replete with a bright fluorescent orange pattern, proved that he would be cool enough to appeal to kids yet attractive enough to ladies of a certain age for them to become regular churchgoers. A people's priest. Those ladies would surely have viewed his celibacy as something of a waste. I watched as he strode from the church's unassuming entrance towards us in the sunshine, purpose and confidence the hallmarks of every step. He was too young to be a priest. Priests had always been old men, with snow white hair, bad teeth and a smell you couldn't quite place. They had trouble walking and bore a ruddy complexion as a result of too much communion wine. When the priests are the same age as you, then you can be sure you're getting old.

We introduced ourselves, shook hands and he escorted us back inside the church. It was dark and cool, which in itself came as something of a relief, though shuffling into one of the pews to the rear of the hall brought back even more uncomfortable memories. Duggan slid in alongside me; the young priest sat in the row in front. Duggan produced the photograph of 'Simon' on the slab and passed it across. There was no discernable change in his demeanour, nor any immediate indication that he was about to volunteer potentially useful information.

"Do you know him?"

He coughed twice into the top of a clenched right fist and nodded.

"Yes, I know him. I saw him a week or so ago."

"But you didn't know that he was dead?"

He shook his head in the same manner as before. There was still no noticeable reaction.

"Can you put a name to him?"

His eyes remained fixed on the face of the deceased, as if he were studying the photograph inch by inch for any sign of life. He spoke without looking up.

"His name's Simon Murrell."

"A parishioner?"

"No, nothing like that," he replied, still staring at the photograph. "We were at university together."

"At university?"

"Cambridge. I read theology. Simon read economics, I think."

"You think?"

"I may look young for a priest, Inspector, but it's still twenty odd years since I went to university. We lost contact after we left Cambridge."

He smiled an engaging smile, the smile of a man who could turn on charm at will and lure someone less certain of himself than me back into the religious fold.

"And yet you saw him again only recently?"

"Yes. We first bumped into each other again a month or six weeks ago when the women's committee of all the local churches held one of its occasional soup and sandwich lunches for the local homeless. I went along to provide moral support and spoon out the odd bowl of minestrone. He recognised me rather than the other way round. It's an occupational hazard when you've got red hair."

"So he was homeless?"

"I can't say that with any authority. You don't need to be that far down on your luck to qualify for a bowl of soup. He may have just been going through a bad spell. You must know the type of thing; no job, his wife or his girlfriend has left him, and he has no home to speak of."

"It happens to the best of us." I shifted a little uncomfortably on the hard, mahogany bench. "You didn't think to ask?"

"I try not to force information out of people, Inspector. I find it works best if I wait for them to decide for themselves that they want to talk."

"I suppose that's one of the differences between us, Father. Yet this man was an old friend of yours. That's different, isn't it? Surely you would have been interested?"

"Perhaps, but Cambridge was a lifetime ago, and when you're a priest, Mr Munday, the dynamics are different whether the person you are ministering to is an old friend or not."

"So what did you talk about?"

"Not much really. We didn't speak for long. I just reassured him that no matter how bad his situation was that the church was here for him."

"I'm sure he found that a great comfort. And what about the last time you saw him?"

The priest shifted nervously on his seat, cleared his throat with another short cough and looked directly at me.

"Do I need a lawyer, Inspector?"

"I don't know, Father, do you?"

"I mean is this conversation official, on the record?"

"Let's just call it a friendly, informal, official little chat. We can put it on the record later. Now when did you last see Simon?"

"Maybe a week ago."

"Was that here?"

"Actually no, we met by accident in a café."

"Were you pleased to see him?"

"What are you driving at Inspector?"

"Nothing particularly. Were you pleased to see him?"

"I was neither pleased nor displeased."

"What did you talk about?"

"I think he said how grateful he was for the support he had received from the church but that now he had some money coming in, he thought he was beginning to get his life back together."

"Did he say how much money or where it was coming from?"

"Sorry, no, and I didn't ask."

"And that was the last time you saw him?"

He nodded.

I leant back against the hard wooden structure of the pew and took time to observe Father Thomas O'Neill. There were moments when his boyish enthusiasm was endearing and then others when he exuded a quiet confidence that bordered on conceit. I found it unappealing; it put me slightly on edge. I wanted to know more about him, get myself beneath the charismatic façade and maybe irritate him a little. I stood up and in what space I had in the pew, I stretched and turned slowly full circle to take in the whole of the church.

"Nice place you've got here, Father."

Duggan sighed in despair. Father Tom just laughed.

"You don't have to be polite, Inspector. We all know it's not the Sistine Chapel, but I like to think it's what happens here between individuals that's more important than the baubles and the trinkets."

"And exactly what does happen here between individuals?"

He smiled again and leant back in the pew, trying to adopt a relaxed pose.

"People come, they spend time with me, with other parishioners or just alone with their thoughts. I don't mind as long as they come. I try and make the church something of a haven where people don't have to wait for organised services to enter. They can come whenever they feel they need to take a short time out from the rest of their life. You should try it one day, Inspector. We have no bars on policemen."

We made eye contact for ten seconds or so without either of us speaking. The conversation had the feel of two boxers moving cautiously around a ring, each waiting for the other to make the first move.

"Don't take this the wrong way, Father, but you see I'm looking at you sitting there and there's a voice in my head that keeps on asking me what makes a young, good-looking fellow like yourself decide to become a priest, and a Catholic priest at that?"

He smiled back at me, calmness personified.

"Do you want the unexpurgated or the abridged version?"

"I'll start with the whistle-stop tour. I can always catch up on the detail if it becomes relevant to the enquiry."

He looked at me, stony-faced for the first time at the thought of even remotely being considered part of a murder enquiry. I let my face fall into a smile and then break into a mild laugh. I think, to his relief, he laughed with me, though neither of us knew if I was genuinely joking.

"I didn't hear a voice or see a bright light shining down on me, if that's what you mean," he began. "Gradually, I began to feel something inside me telling me to make my relationship with God stronger. My parents were always churchgoers without being especially religious. I think they liked the social side of it. I used to be quite half-hearted in my attendance. I went because it kept them happy but I wasn't especially interested. Then, while I was studying for my A-levels, I was out with some friends one night, one very wet night, and we were involved in a car crash. The other three were killed and I survived with just cuts, bruises and a fractured leg."

"So don't tell me, you felt a debt to God for protecting you?" I tried to summon up all the clichéd, religious mumbo-jumbo stuff that we atheists adore.

"Not so much that but the longer time went on and the shock wore off, I did find myself wondering why I had survived rather than the others. I became obsessed with understanding why and I began to use the crash to try and put my own life into some kind of perspective. I found that my willingness to attend Mass with Mum and Dad on a Sunday became a real need to attend Mass every day. I began to pray as part of my daily routine and soon I was reading less Frederick Forsyth and more and more of the Bible. It's actually a really good read."

"I'll take your word for it. So you went to read theology at Cambridge."

"I originally applied to read English. I wanted to be a journalist, but I changed my course soon after I arrived, though I don't think at that stage I had decided to enter the priesthood. I thought that was something you felt as a calling and, though I toyed with the idea in my head, I can't say that I felt a calling."

"So what changed your mind?"

"I was back home with my parents for the summer at the end of my first year when their local priest asked me if I had ever thought about the priesthood. I didn't really know what to say to him but it struck me for the first time that other people were beginning to see me in this way. People started to tell me that I would make a good priest and when I went back to Cambridge at the start of my second year, I began to think seriously about it."

"Had you met Simon Murrell by this point?"

"Met him? Probably. Friendly with him? I don't think so. We had divergent lifestyles. I began doing voluntary work through the churches in the town and helping out as much as I could. Simon was living your typical student life. You know, the original good time had by all. We only became friends, strange as that may seem, when our paths crossed later that year through mutual contacts."

"Maybe we can go back to those later?"

He nodded.

"As time went on I began spending more and more time in Cambridge helping a young priest there. I began to be impressed by how much of a difference he seemed to be making to the lives of his parishioners. I explained to him how

I felt and he convinced me that God had brought me there to show me the life of the priesthood. That was probably the point that I decided it was for me."

I listened to him speak, with passion, pride and plausibility and yet the atheist in me still looked at him as if he had in some way been duped, another victim of a giant theological con trick.

"So how did you move things forward?"

"I finished my degree and then explained to the pastor at my parents' church that I wanted to enter the priesthood. He was pleased for me and not at all surprised. He spoke to the Diocesan Vocations Office on my behalf and I entered a year or so of formal discernment with the Diocesan Vocations Office. I spent some time at a seminary after graduation and was ordained just before Easter in 1987."

"And is it a good life?"

"It suits me. Every now and then I sit back in amazement and look at where I've come from."

"Particularly when you meet someone that you haven't seen for years? Someone down on their luck, like Simon Murrell?"

He smiled that smooth, charming smile again.

"It's not about one-upmanship Inspector, if that's what you're driving at."

"Not necessarily, Father, but it must give you a sense of satisfaction, even power, having so much influence over these people's lives, healing the sick, nursing the poor and all that."

He laughed out loud.

"I'm a diocesan priest, Inspector, not Jimmy Swaggert. I can't make the blind see or the crippled walk."

"So tell me more about Simon," I tried to bring the tone

of the conversation back to my business-like territory. "What did he like? Who did he hang around with? What do I need to know about him?"

Father Tom thought quietly for a few moments, before breaking his silence.

"Let me see. He played rugby when he wasn't hung over. But then most of us did. Played rugby, that is, not get hung over."

"But you weren't great mates?"

"Not great mates, but we had friends in common."

"Tell me about these mutual friends."

"I'm not really in touch with any of them any more. Most of them went into very commercial careers. I think they found my vocation a little incompatible with their own. Perhaps they thought I'd always be making judgements about them."

"Do you know if Simon was still in contact with any of them?"

"I don't, sorry."

"Well, do you remember any of their names? Perhaps I can track them down and maybe throw a big reunion party for the lot of you."

"You could try Crispin Monk."

"The politician?"

He nodded.

"My my," I smiled, "friends in high places."

Even *I* knew the name. Crispin Monk was the darling of the Conservative right. Bright, forthright and telegenic, he was a throw-back to Thatcher, espousing the kind of right-of-centre views on Britain's moral decline that many of his contemporaries expected would eventually lead him to the party leadership and, after two thumping election defeats, sufficiently rouse the electorate to enable him to guide his party out of the wilderness and into the political promised land of government.

"Anyone else?"

"You could try Seb Brown. Last time I heard of him he was working for one of the big corporate law firms in the City."

"I don't suppose you know which one?"

He shook his head again.

Father Tom looked thoughtful, giving the appearance of searching mentally for information, before finally shaking his head.

"I can't be sure but I think it was also something in the City. He was quite close to Seb."

"All this was a bit of a come down from the City, wasn't it?" I waved the post-mortem photograph in his general direction.

"Like I said, Inspector, I don't know any of the details. Obviously I'm very sorry about it."

"Obviously. I don't suppose you know where he was staying?"

"We don't ask those who come to the church for help to register or sign in. They're not applying for a credit card or an overdraft. That's why so many of them feel comfortable here. It's how we build their trust."

"And you didn't have that kind of trust with Simon?"

"No, not yet. Like I said, it takes time."

"Did he smoke, Father?"

He seemed a little startled by the switch in the questioning.

"I think so."

"Did he drink?"

"I wouldn't be surprised."

"Heavily?"

"I couldn't say."

"What about drugs?"

"I have no idea Inspector, but again I wouldn't be particularly shocked. When people are down they seek solace and escape in all manner of things."

"Actually, Father, I'm not sure I would be. Believe me, once you've seen some of the sights that I have, there's not much left that can shock you."

Father Tom leant back in the pew and stretched back his shoulders for relief. He glanced anxiously at the Tag Heuer watch on his left hand.

"Are we keeping you?"

"I'm sorry, Inspector. I'm on the board of a Catholic children's charity and we have a board meeting in Westminster at five. I will have to go soon."

"Of course," I tried to be polite enough to make my mother proud. "Just one last thing. As you're the only person to have so far named the deceased, we may need to call on you in the next few days to undertake a formal identification of the body. I'm sure that wouldn't be a problem for you, would it?"

"Of course not. Just let me know where and when."

My back had stiffened by the time we rose, exchanged firm handshakes, and thanked him for his time. Father Tom ushered us towards the heavy wooden door and accompanied us back into the warm sunshine and down the pathway towards the main gate.

"Don't forget," he called after me, "you're welcome any time."

Chapter Sixteen

I KNEW FROM my previous experience that now the 'body in the bag' had a name, press interest would intensify rather than diminish. There would be a scramble to find photographs of Simon Murrell, to interview the same friends and acquaintances that we would ourselves be desperate to meet and to flesh out for the readers every detail of his life and death. I didn't necessarily have a problem with that. I'm long enough in the tooth to know that if you want the press to help you catch a killer, you have to allow them their moment in the sun. I also knew we could use it to our advantage to bring people from Simon's past out of the woodwork and help us piece the puzzle together. The downside, of course, is that if the situation is not managed properly it can place a heavy extra pressure on the investigating team to come up with the answers before the journalists do. Otherwise, they'll just run rings around you.

The team reconvened in the Incident Room a little after nine on that bright Friday morning, four days after the discovery of Simon's body. An overnight storm had broken the oppressive humidity and for the first time in days a gentle breeze navigated its way through the venetian blinds to refresh the previously stale atmosphere in the room. If you were the type that believed in that kind of thing, you might have argued that the renewed freshness mirrored a similar feeling among the enquiry team and was in part responsible for the lift in our morale.

I balanced myself on the corner of a desk adjacent to the pin board that held every photograph and a note of every clue that had been gathered since the previous Tuesday morning. Around the room, members of the team either sat alone waiting for the meeting to begin or stood in small clusters, huddled in conversation. Shaw, Price, and Lesley Hilton talked animatedly to one of the young uniformed officers assigned to the team for CID experience. Danny Thorne, in contrast, was slumped back in a swivel chair, feet crossed casually on the top of the desk, his number two crew cut just visible above the top of that morning's "Racing Post". To the right of me Mike Sheridan studied the incident board with the intensity of someone revising for an important exam. Duggan entered the room, folder under one arm, his fingers struggling to hold on to two obviously boiling cups of vending machine coffee. He placed the plastic beakers down on the table next to me and we looked together at the strangely coloured brown liquid that was topped by a definitely unnatural looking froth. Harry shrugged his shoulders as if to say, "it's the best I could do."

A loud cough was enough to secure the team's attention. Most turned from what they were doing and moved slowly towards the front like a pack closing in on its prey.

Thorne removed his feet from the top of the desk, folded his newspaper and stretched to the point where his shirt came out of the top of his trousers. He let out a loud and exaggerated yawn. I stood up from my position on the desk and looked back at the mass of faces waiting expectantly for instruction. I clasped my hands together tightly before starting.

"Okay, so even I'm prepared to admit we've had a couple of good days but let me tell you, it will mean sweet FA if we don't keep our feet down on the gas and try and put this thing to bed as soon as we can."

I glanced around to see nods of agreement.

"Let's recap on what we know and then we'll talk about what we don't. Simon Murrell was thirty-eight years old. He had an economics degree from Cambridge. He graduated in 1984 after which, we believe, he went to work in the City. Precisely what he did there and for whom, we don't know. Sometime between then and now, he has fallen or at least given the appearance of having fallen on hard times. He has been hanging around with the local homeless and attending soup kitchens run by local churches. It was at one of these soup kitchens that he bumped into an old university friend, a Catholic priest, Father Thomas O'Neill…"

As I spoke, Harry pinned a picture of Father Tom onto the incident board adjacent to the crime scene photograph of Simon's body.

"Father Tom was seen in conversation with Simon in a café in Tottenham by a homeless lad called Ben Hailey and by the café owner as recently as last week. He confirmed to DS Duggan and I that he and Murrell were at university together, though he was coy to say the least about just how close they were."

Sheridan was making copious notes.

"I am accompanying Mr Morgan to a press conference later today at which he is under strict instructions to give out only limited information about Simon Murrell and what we do or don't know. My hope is that once the press splash the story, we will get some people who knew Simon more recently than university offering to come in and help us fill in some of the blanks."

"Like a wife or a girlfriend?" offered the uniformed constable.

"Or a work colleague, or a friend, or the bloke he bought his newspaper from every morning. We have to find out who he's been hanging around with, who he plays with, drinks with, eats with and sleeps with. He needs to become the best friend you never had. We need to know everything there is to know about his life. In the meantime, Mike, contact the Family Health Practitioners' Association and see if you can find out who his doctor was. I want to know anything that was wrong with him. Was he getting treatment for drug addiction? Was he using one of these needle exchange centres? You know the kind of thing."

Sheridan wrote the instruction down.

"Then see if you can run him past the Revenue and find a National Insurance number or something that will help us put together his employment history. It's also worth running a check on our own system to see if he has a record."

Sheridan only nodded this time. He was obviously getting more confident.

"Rob, Paul, if this guy wasn't homeless or living in shelters, then we need to know where he *was* living. It's feasible, even likely that he was murdered at home and then moved. So find me an address. Visit letting agencies, check the electoral roll, and keep in contact with Sheridan in case any of his enquiries throw up some pointers."

Lesley Hilton preened a little, expecting to be the next to

be instructed. Thorne, in contrast, yawned again.

"Danny, you're good with money, find out where Simon Murrell banked and get hold of his statements for the last year or so."

"I'll do my best, but you know what banks are like if I don't have a bit of paper that says he's dead."

"I'm sure you'll think of something. You know, offer them sexual favours or an afternoon in the mortuary with the corpse."

Thorne smiled again.

"By the way," I confirmed. "The sexual favours thing was a joke. We'll get nowhere if you offer them your body."

"What about me, guv?" piped up Lesley Hilton, from the back of the group.

"The homeless kid, Ben, mentioned that Simon used to talk about visiting Internet cafes. Could be local, could be in the West End. I don't know how you'd find out if he was a regular, but start locally and work your way closer to the lights. Then, and I know it was all a long time ago, but find out what you can about Father O'Neill and the rest of the university set. Call Cambridge if you need to. See if there's anybody still there who remembers Simon."

"Do we know who else he hung around with at Cambridge?"

"Well this is where it all starts to get potentially interesting and where we may have to start treading on eggshells. Although Father Tom went to great lengths to insist that he and Simon weren't close…."

"You think he was protesting too much?"

"Perhaps. He listed one Seb Brown…"

"He's not the most interesting one, though, because the

priest also mentioned Crispin Monk."

"The politician?" chipped in Hilton.

"Uh huh, the politician. Mr Family Values. So, we need to be a little diplomatic and a little discreet in the way we handle this, which I know is not exactly second nature to some of you. Get me more names and then try and find out if any of them are still in contact with each other. But for Christ's sake be subtle about it. Also, start putting together files on Mr Brown and Mr Monk, just in case the need arises to pay either of them a visit."

Hilton fastened her black leather personal organiser shut and slipped it back into the matching shoulder bag that she carried everywhere with her. For a few moments the group stayed in the same position, like a class waiting to be dismissed.

"Come on, we've got work to do. And remember what they said in *Hill Street Blues*."

"Be careful out there," they replied as one, in a tone that acknowledged that the joke was wearing thin, scattering in different directions as they did so.

Chapter Seventeen

I T WAS ONE of those difficult decisions; the type if you get just slightly wrong can cause horrendous repercussions. Wine was clearly inappropriate, Belgian chocolates too romantic, an ordinary box just too miserly, and flowers I thought would smack of trying too hard. At any rate, Elaine had never been one for flowers. Knowing my luck they'd probably set off her hay fever and that would be the end of that. But, as I stood in the local 24-hour "we-sell-everything-you-can-possibly-think-of" convenience store surveying the options open to me, I was more convinced than ever that I couldn't go empty-handed. Harry thought it looked like weakness on my part.

"So what did you settle on?"

I slung my jacket over the hat stand in the corner of the office and rested the bulky carrier bag on the edge of my desk.

"Biscuits."

"Biscuits," he repeated with incredulity, "biscuits are just so…shite."

I was a little put out by such a summary dismissal of my gift.

"Nice biscuits though, with chocolate, in a box with foil

wrapping and the word 'luxury' slapped all over the packaging. I'm not talking about a pack of custard creams here."

Harry's expression was midway between despair and pity.

"Well *you* come up with something better."

"Did you get anything for Connor?"

"DVD." I bit into an oozing but ageing prawn sandwich bought from the same convenience store. As I tried to hold the two slices of bread together with one hand, I reached into the carrier with the other and pulled out a marked down copy of *Apocalypse Now*.

"Is that appropriate viewing for a boy of his age?"

I shrugged my shoulders in ignorance. "Tonight's more about mending fences than what's appropriate."

"And what if Elaine doesn't approve?"

I pointed the prawn sandwich towards him for emphasis. "She couldn't disapprove of me any more than she does at the moment, so what have I got to lose?"

I LEFT THE station early on the pretence of a meeting with a contact, leaving details that were so vague as to be unverifiable one way or the other, and switched my mobile off. Despite the questionable plumbing in my present accommodation, I returned to the bedsit to shower, wash my hair, and shave. Choosing what to wear was almost as difficult as deciding what to buy. Too formal and it would look like a job interview; too scruffy and it would reinforce all those negative thoughts in Elaine's head. I settled on a pair of black chinos, boots and a plain black shirt. Who could possibly take offence at that?

"My God," yelled Elaine as she opened the door and ushered me in to my own porch, "it's Captain Black. Have you got the Mysterons with you or did you come on your own?"

"Couldn't you have just said good evening?"

I passed over the box of biscuits and she just smiled.

"What? What's wrong with biscuits?"

"Nothing, I suppose, if I was your grandmother or maiden aunt."

She apologised and made light of the crack as she took my leather jacket and hung it over the banister. She stopped herself from pointing me in the direction of the lounge, both of us giving each other a slightly self-conscious smile. That was when I realised that all this was as awkward for her as it was for me.

"Are you well?"

Although she nodded and forced a smile, I could see she was doing so through a body tense from anxiety.

"Not too bad," she lied, "I'm bearing up."

I followed her into the lounge. Instantly I knew that the room was not as I had remembered it. I had to check and then check again to be sure where the changes had been made. The furniture had been moved around, a coffee table added and the warm cream wallpaper changed to a rather vapid, pale blue. A quick scan confirmed that our wedding photograph, which had once been pride of place on the waxed pine mantelpiece above the fire, had been removed, together with any other family pictures in which I had featured.

"It looks nice in here." I helped myself to a clutch of salted peanuts from a bowl on the new coffee table. "But I see you've got rid of any evidence that I ever existed."

Elaine slumped wearily into the armchair facing my position on the well-worn sofa.

"It wasn't like that." She looked at me as if I was being unreasonable to even make the observation.

"No? Was I just put into storage and forgotten about?"

"Jason thought the place needed freshening up."

"Oh, Jason thought, did he? Well that must have been a first. And what did you think?"

She didn't reply. I started to laugh.

"What's funny?"

"I've never been the victim of a spring clean before."

"I don't want to row with you, Jack."

"What's wrong; lost the stomach for a fight?"

"I just want us to be civil to each other, friendly if we can manage it. For Connor."

It was admirable if it was true. It's just that I wasn't sure if it was.

"Where is Connor?"

"He's at a friend's, Danny." The additional information was clearly thrown in to confirm how little I actually knew about my son's life.

"I thought you wanted the three of us to talk. We can't do that if he's at Danny's."

"I do. I mean, we will. He'll be back any time. I wanted us to speak first. Do you want a drink? I've got cold beers in the fridge."

I nodded. She fetched a cold bottle of Rolling Rock and a glass of white wine for herself. What with that and the nibbles on the table, it was all horribly civilised. So un-us. The silence was like sitting in a doctor's waiting room or being trapped on an underground train surrounded by strangers, and punctuated only by the occasional sipping of wine or slurping of beer. It was beginning to get to me.

"So how do you want to handle this?"

She shrugged.

"I haven't got a plan. I thought we'd just play it by ear."

I nodded and the silence resumed.

"Do you want me to talk to him alone or should we do it together?"

She thought for a moment. The conversation was becoming stilted and more difficult.

"I think, for once, he needs to see the two of us together, getting on, instead of arguing."

"And can we do that?"

She took another sip of the chilled Chardonnay. "We have to. We can't argue all our lives."

The conversation ebbed and flowed for a while in the same uneasy manner, with each of us forcing ourselves to converse when we had to, before reverting to looking at the walls rather than looking at each other. Three or four minutes after our last snatch of conversation, I slumped back on the settee and threw my arms behind my head. I stared directly at her. No matter how hard she tried, she had to turn her head and look at me. For a second there was the faintest spark of a smile that broke through all of the mistrust and the hurt that I had inflicted on her.

"Do you miss me? At all? Be honest, do you miss anything about me not being here?"

She swilled the wine repeatedly around the glass, trying to get the liquid as close to the rim without pushing it over, while she considered her response.

"I suppose so. It's just that the bits that I miss don't really come close to all the stuff that I don't."

"So tell me, what is it that you miss?"

She thought again, shaking her head and shrugging her shoulders at the same time.

"I don't know, just a bit of everything: the way you used to wrap yourself around me in bed at night to keep me warm and the fact that you always knew what I was thinking when I was thinking it. I miss that."

"What, like, *where's this conversation heading?*"

"Exactly. Do I get to tell you what I don't miss?"

"I think you've made that clear enough already. I thought we were trying to be nice to each other."

"Yep, you're right." She took three tortilla chips from a second bowl on the table.

"You know, when we were good, we were very very good."

"Exactly, but when we were bad we were awful. Isn't that how the rhyme goes? And, let's face it; for the last couple of years we were bad more often than we were good. Even you have to admit that."

A few seconds later she rose to put some music on. Van Morrison. Good choice. It broke the formality, the way music does, and she settled back in her seat seemingly more relaxed than she had been when I had first arrived. I was still wondering where Connor was. I waited a few minutes before speaking again. I was keen to show her that I, too, was moving on. Emotionally, of course, that was a pack of lies.

"I've been told on the QT that my promotion to DCI's going to come through."

"Congratulations."

I nodded my thanks. She seemed genuinely pleased.

"This calls for another drink." She topped up her Chardonnay and fetched another Rolling Rock from the kitchen.

"But there's no job for me here," I called out.

"So what are you going to do?" She placed the bottle down in front of me on the table.

It was my turn to shrug.

"I could look for a DCI's job somewhere else or stay here as a DI and wait for something to come up."

Where I had expected her to betray some enthusiasm at the prospect of me being out of the picture, instead she seemed concerned at the thought of me moving away, and not, I detected, just for Connor's sake.

"We wouldn't want you to move away."

"We?"

"Connor and I. He needs you around, particularly now, when so much between us is up in the air, and I wouldn't want you to go if it was going to make him any more unhappy."

"It's good to hear you say that."

I let her comment hang in the air without further response.

As Van Morrison came towards the end of "Dark Side of the Road", I heard the doorbell ring and waited as Connor bounded in, displaying more energy as he did so than I can ever remember having at his age, or at any time since. He raced into the lounge, dropping a sports bag just inside the door, and then leaping from a distance to hug me on the couch. I grasped hold of him, his head resting conveniently at an angle on my shoulder, and pulled him close. I felt a kind of euphoric surge, as if I suddenly realised that this was what I had needed more than anything.

"So how are you, hooligan?"

"Who are you calling a hooligan?" He landed a series of

mock punches to my upper arms, before sliding down the side of my body and tucking himself into me.

"Hungry?"

Connor nodded vigorously.

"How about you?" asked Elaine.

"Me?"

"You. Are you hungry? It's not a loaded question."

"Me, hungry? Always."

"I've got pizza and garlic bread I can pop in the oven. There's enough for all of us. I'll bring it in when it's ready."

And with that Elaine moved out into the kitchen, leaving Connor and I alone on the couch. I pushed him gently away from my side and then turned myself side on to face him.

"Did you have a good time at Danny's?"

He nodded without lifting his head from my chest.

"We played World Rally on the Playstation and I got through one whole race without driving over a cliff once."

"Hey, that's great. I've got guys at the station who are trained and paid to drive fast, and I don't think they could do that."

As I sat with his head nestled still against my chest I thought how best to ask him how he was really feeling. I wanted him to know that he could open up to us – well, preferably to me – but knew I needed to tread gently.

"Mum tells me you've been a bit upset lately," I said. "She says she's heard you crying in your room at night."

He shook his head as if the denial would in some way stop me from being disappointed in him.

"You don't have to shake your head." I ran my fingertips through his perfect hair. "It's okay to cry and to be upset. If you can't talk to me or Mum about it, then who *can* you talk to?"

"It just hurts," he said falteringly a few moments later.

"What hurts?"

"Seeing Mum cry all the time when she thinks I can't see her, and thinking of you going home to that room on your own every night when you could be here with us. That's what makes me cry."

The maturity of youth can be a remarkable and humbling force. I felt ashamed. Kids like Connor shouldn't be required to grieve the way he clearly was.

"You know, none of it is your fault."

He instantly became more subdued. He pulled away from me, sat up and looked down into his lap. I put my hand out under his chin and gently lifted his face with two of my fingers until our eyes met.

"None of it," I emphasised. "Nothing that's happened between Mum and I is a result of anything that you have or haven't done. You understand that, don't you?"

"But I'm always going to get caught in the middle. And I don't want to any more."

Sometimes, I guess, you just have to accept that a question can't be given a satisfactory answer. I had it within my power to make things right for him, and I couldn't. That's a cold and lonely place to be.

"You know we both love you?" I added "very much," for emphasis.

He nodded again. And then he spoke.

"So why don't you love each other any more?"

"I think we still love each other, but maybe in a different way. I just think that we're having a bit of trouble liking each other at the moment."

"Why?"

I breathed in deeply before exhaling again loudly.

"Sometimes, just because you're an adult, it doesn't automatically mean that you're going to have all the answers. When you grow up, if you're not careful, you lose sight of what's really important to you. You start to take for granted all the things that are valuable and you put your time and your effort into other things instead. It's a bit like that plant over there. If you water it every day, it will always be there for you, looking just as great as the first time you bought it, even better perhaps. But if you forget to water it because you're too busy doing other things, then one day when you want to look at it, you'll turn around and it will have withered and died."

He stared directly at me, his deep, chestnut brown eyes seeking further clarification.

"I guess I forgot to pay Mum the attention she needed. I did some silly things that upset her and by the time I realised just how much, it was too late for her to forgive me."

"But can't you just say sorry?"

I smiled. The innocence and simplicity of a child's mind is also a beautiful thing.

"Sometimes saying sorry isn't enough. You have to make sure you don't do the thing in the first place."

"You must have done something really bad for her to throw you out."

"It was more about us doing what was best. Having the two of us arguing all day isn't a whole lot of fun for any of us, especially you."

We sat quietly for a few minutes as Connor absorbed that part of the conversation and tried to make sense of it in his own mind. I was keen to wait for him to restart the discussion, which he did after helping himself to some nuts from the table. He spoke quietly, as if the questions had taken genuine courage to ask and as if he was fearful of the answers he might receive.

"Does this mean you're going to get divorced?"

"Would that worry you?"

He nodded.

"Why would it worry you? You'd still have a mum and dad that loved you. It's just that we wouldn't live together any more and that's no different to how it's been for the past few months anyway."

Connor took a deep breath, as if to stave off rising emotion, and looked into my eyes.

"Liam, this kid in my class, his parents got divorced and his dad moved to Edinburgh. He only gets to see him during school holidays and sometimes not even then."

"So?"

"So, if you get divorced, will I only get to see you in the holidays?"

"Not if I've got anything to do with it."

We smiled at each other.

"If we get divorced, and we don't know at the moment what's going to happen, but if we do, one thing's certain, nothing will be done unless we're sure that it's what's best for you."

"And we both know how important it is for you to see your dad," interrupted Elaine, laying a platter of sliced pepperoni pizza and three plates down on the table in front of us.

Connor leapt forward off the seat and helped himself to the largest of the unevenly cut segments, using the tip of his tongue to hook a hanging thread of melted cheese into his mouth. For some reason, I waited to be offered. Elaine quickly picked up on my reticence, said nothing, but just gently nudged the plate of pizza closer to me. I helped myself.

"You know, Connor, just because your dad won't be living here any more, it won't necessarily stop us from doing things together as a family."

I could see instantly in her eyes that Elaine had thought this maybe a promise too far. I felt a curious obligation to come to her rescue.

"What Mum means is that we'll still go to all your school things together. I'll still come to watch you play football. Nothing like that is going to change."

"Will you tell them at school?" Connor asked, a moment later, as he reached for the can of Diet Coke that Elaine had placed on the table for him.

"Do you mean they don't know?" I asked Elaine.

"Of course I told them. I had to tell them. After all, I couldn't rely on you to do it. What do you take me for? I wanted them to watch for any changes in his behaviour. But I don't think we need to tell them anything else until…well, at least until we've *got* something else to tell them."

I immediately realised that not only had we slipped back towards our former, more entrenched positions, but also that we were speaking over Connor rather than with him, cutting him out of the conversation completely. It was, perhaps, symptomatic of how far our relationship had deteriorated that it had become such a mass of contradictions to the point where I still couldn't judge how Elaine would react from one second to the next.

CONNOR LOOKED AT me quizzically, as if to ask how this situation could lead to anything positive. I have to say, from my position; I tended to agree with him.

"You have to try and not let this affect you," I found myself saying to him with monumental naiveté. "You've got a big year coming up at school, what with your SATs and that. You need to try and stay focused. I realise that's okay for me to say, but you have to try and put all this to one side. What do you say?"

"No more fighting between you two?"

"No more fighting. I'll make you a deal. We'll try and make sure that everything stays as stable as we can, providing you try and do your best. That's all we ask. Deal?"

He thought for a second.

"Deal." We shook on it.

FORTY MINUTES LATER and with dusk just falling into darkness, Elaine and I stood on the front drive. Connor was in bed in his room at the back of the house and a cursory glance five minutes earlier had shown that he had quickly succumbed to the need to sleep. As with most children, he looked much younger then than he did when he was awake. I stood for no more than a minute, looking at the downy hair on the back of his neck, and was able to recall exactly how he had looked the night we had first laid him in his cot at home. It was a lifetime ago.

I had come back downstairs happier than I had expected to be with the way the evening had gone, galvanised by the fact that our relationship seemed to be as important to Connor as it was to me and reassured by Elaine's apparent recognition of the fact. When Connor threw his arms around me and kissed me goodnight, he seemed more comfortable than he had been at the start and, as far as I was concerned, this had been achieved without us having to resort to any rash or unrealistic promises. Honesty had to be the order of the day. Elaine, I think, saw it differently.

"How could you make him a deal like that?" shuddering a little from the chill of the night. She wasn't angry, but weary, the stress of the situation manifesting itself in tiredness.

"Like what?"

"You know, all that stuff about us not doing anything that would unsettle him this year. How could you make him a promise like that?"

"I can't believe you have a problem with it. All I've said is that we'll keep things as they are."

"We should have agreed that between ourselves before you started making promises to him."

"Why, did you have something else in mind?"

She shook her head.

"Because if you did, I'm afraid the divorce will have to wait. We've both got a responsibility to put him first and I'm not going to apologise for telling him that."

"I don't think you're in any position to start telling me how to put him first."

As we stood there – conversation aside – like two lovers saying goodnight on a warm summer night, the light from the street lamp adjacent to the house threw a pale orange wash across the front of Elaine's face, picking out some of the redder highlights in her shoulder-length blonde hair. I sensed this might be a turning point. With Connor's acceptance of my words, the balance of power for his trust had evened out. I detected that Elaine recognised she no longer had first claim on his affections. With the shake of a hand Connor had signalled that he trusted me, and providing we gave him the stability he craved, that he was ready to move on.

I pulled my leather jacket over my shoulders, "You know the reason I always put the job first? I thought it was the only place I'd ever achieved anything."

She looked straight at me.

"Now I know that I was wrong and that my greatest achievement was around me every day. I just never saw it."

She smiled a sad, reflective smile.

I continued with a single breath. "I wanted you to know that," I added.

She returned inside the house without waiting to see me to my car.

Chapter Eighteen

A FTER A WEEKEND of intensive press coverage, it was an unexpected visitor on the following Monday morning that provided us with our most significant development since the identification of the body.

The woman had presented herself at the front desk and asked to see the officer in charge. In her early thirties and at no more than five feet five, she was of slight but elegant appearance, dressed in a tailored blue suit and matching navy leather shoes. Her contrasting Prada handbag looked out of place in front of her on the functional wooden table in Interview Room number two. The delicate gold chain around her neck brought out the colour in her olive skin; earrings peered through from behind cascading ebony hair, all of which betrayed her Mediterranean roots ahead of her accent. She was making last minute adjustments to her immaculate appearance in a small hand held mirror as I entered the room and introduced myself. She clasped the mirror shut and returned it to its place inside the bag.

"Now that's not a London accent." I smiled as I removed my jacket and laid it casually across the spare chair to my right.

"Indeed not," she replied, in impeccable English. "I come from Spain."

"Ah, Spain, I love Spain," I found myself saying without giving it a second thought. "Whereabouts?"

"Alicante." She saw my blank expression and picked up on my need for further qualification. "It's about midway between Barcelona and Malaga."

I apologised. "Geography was *not* my strongest suit at school."

She smiled. "So which part of Spain is the part that you love?"

I had to admit she had me there. I had only been to Spain once in my entire life and that was on a last-minute package holiday before Connor was born, and I spent most of that trip in an alcohol-induced haze. I had soaked up more of the sangria than I had of the culture.

"I don't recall exactly. I was there on holiday."

"The Cost Brava, Costa Blanca or perhaps the Costa Almeira," she offered helpfully.

"Probably," I smiled.

With my ignorance exposed, I was spared total humiliation by the timely entry of a young uniformed officer balancing two cups of tea and a rather meagre plate of biscuits.

"So…" I started, fishing for her name.

"Maria."

"So Maria, what brings you here this morning?"

She considered the question carefully and took time to respond.

"It's about the man in all of the newspapers this weekend, the man you found in the bag."

I nodded.

"He is my husband."

I swallowed hard and put the mug that was halfway to my mouth back on the table.

"You're married to Simon Murrell?"

I asked for the sake of clarity. She nodded in confirmation.

"Can I ask why it has taken you almost a week to come and see us?"

"We were no longer together. In fact, I have not seen him for more than a year. I only saw the picture yesterday in the newspaper. That's why I have come today."

"Were you divorced?"

"No, we were separated. Our relationship ended rather messily, I am afraid. We haven't spoken to each other for quite some time."

"But surely you would still need to be in contact? I mean, what if you wanted to get married again and needed to organise a divorce?"

"It may be a year since I last saw him, Inspector, but believe me it all feels a lot more recent than that. I know I would have eventually forced myself to cross the divorce bridge but I wasn't ready for it yet."

She took her tea without sugar, declined the offer of a biscuit and sipped slowly and gently from the cream-coloured mug. She rested it back down in front of her after each taste. I watched her carefully and, though she had made it clear she no longer had any relationship with Murrell, the decision to present herself at the station had clearly been the result of more thought and soul-searching than she was prepared to admit. She knew that it would require her to revisit painful memories, something that may take more courage than one would think possible to squeeze into a body of her size. She shifted her position on the seat as if readying herself for what she knew would be an uncomfortable experience.

"Can we go back to the beginning of your relationship with Mr Murrell?"

She took another sip of tea, gave momentary thought as to what she wanted to say and then looked at me and nodded nervously.

"Simon and I first met when he was working as a trader in the City. We were both employed by the same bank, the Osaka National. I was a personal assistant to one of the managers, and we worked on the same floor. He was older than me but handsome in a young Harrison Ford kind of way, very funny and, what I liked best about him, he always seemed to have time to stop and say hello."

She looked up, I suspected, for some kind of confirmation that this was the type of information I was expecting. My return smile gave her the signal she was looking for.

"Gradually I started to join the traders when they went for a drink after work. I had only been over here from Spain for a matter of months and I needed all the friends I could get. Well, you know, the way these things happen, we began to spend more and more time in each other's company and we began to realise that we were attracted to each other. So we began a relationship."

"When was that?"

"That would have been in the late summer of 1993."

"Tell me how the relationship developed."

"Well, the following New Year's Simon asked me to move in with him. To be honest it wasn't entirely unexpected.

I had basically been living half of the week at his place anyway, so I didn't give the decision too much thought. Although we had only been together for a matter of months, I knew I was in love with him and the chance to be with him all the time was exactly what I wanted. He has-had-a kind of magnetic personality that you can't help finding attractive, seductive even. Plus, of course, he had a fantastic apartment in Docklands overlooking the river while I was living in a cramped studio apartment in Wembley. Believe me, there wasn't too much to consider.

"Things were really good for maybe eight or ten months. He was earning more than you can imagine and we were living the kind of lifestyle that you would associate with a successful City trader. We ate in all the best restaurants, stayed in all the best hotels. I'm not pretending it wasn't fun. It was intoxicating."

"But?"

"But, by the end of 1994 and into 1995, things seemed to be falling apart. I would never know what time he would be coming home and there were nights when he wouldn't come home at all. Although I had left the bank by this time, I still had friends there and they began to warn me that they thought something could be seriously wrong."

"And was there?"

"Well, yes, obviously. I mean, there must have been, particularly as so many people had noticed it. You only had to look at the way he was living in the cold light of day to see that something untoward was going on. So I plucked up the courage and confronted him and eventually, after I had threatened to leave him a hundred times, he apologised. He told me he had been anxious over money problems and had been drinking and taking tranquillisers to calm himself down."

"You believed him?"

She shrugged her shoulders.

"What can I say? I was like putty in his hands. He promised me he would clean up his act. And I, being an idiot, believed him. He apologised, we fell into bed, made love for a weekend and then, to cap it all, he asked me to marry him."

"And you did?"

She nodded.

"Madness, I know," she continued, "particularly, as with hindsight, he hadn't really given me an explanation at all. But I didn't want to see the negatives."

"Hindsight's a wonderful thing," I smiled. "We all have something we'd like to be able to turn back the clock on and do differently."

She gave no sign of detecting that I spoke from personal experience. Throughout our meeting she sat pensively and answered each question in turn deliberately and with considered caution.

"Despite all the money it wasn't a fancy wedding. In fact, it was just the two of us, one of his old friends from university as his best man and the clerk from the registry office as a witness. We just climbed in a taxi and went to the registry office in Chelsea and did it there and then. I got into terrible trouble with my family for not telling them, but to me the spontaneity of the whole thing was terribly romantic."

"A spur of the moment decision?"

"Exactly," she smiled, enjoying these happier reminiscences.

"When was this?"

"September 20th 1996."

"The friend, what was his name?"

"Patrick Ramsden. He left London about a month later to go and work abroad. Canada, if I recall."

"Was Simon still in touch with him?"

"I really couldn't say. Simon wasn't a great one for working at his friendships. He expected every relationship to be one-way traffic. Perhaps that's one of the reasons why we never stood a chance."

I turned to the constable just inside the doorway and ordered refills of our tea. I stood and stretched, took a pack of mints out of my pocket and offered one to Maria. She refused, at which point I simply closed the pack without taking one myself and returned to my pocket.

"You know, Maria, I realise there is a lot of bitterness there, but when you speak about him, there also sounds like there's still a great deal of affection."

She nodded enthusiastically, as if pleased for the first time that somebody else had recognised this in her.

"Frustrated affection, I suppose. Frustrated because of what might have been, and because I fell in love with a small but very beautiful part of his personality. My sadness is that the rest of him was not as beautiful and no matter how much I kidded myself that I could, it wasn't possible to have that part of him without the rest."

I began to slowly pace around the room, Maria's head turning to follow me as I moved. It helps me think. She said she didn't mind.

"You said there were other reasons that your relationship collapsed, apart from Simon's selfishness."

She nodded, but more despondently now.

"What were they?"

"Where do you want me to start? During the following eighteen months I became increasingly suspicious that Simon's financial problems were more serious than he had led me to believe. His car was repossessed and we started getting calls from, let's say, unwanted visitors. It made him very depressed because he was basically a show off and the money troubles were steadily stripping him of everything that he regarded as a status symbol. That, I think, was one of the main contributors to his heavy drinking and his drug use. Then, of course, there were the affairs. They were really the last straw. But every time I asked if I could help, he just became more abusive and more self-centred."

"Can you tell me more?"

"Shortly after I took the decision to leave him in mid-1998, I understand that his apartment was repossessed. It had been coming for a while, to be honest. From what I was able to piece together afterwards he had invested heavily in Lloyds, been persuaded to become a name and then, like so many of them, had been badly stung by the crash. This was the fall-out from all of those losses. He had tried to maintain his lifestyle rather than admit to the problems but he was living on air. There was nothing to maintain the lifestyle *with*. Unlike many of his friends Simon had no massive family wealth to fall back on. He came from a very run-of-the-mill middle class background and so he was unable to take the losses in the same way that some of his contemporaries were. He basically lost all that he had."

"So he became depressed?"

"Depressed doesn't come close to it. I think he felt very let down and very embarrassed, ashamed even. I think the people he had looked to for guidance hadn't guided him well and now when he was really in trouble, really down, he felt they were washing their hands of him. He wanted them to support him until he got back on his feet, but they turned him away. He started using drugs. Heavily. I was aware that he had been using cocaine for a while, but then so many of them did at that time. By the time I left him, I strongly suspected he was dabbling in heroin as well. And, of course, he had no money to pay for his habit, so it all began to get very nasty. It was beginning to scare me."

"When you left him, was there a big fight? Did he try to stop you?"

"He was finding it difficult enough to remember basic everyday things. I waited until he was out doing who knows what and I simply packed, wrote him a note and went to stay with a girlfriend."

"Do you know how he paid for the heroin or where he got it from?"

"Getting it wasn't difficult. There were always people hanging around willing to get whatever you wanted. How he paid for it is harder to answer. I suspect he did favours of one sort or another."

"Heroin wouldn't have done much for his performance at work."

"Well, someone blew the whistle on him. As far as I know about four months after we split the bank confronted him about his heroin use. They presented him with proof, he had no option but to admit it, and he was escorted out of the building there and then. That kind of finished him off."

"And you lost track of him after that?"

"Kind of. I tried to get hold of him to see if I could do anything to help but he was too busy wallowing in self-pity to return my calls. So I returned to Alicante for a while to see my family and generally restore my faith in human nature and I came back to the UK about a year ago. I thought long and hard about staying in Spain. I had lots of offers of work from family and friends out there keen to see me stay, but I figured that to do so would have looked like failure on my part, and I'm too stubborn to give up like that."

I looked down at the notes I had been taking so I knew where to dig deeper in my conversation with her.

"Would you say Simon was a violent person? I mean, was he ever violent towards you?"

She shook her head.

"No, never violent. He could be abusive, particularly when he'd had too much to drink, but it was only ever verbal, shouting and screaming and so on. He never lifted his hands to me. That would have been too awful for words."

I nodded awkwardly before looking hastily back down at my pad.

"And you mentioned affairs. Were these with women from work?"

"And men."

"Men?"

"Simon was a very sexual person," she replied wryly. "He didn't believe that monogamy was a realistic way to live your life, nor did he see anything particularly wrong with climbing into bed with somebody of his own sex, if that was the way the feeling took him at any particular moment."

"Did you know about this when you married him?"

"Of course not. We had row upon row over it once I found out. He used the old argument that it was just sex whereas what we had was a proper relationship. He couldn't grasp at all that I could see it as a betrayal, whether he was sleeping with a man or a woman, let alone be concerned about any of the health implications that went with it."

"How did you find out?"

"About the men or the women?"

"All of it."

"You know what girls are like. Simon was a very sought-after commodity and, if you're young and you've just bedded one of the hottest traders at the bank where you work, you're not going to miss the chance to brag to your friends, are you? I know I didn't. So word goes around and eventually it reached me. Remember I was young and in a foreign country and he was treating me very well, so for a while I turned a blind eye."

"To the men as well?"

"I didn't find out about that until much later, though of course I had heard the rumours. It was only when I found an old photograph from his university days that I began to think there might be something to it. It showed him, Patrick, and some others in, shall I say, a compromising position."

"Is Patrick gay?"

"Patrick, yes. The others? I never met them. I don't even know their names. All I know was that he was part of a very close circle of mostly male friends at Cambridge and I think they lived – how can I put this – a very hedonistic lifestyle."

"Do you know where Simon was living?"

"Not for certain."

She unclasped the Prada handbag, which by this time I had deduced was a trophy of her former life with Simon Murrell, reached inside for a neatly folded piece of Vellum notepaper and handed it across.

"That's the last address I had for him. It's about a year old."

I glanced down. It was local, in a part of the area renowned for rented accommodation suitable for students, nurses, teachers, and others on a relatively low income. I thanked her.

"One of the people that we have spoken with made mention of the fact that Simon had recently come into some money. Are you aware of that?"

She smiled.

"I haven't seen him for a year. I wouldn't know."

"Of course."

I looked down on my notebook again just to be sure that I'd covered everything, and to give her time to add anything more to what she had already provided.

"Does Simon's death shock you, Mrs Murrell? Are you upset by it?"

She answered quite routinely to what was not a routine question.

"Did it shock me? Not particularly. Did it upset me?" She thought for a second. "A little, when I think of the man he *was* rather than the man he became."

"Are there any questions that you would like to ask me?"

She shook her head.

"One thing that does surprise me is that you haven't asked me how your husband died. Sometimes bereaved relatives need to know more of the details."

"Mr Munday, I don't feel bereaved. I came to tell you what I know."

She closed the handbag again and began to rise out of her seat.

"Now, if you've no more need of me, I have a train to catch."

"We may need to speak to you again."

"You have my contact details. I'm not planning a holiday."

I escorted her towards the door of the interview room, delaying her while I turned back to retrieve my jacket.

"Just one final thing," I asked, "we have yet to formally identify the body. I mean, we know it's Simon, but it still has to be done. It's only a formality but, with you being his next of kin…"

A look of horror moved across her face. She asked if it was absolutely necessary and whether it had to be her, to which I nodded my confirmation. Despite the history she had set out, I was still keen to know how she would respond to coming face to face with the body of her husband. It was the only way to find out.

"It shouldn't take long. In fact, I can arrange for it to be done immediately and then I'll get one of my officers to drive you back to the station in time for your train."

Left with little choice, she agreed.

"I appreciate that, Mrs Murrell, really I do."

Chapter Nineteen

I T WAS LATE afternoon, the sun was warm without being oppressive, and in a narrow street of terraced Victorian housing, four helmeted children on scooters and bikes ignored the pleas of their mothers to be careful as they rode a circuit across both pavements and back again between densely packed lines of parked cars. They were pursued relentlessly as they did so by a scruffy pet dog keen to join in the fun.

It was a typical suburban setting, whose soundtrack was the gentle but consistent rumble of traffic on a major road about a quarter of a mile away. In their eagerness to play the children paid us little attention as Harry and I propped ourselves against the garden wall and waited for colleagues to arrive. In their innocence the children were oblivious to the fact that behind the discoloured net curtains of the third house in from the end of the row – the one on the second corner of their circuit – it was likely that a murder had been committed. But they wouldn't be oblivious for long.

At first I hadn't been convinced that this, the address supplied by Maria Murrell, would yield anything at all. The street itself was neat and tidy; the houses, which were mostly of uniform age, were well kept, with gardens tended and baskets hanging. The avenue of trees adjacent to the road filtered the sunlight so that it shone through the branches like tiny spotlights, casting a mottled shadow across the pavement. The close proximity of the houses to the roadside meant that only the smallest of cars could fit comfortably on a driveway without spilling onto the pavement and becoming an obstacle. As a consequence, most householders seemed content to leave their vehicles on the street, their wing mirrors turned inwards, which in turn made the road feel narrower than it really was.

Simon Murrell's one bedroom flat occupied the lower half of a small converted house. There was little to set it out from the crowd, the type of house you could walk past every day of your working life without giving a second thought to who or what went on behind the façade. We gained access via an elderly neighbour who, a little intimidated by having the police come calling, sensed trouble and scurried back to the sanctuary of her own home, leaving our entry to the property impeded only by the lock on the door.

"Don't you think it might have been worth getting a warrant to search the place?" asked Harry, straining and bent double by the lock as he patiently manoeuvred his Swiss Army knife back and forth inside until the door slipped open.

"What's he going to do, sue us for breaking and entering?"

"What if it's not his flat?"

"Trust me, it's his flat."

"How can you be so sure?"

"The lady upstairs for a start," I whispered. "She didn't ask what we wanted, she didn't have to. She knew exactly why we were here. She's read her papers; she knows he's dead.

Probably just doesn't want to get involved."

"Do you blame her?"

I shook my head. Harry folded the Swiss Army knife back into itself, slipped it into his left trouser pocket, and pushed the door gently open to reveal the wreckage of a room apparently turned completely on its head. It was a dark, spartan room with long, outmoded brown curtains which connected only haphazardly to the rail above. They had been pulled roughly together to the centre of the window, exposing sunlight where they stopped meeting two thirds of the way in. The drawers on a badly scratched mahogany chest had been pulled onto the floor and their contents strewn about. Every cushion from the sofa and the armchair had been pulled away and now lay chaotically wherever they had landed. The furniture was clearly second hand. Even from a distance it was obvious that the faded green and beige velour sofa desperately needed reupholstering. From my position just inside the door, the scene offered few noticeable clues to the personality of the man for whom it had been home, or the fate that had befallen him.

"You know, you should speak to the landlord," said Harry, pulling on a pair of surgical gloves he kept in his pocket.

"Why?"

"Well, it's vacant," he laughed, his arms outstretched to indicate the flat, "and even in this state it's better than your place."

"Mine's not this bad," I refuted.

"Yeah, right." Duggan moved across the main body of the room, tiptoeing like an out-of-condition ballerina to avoid treading on debris. He moved carefully around the front of the sofa and across to a small dining table in the far corner, pointing out a series of aluminium containers.

"He's got the same crockery as you, too."

"Stop taking the piss and tell me what you see."

He placed a gloved hand on the corner of one of the foil containers and tipped it towards himself. He bent lower to get his face closer to the object and sniffed twice before rearing back like the recoil on a gun. He turned towards me, still holding the foil container between his right thumb and index finger.

"It was Chinese," he confirmed, "once."

"Okay, that's all I need to hear. Seal the door, call SOCO and let's wait outside until they arrive. I want every fibre on this cheap and nasty carpet examined, every square inch of this hideous wallpaper looked at and every single thing removed, inspected and catalogued until we know exactly what happened in this place last Monday. And I mean *everything*."

Harry, relieved to be able to return the foil container to the table, nodded and followed me out.

BY THE TIME the children were called in for their tea, Addison Road looked completely different. Where their circuit had stood earlier, now patrol cars and police transits blocked entry to the road at one end and halfway down the other. White screens identified the house as a crime scene and officers covered from head to toe in protective clothing moved relentlessly around like ants drawn to something sweet. Occasionally a bag or a box would be removed and placed carefully in the back of one van or another. Harry and I watched from our position on the wall.

"Cup of tea?"

The unexpected voice from behind came from a small, plump woman in her late forties who was balancing a tray on the post at the end of the garden wall on which we sat. She ran an eczema-covered hand through her dyed copper-coloured hair, exposing the dark roots that indicated the need to return to the hairdresser. She smiled an unattractive smile.

"I made two cups but I can always make more."

"That's very kind of you, Mrs...?"

"Bannister. Ruth Bannister."

"It's very kind of you, Mrs Bannister, but really you need to stay on the other side of the tape."

Ruth Bannister smiled, nodded, but made no effort to move anywhere. Instead she folded her arms across the front of her floral vest top, in so doing accentuating the size of her obviously substantial chest. A black bra strap on her right shoulder peeked out from underneath the top. Beads of sweat that had begun to trickle slowly down the side of her face, whether through nerves, the heat or a combination of the two, were casually removed with a paper tissue taken from the pocket of her calf-length denim skirt.

"It was him then?" she said after a few seconds.

I swung myself around to face her and, to her obvious satisfaction, picked up one of the mugs of tea from her tray.

"What was him?"

"The body in the bag; the one that's been in all the news-papers. The body in the bag was his."

"Surely that depends on who 'he' is?"

"We all thought it was him. The picture in the paper looked like him, so we thought it probably was, plus the fact that none of us had seen him around since it happened. Not that all we do is talk about it," she added hastily.

"Of course not." Harry smiled.

"So what was he like?"

I was aware that none of us had yet mentioned Simon Murrell by name.

Ruth Bannister shrugged her fleshy shoulders, the realisation moving across her face that perhaps she was at risk of being drawn in deeper than she had originally intended.

"We didn't really have much to do with him."

"So how can you be so sure that it is him?"

"You know," she hesitated, "word gets around."

"And what does 'word' say?"

Unease seemed to be settling in with Mrs Bannister. She turned away from us towards a clutch of her neighbours who were observing every word of our conversation from a distance, no doubt keenly waiting for her to return and report back. I leant forward and returned my mug to the tray, picking up a biscuit and snapping it in half in front of her face. I deliberately spoke in an undertone:

"Look, Mrs Bannister, we can chat about this here, right now, or we can put you in one of those patrol cars and take you down to the station as a potential witness."

She swallowed hard, the beads of sweat gathering pace on her forehead.

"You don't want to give your friends over there any more to be talking about, do you? Otherwise, mark my words, by the time we drop you back, *you'll* be the word on the street round here, not him."

She nodded in an artificially relaxed manner.

"So let's start again, what do you know about Simon Murrell?"

"Not too much. You have to believe me, not too much. We'd occasionally see him in the street, that's all. He'd pass the time of day, a nod good morning, pat the kids on the head, that kind of thing, but mostly he'd keep to himself."

"Have you ever been inside his flat?"

"No."

"So what impression did you form of him from the contact that you did have?"

"No impression really other than he just looked like he'd let himself go a bit. His clothes were always shabby. He was never filthy, but never clean either, do you know what I mean? And he looked sad, lonely really, like everything had gone wrong and he was trying to pick up the pieces."

"Do you know if that was true?"

"No, that was just what he looked like. I used to think that the neighbourly thing would be to go in and cook him a meal, but he always seemed to want to keep his distance. He'd walk down the street and talk to himself, shout to himself almost, like he was having a go at himself or psyching himself up about something."

"Did you ever hear what it was he was saying?"

Again, she shook her head.

"Was he always on his own or did you ever see him with people?"

"No, he was a loner, that one. Always on his own. Except, of course, for that party last weekend."

"Party?"

"Well it sounded like a party anyway. The music was loud enough. I mean you could hardly hear yourself think. I was trying to put my two to bed and I could hear every line of every song in their bedrooms, and they're at the back of the house."

"Did you see any guests arriving for this party?"

"Now that you come to mention it, I didn't. But we never ever heard a word out of him normally, and that's what made me think he must have had friends in."

"And the noise disturbed you?"

She nodded.

"So why didn't you complain, knock on his door or call the police or something?"

"I thought about it and if it had carried on really late, then I suppose I would have gone over there and asked him to turn it down a bit. I just didn't want to come across as the heavy neighbour."

"But it stopped?"

"Yeah, it stopped about nine, I think. Maybe a bit later."

"And did you hear the party guests leave?"

She shook her head.

"Not straight away. I did hear a car leaving a little while later but I can't be sure if it was from his place or from somebody else's."

"Did you see what type of car it was?" interjected Harry.

"I didn't look."

"What about the lady who lives in the upstairs flat?"

"Mrs Skelton? What about her?"

"Well, if the sound of the music was so loud that it was making it difficult for you to get your kids to sleep across the road, she must have felt she was living on top of a disco or something."

Ruth Bannister smiled.

"Mrs Skelton wouldn't have heard if anything if Iron Maiden had been playing live in her living room. She's as deaf as a post."

"Completely deaf?"

"Totally. And it's all through vanity. She's got hearing aids alright; she's just too vain to wear them."

Ruth Bannister took possession of her tray and returned back towards her house, resolutely refusing to answer the questions of her enquiring neighbours as she passed them. SOCO completed their trawl through Simon Murrell's property soon afterwards and Harry and I watched as the flat was sealed and the last crate of personal effects were loaded into the back of a police transit before we called it quits for the day and went our separate ways.

Chapter Twenty

OCCASIONALLY – WHEN HE knew he had a piece of particularly important information to impart – Mike Sheridan could be very reminiscent of a Labrador puppy. At the front end he'd be up on his paws, panting hard and eager to please, holding out the information for you to take from him and then waiting for the reward that your appreciation represented, whilst at the back his tail would wag so fast it would knock over everything within an arm's length, leaving a trail of devastation in its wake. I had that kind of enthusiasm once.

I returned to the station after breakfast, already feeling early signs of the indigestion that would plague me for the rest of the day. Sheridan had not only met me in the car park, he had held the door open for me, carried my briefcase and then pursued me vigorously all the way through the building and up two flights of stairs to the door of my office which, perhaps harshly, I had then closed firmly behind me leaving him isolated on the other side. The only thing he hadn't done – thankfully – was hand me a highly polished apple.

Throughout the brisk walk from car to desk he had fed me incoherent snatches of information, the way an excited child might when he simply can't get out the details quickly enough or in the correct order. As I expected, he waited barely long enough for me to reach my desk before tapping twice on the frosted glass and then awkwardly letting himself in. He set my briefcase down in the corner and coughed a nervous cough.

"Was that a bit too much?"

"A bit."

"Sorry. I'll try and tone it down."

"No need to apologise."

He watched as I watered a neglected rubber plant whose wilting leaves had brought on sudden pangs of guilt. I plugged in and switched on my illicit kettle and rummaged through my over-spilling in-tray to locate a copy of the transcript from my interview with Maria Murrell, all the time having to work my way around Mike Sheridan, who stood statuesque and silent in the centre of the office. The excitable child had become a mute and it was irritating me.

"For Christ's sake, Sheridan, either tell me what you've got to tell me or just piss off out of my office. If you're staying, sit down. If you're not, get out."

"Sorry."

"And don't fucking apologise."

"Sorry."

The glare was enough to tell him that this was a final warning. I poured steaming water onto the tea bag in my mug and watched as the colour slowly seeped out to turn the liquid brown. I dropped in some milk that looked as if it may be on the turn, took the tea back behind my desk and sat down to face the young officer.

"Right," I sighed, "I'm all yours. Begin."

He nodded uncertainly.

"It's about bank statements, sir. Simon Murrell's bank statements."

"I had a feeling it wouldn't be about your own."

He was too on edge to recognise the glib remark; too unsure of our relationship to know whether he could laugh or not. I dipped a Rich Tea biscuit halfway into the mug, pulling it out again and lifting it quickly to my mouth before the sodden half had a chance to detach itself and fall to my desk. Sheridan continued to regard me with a mix of reverence and horror, like he wanted to tell me he thought I was a waster, but didn't have the nerve. Perhaps he envied that as much as he disapproved of it. At last, though, he relaxed enough to sit down.

"The bank statements show that, far from being down on his luck, Simon Murrell had been receiving a steady stream of income for the past six or eight months. It started off at a thousand a month and it seemed to grow to around seventeen-fifty."

He had my interest. The rubber plant would have to wait for a further top-up.

"Do the statements say where the money came from?"

"The most recent stuff appears to have been cash deposits but paid in fairly regularly and mostly into the same one or two branches. It was always paid in the same amounts, one deposit of five hundred a month and one of two-fifty. I thought maybe it was cash in hand for doing a bit of work for a mate."

"Seven hundred and fifty a month is a lot of cash for helping out a mate. At least it is if he's getting it *every* month. What about the other thousand?"

Sheridan glanced down at some notes that he had made to reassure himself of the facts before imparting the information.

"The other thousand was paid regularly on the 27th or 28th of every month, always by BACS transfer and always from a company called Santuary Holdings."

"Santuary Holdings?"

Sheridan noticeably grew in stature. His body seemed bigger in the chair, his back straighter and, as the confidence flowed into him, he became more lucid and more relaxed.

"I ran a quick check on them this morning. They're a firm of insurance underwriters, active on Lloyds and seemingly quite legitimate. I tried to speak to their accounts department but they wouldn't tell me anything over the phone. They wouldn't even confirm that they had a Simon Murrell on their payroll."

"So make an appointment to go see them. Rattle the senior partner if you have to."

"Already done. I'm seeing him at three."

I nodded in genuine approval.

"And get me some information about them: a recent set of accounts, a list of the directors, go talk to some people in the City. I want to know anything about the company that might, just might, make them feel a little edgy or uncomfortable if we have to start playing hardball."

"In relation to Simon?"

"In relation to anything. I want to know about any unpaid tax bills, pending sexual harassment cases, curb crawling allegations against any of the partners, unfair dismissal tribunals... anything that might give me a bit of leverage if we need them to co-operate and they're reluctant to do so."

"Got it."

I was so taken aback by the young man's uncharacteristic pro-activity that the dipped biscuit I was holding inches above my mug severed in two and plummeted into what remained of my tea. A large splash-back landed on my only silk tie; another trip to the dry cleaners. I cursed under my breath.

"Good," I wiped my fingers on a paper. "I'm going to get DS Duggan to meet you there, but it's your gig, Mike. You do the talking, you do the ferreting, you bring me back the information. He's just there to make you look good."

Sheridan now almost looked the part. He nodded in a business-like manner and waited to be dismissed. I wasn't quite ready to let him go.

"There are a couple of other things I want you to do for me."

He opened his notebook again and held his pen poised a quarter inch above the paper. I wiped some biscuit off the corner of the Maria Murrell transcript and handed it across.

"This is what Simon Murrell's wife told me when she presented herself for interview."

He nodded again.

"Her contact details are on there. I want you to get on to her, in person if you can, by phone if you can't. Mrs Murrell told us that Simon had been having affairs throughout their relationship. His secretary at the bank was a woman called Gail Weaver. I will lay down a fiver that they had been doing the deed as well. Find out what you can about her and whether Maria knows anything about an affair between the two of them. Any little detail could be useful. I also want to know what Maria's relationship was like with Gail. Were they best buddies at the office or were they ready to scratch each other's eyes out? Are we talking macramé or mud wrestling? You know the type of thing."

For the first time he allowed himself to enjoy the comment.

"And the other thing?"

"I want you to find me a school in Folkestone."

Sheridan looked puzzled.

"Not just any school. I'm looking for a particular 14-year old girl and I want to contact her through her Head Teacher."

"Is she to do with the enquiry?"

"Loosely. Her name's Chloe Hailey. All I want is the telephone number of the school and the name of the Head Teacher. I don't want her picked up, followed, or tipped off. In fact I don't want anyone knowing that we're even looking for her. This one has to be handled sensitively. Got me?"

"Leave it with me."

"Now call me once you're done at Santuary and maybe we'll meet up later and get our heads together. You never know, we might even get DS Duggan to buy us both a drink. In the meantime I've got to visit a man about a car," I finished, ushering him out of the office as his expression changed from mildly puzzled to completely perplexed.

UNLESS YOU KNEW the location of the garage where Dean Weaver worked, you would have been hard pushed to find it. Tucked in the service road behind a parade of small shops less than half a mile from where Simon Murrell's body had been dumped, I found myself wondering how it could possibly hope to pull in any business from passing trade. The only pointer to its whereabouts was a rusting metal sign, not much bigger than an average sheet of company letterhead, screwed to a fencepost at the entrance to the service road. If you got close enough, you could just make out that the garage offered full services and regular checks, but it was surely illegible from a passing car and still a challenge to the eye at a distance of only inches, rendering its marketing value virtually nil.

I wandered farther down the service road, turning right at the bottom so that I was now walking parallel to the backs of the shops on the parade. The disembowelled bodies of five or six old run-arounds were evident as were a similar number of young men in heavily oil-stained, navy blue overalls. One of them caught my eye as he emerged from underneath an old Ford Granada. He lifted himself off the floor to enquire if I needed help.

"I've got a car that needs servicing," I replied above the din of a cheap radio playing Kylie Minogue.

The man, tanned and in his late twenties, wiped the grease off his hands with a scrunched-up piece of newspaper and rolled the sleeves of his overalls down to his wrists to conceal tattoos on each forearm. He went to offer his hand for me to shake before thinking better of it, turning it instead to usher me into a small room that doubled as a reception. As I entered, my foot clung to a patch of something sticky on the cheap kitchen linoleum that they had laid on the floor. On my side of the counter was a bench seat that looked barely cleaner than the mechanics' overalls, a free vend coffee machine out of everything except for hot chocolate and a pile of old magazines. Mostly "Auto Express" or the like. To one side of the counter was a poster-sized calendar from a local tyre supplier, to the other a second, well-thumbed alternative from which the tanned, and probably silicon-enhanced, breasts of young topless girls stood out ahead of their faces.

"So you need a service?" he asked, opening to the following week a grimy desk diary, whose dog-eared pages were almost obliterated by unintelligible ballpoint scrawl.

"No, I need a price for a service."

He glared at me, as if this was the type of insolent remark to which he would normally put right with a fist. For whatever reason, and it couldn't have been my bearing for he was at least twice my size all over, he thought better of it.

"What car, what service?"

"Vauxhall Cavalier, 72,000 miles."

"What year?"

"This year."

He looked confounded. I decided to help him out.

"Oh, I see, you mean what year's the car, not what year do I want the service done."

He kept whatever sense of humour he had well hidden.

"1992."

He hammered the buttons on an ageing calculator before turning the calculator towards me to confirm his arithmetic.

"A hundred and twenty, a ton for cash."

"And the VAT?"

He smiled.

"Give me cash and we can lose the VAT."

I smiled again, reaching into my pocket for my warrant card, opening it slowly in the palm of my right hand before slapping it down on the counter top with a ferocity that made his calculator jump.

"Taking cash and not declaring it is an offence," I smiled. "Trading Standards and the Revenue would be very interested."

"Every garage does it."

"Yep, but you're the ones I caught," I confirmed, making a grand gesture of switching off a hand-held tape recorder that had no batteries in it anyway.

"What do you want?"

"I want to speak to one of your guys."

"Who?"

"Dean Weaver."

"Why do you want him?"

"I want to compare tattoos," I whispered. "It's none of your fucking business."

"Dean's in the last bay, working on an old Renault."

"Thank you. Now I want you to go and get him for me and bring him in here. I don't want you to tell him why or who I am. Just bring him in here and then go and get on with whatever it was you were doing when I arrived."

I watched as he left the office and walked back down the right-of-way to where he had indicated Dean Weaver would have been working. I helped myself to a drink from the free vend machine while I waited.

I watched out of the grubby window as Dean Weaver approached the office, wiping his hands on a green paper towel. He was tall, over six feet, and had clearly pumped more iron in his life than I'd had hot dinners. As he entered the office, he dipped to fit through the door, his frame filling the space between me and the counter, accentuating his size and stature. He peered down at me through narrow, dark brown eyes, his eyebrows all but meeting at the top of his nose, his face framed by close-cropped hair on top and a significant growth of stubble around the bottom. His overalls were undone down to his waist, the arms tied into each other to secure them. Tattoos cascaded down both forearms and up towards his shoulders, disappearing beneath the fabric of the navy blue tee shirt that was taut against the girth of his upper arms. A second tattoo – an eagle in flight – drew your eye immediately to the right hand side of his neck, one wing tip touching just beneath his right ear, the other curving round towards his Adam's apple.

"Hello, Dean." I gestured for him to sit down. He remained standing, his gaze fixed and impassive.

"Who are you and what do you want?"

I introduced myself, showing him my warrant card, which he studied in finite detail before passing back. My mouth dry, I took a sip from the lukewarm drink in my hand.

"Do you want a hot chocolate?" I offered.

He shook his head, but said nothing.

"Wise choice." I dropped the half-empty cup into the bin in the corner. "I just wanted to ask you a few questions, if that's okay?"

He continued to stare down at me, shrugging his shoulders in the manner of an insolent, disinterested teenager. I took his silence as agreement.

"Do you know anyone called Simon Murrell?"

He continued to look straight at me, a smile slowly breaking out across his face as he began to shake his head again.

"Have I said something that you find funny?"

"She put you up to this, didn't she?" he replied, quietly, without hysteria but with no little menace.

"She?"

"Don't give me that. You know exactly who I mean, that lovely bitch of a wife of mine."

"We've spoken to your wife, yes."

"I knew it. I'll fucking kill her."

"From what I've heard, Mr Weaver, you've already had a pretty good go at that."

He smiled again.

"Is that right? And what else have you heard?"

"Why don't you answer my questions before you starting asking ones of your own?"

He leant back against the service counter and folded his arms across his chest. He was going to volunteer nothing. I was determined to jolt him out of his complacency and make some kind of headway without having to go the whole hog of arresting him. After all, at the moment, I had nothing to arrest him on.

"Play ball with me, Dean, and we can have you back under that Renault real quick. Mess me around and it becomes a whole new ball game."

He remained emotionless.

"So can I take it that you've heard of Simon Murrell?"

No feedback. Perhaps the man-machine did not compute. I sat myself down on the bench seat, crossing my left leg over my right, and sitting back in as relaxed a position as the furniture would allow. His narrow eyes followed my every movement. I reached into the inside pocket of my jacket, and pulled out the creased autopsy photograph of Murrell and passed it across. It elicited the first flicker of recognition. Perhaps, I reflected, he had never known Murrell's name.

"I tell you what," I began. "Why don't I tell you what I know, and then maybe we can talk?"

Still no reaction. I carried on regardless.

"Okay, so I know that your lovely Gail and my friend Simon Murrell had been engaging in a little horizontal gymnastics while you were, shall we say, away on your recent business trip. I also know that when you found out about their little relationship, you weren't best pleased. Doesn't do much for your self-image, I can understand that. Can't say I really blame you there. But, you see, where you and I are different, I don't think I would have throttled her half to death and tried to do the same to him."

"Why not?"

"Because you see, when a policeman like me is forced to investigate how Mr Murrell here came to be murdered and then dumped outside a charity shop in a black plastic bag, it kind of puts somebody with your motive and track record firmly in the frame."

"I want a solicitor."

"Do you need one?"

"I'm entitled to one."

I nodded.

"Okay. Let me call a squad car with its siren blaring and its lights flashing and we can call you a brief after we've decamped to the station. But I know they're awfully busy at the minute so it might be a few hours before we can actually get to sit down. You never know, you may end up being our guest overnight."

He looked at me and then at his wristwatch, two beads of sweat just beginning to bubble up below his tightly cropped hairline.

"Alternatively we could just carry on our chat here for now," I offered helpfully, "and then do the formal interview bit later. If we need to."

He nodded. I gestured again for him to sit down and this time he responded, but not happily and rather in the manner of a chastised toddler reluctantly doing what its parent wants.

At last I felt in control.

"When did you first find out that Gail and Murrell had been having an affair?"

Dean Weaver stared straight down at his hands, picking grease and engine oil out from beneath the fingernails on his right hand with the nail on his left index finger.

"Before you got out of prison?"

He nodded and then looked up from his hands.

"I kind of had a feeling when I was inside. You know, the visits and the letters got more infrequent and when she did visit, she seemed more distant than usual, like she was doing it because she had to, rather than she wanted to. But also she was dressed really nicely, make-up, good perfume and that. It seemed fairly obvious that none of that was for me."

"And so you came out and… then what?"

"I came out and she kept on saying she was busy, working late. We hardly ever saw each other. I got this job here through a mate, so when I got home I wanted something to eat and, you know, a bit of female company. But she was never there, and there was never anything in the place to eat."

"So?"

"So I decided to follow her."

"And?"

"Work it out for yourself, detective. I followed her back to his place and waited until the following morning. I don't think they were playing cards all night."

"So you smacked her about a bit to teach her a lesson?"

"I kept tabs on them for a couple more weeks, until I was sure that they were together and that I got a proper look at him. Then I confronted her."

"With your fists?"

I knew I was on slightly shaky ground here but there was an investigation to be conducted and I wasn't about to let it drop simply because it made me feel bad about myself.

"It got out of hand. She'd been drinking and so had I. We're both strong characters, probably too strong, and things went too far. But I couldn't let her carry on pissing all over me without letting her know that I had disapproved."

"Fractured eye socket, compression fracture of the right cheekbone, multiple bruises to the face and torso, what looked like attempted strangulation," I read from my notebook. "I think it's safe to say you let her know you disapproved."

The litany of injuries sustained by Gail Weaver at his own hands left Dean quiet and contemplative and me determined to call Connor as soon as the interview was over.

"So if you did that to Gail, I can't imagine what you wanted to do to Simon."

Dean wiped his nose against the back of his right hand and then caressed his five o'clock shadow with the palm, shaking his head as he did so.

"Nothing. I did absolutely nothing to him."

"And how am I meant to believe that? You've got all the classics stacked in your corner. Form, motive, opportunity. It doesn't come a lot better than that if you're a copper like me and it can't look a lot worse if you're a scrote like you."

"Maybe so but I didn't touch him."

I got up from the bench seat and joined him at the counter.

"Okay, I believe you for now. Let's just hope a jury will too. I strongly recommend that you call me if anything should suddenly come back to you. Otherwise, I shouldn't book a holiday in the near future. We'll need to speak again. And make sure your mate starts charging VAT. I think he might find there's a lot of interest in his books over the next couple of months."

I left a contact card on the counter and watched as he picked it up, leaving a greasy thumbprint in the top right hand corner as he slid it into a pocket of his oily overalls. I turned back as I reached the half-glazed door to leave. He hadn't moved an inch.

"Just one last thing," I said, turning back. "Did you ever speak to Simon Murrell face to face? Confront him about Gail, go round to his house for a chat? Anything like that?"

He shook his head.

"Certain?"

He nodded again. I left.

Chapter Twenty-One

INVESTIGATIONS NEVER PROCEED at a constant pace. That's another fallacy from TV cop shows. Not getting carried away with the ups, managing expectations through the downs and holding fast to the belief that, sooner or later, you're going to get a break are all important staging posts on the road to catching a killer. Where TV cops speed their way to an arrest via a dramatic car chase down a back alley strewn with empty cardboard boxes, the reality is more mundane, more painstaking, and based more heavily on making sense of apparently random snatches of information and then stitching them together to create an accurate pattern of events. It is time-consuming and frustrating and is usually as dependent on good fortune as it is on good detection. But never tell anyone I said that.

"Be a good copper for sure," Henry Raven once told me, "but be a lucky one as well."

The result is the end product that we all strive for, but it is not the process itself. The process is something that is constrained by procedure and weighed down by paperwork to ensure that nothing can come undone at the hands of some preppy, sharp-suited lawyer. So, when luck does come our way, we greet her like an old friend.

On the way to meet Duggan and Sheridan, I received four pieces of information. Three had buoyed me up; the fourth had threatened to drag me under. Door to door enquiries that Danny Thorne had undertaken among Simon Murrell's unneighbourly neighbours had thrown up two potentially interesting nuggets: a sighting of what sounded like Dean Weaver outside Simon's bedsit the week before he died, though Weaver had categorically told me he had never met him, and more interesting still, reports of a heated argument between Simon and a woman both inside and outside the property on the Saturday of the weekend that he died. Having been shown a number of photographs, the neighbour had identified the woman as Maria, the estranged wife; the same estranged wife that had claimed it had been more than a year since she had seen her husband. I sensed, for the first time, real flesh being added to the bones of our enquiry.

The third piece of information was an update from Sheridan that Santuary Holdings had confirmed paying Simon Murrell as a consultant, but that there was further information he wanted to give me in person.

The fourth – a text message from Elaine – robbed me of my temporary elation. She was considering moving to the Peak District to be nearer to her parents and wanted to take Connor with her. Could I call her to discuss? Presented like that, I wondered what there could be to talk about.

Holding on as tightly to my bottled beer as I was to my bottled-up anger, I sat at a corner table in the dimly lit bar, swirling the remaining half of Budvar as I waited for Duggan and Sheridan to arrive. An e-cigarette was propped between my index and forefingers and every few minutes I drew it closer to my mouth and let it flavour my lips before expelling it again to the satisfying annoyance of those on the table next to me. God, I wished it had been a real cigarette.

After arriving at the bar twenty minutes earlier, with the exception of the barman who had charged me a sip under three quid for a cold beer, I had spoken to nobody of note. Occasionally some of those disturbed by my smoke would comment to each other on the dishevelled, besuited individual who sat on his own, through expensive hair extensions or with hands muffled across manicured goatees. I merely smiled and tipped my bottle in their direction in polite acknowledgement of their interest.

Elaine's text, coupled with the way we had parted after our talk with Connor, had winded me and after leaving Weaver I had found myself in desperate need of an objective view. Duggan had been pushing me to see a counsellor and, without telling him, I had made contact. I had only seen her once before but had called her from the car and pleaded for a half hour to talk. I offered double her going rate, which offended her, and she reminded me that it wasn't possible to simply shoe-horn me in whenever I felt like it. I, on the other hand, thought that was the whole point. But then she did exactly that and I had come directly from her to the bar.

BRENDA WAS IN her late fifties, a Mother Earth type, with attractive auburn hair cut flatteringly into a soft bob. She had a gold ring on almost every finger and two on her slender wedding finger, one of which bore a ruby that caught the sunlight coming through the south-facing window of the room in which we sat. A gold locket, whose copperplate inscription I couldn't quite read, hung on a long gold chain and rested at the apex of her fulsome cleavage. I have never been told her surname.

As soon as I arrived, she had ushered me upstairs into what would once have been one of the house's three bedrooms and which was now rather grandly signposted as a 'consulting room'. It was a portrait of everything inoffensive. A brown velour three piece suite and a small teak coffee table were the only notable items of furniture, together with some ready-made floral curtains that hung loose from the tracking that ran across the top of the bay window. The room looked identical today to the first time I had seen it. We took the same places as last time in facing armchairs. Brenda placed a glass of water on the corner of the table nearest to her, before reaching into a large black leather bag to take out a spiral-bound notebook and a white travel alarm clock. She placed the clock at her end of the table, facing her.

"Half an hour. I can only give you half an hour."

"Thanks for seeing me."

"So what's happened that couldn't wait until the week-end?"

We'd only known each other for a week and yet I had probably told her more about me in that first hour than I had anyone else. She knew the real reason for the break-up and had cut me no slack in her assessment of the situation. She had challenged my conscience and had asked me to prove that I wasn't simply somebody who couldn't keep his rage under control and was fearful that he would hit out again if the circumstances were similar. It was tough love. Being forced to listen to a dissection of my character and all its flaws – and God knows there are plenty of them – was painful. More than once I had thought of leaving the session and not returning.

That I had come back, Brenda told me, was proof that I believed in the process. I deserved credit for coming back. I didn't feel the same way. Nobody knew I was seeing Brenda and I wanted to keep it that way.

"Elaine sent me a text an hour ago to say she wants to take Connor to live in the Peak District."

I offered her my mobile with the message still on screen. She waved it away.

"And you don't want that?"

"Of course I don't. I thought I was just beginning to win him over."

"Is that how you see it? A competition. Winner takes all?"

Her gentle Irish brogue lent a softness to the question that belied the fact that she was waiting for an answer.

"That's what it's become. A competition."

"So, she's sent you this message which, presumably, you haven't discussed with her because you've rushed straight here. And you feel that suddenly you've lost what little control you thought you'd regained?"

I nodded.

"The question is what are you going to do about it?"

I looked up.

"What are you going to do about it?" she repeated. "Are you going to sit here and wallow, or are you going to tell her it's not what you want? Are you going to suggest an alternative? Are you going to offer her something positive? Wouldn't that be a sensible place to start?"

She made everything sound so damn obvious.

"And what does Connor want? Maybe he doesn't want to go to the Peak District. Then again, maybe he does. Maybe he'd like to stay close to you. Maybe he doesn't know it's part of a plan. Maybe nobody's asked him. Maybe—

"Jack, you need to ask yourself if you're reacting to events instead of shaping them. Are you responding sensibly or are you responding too dramatically to every twist and turn, every snippet of information or suggestion that comes your way?"

I chose not to answer.

"If you want to have a relationship you need to take more responsibility rather than taking too much control of it. It's all in the balance. Instead of flying off the handle at Elaine, which is probably what she expects you to do, why don't you take her out for dinner and discuss her plans?"

"Dinner?"

"Dinner. You were in a relationship with this woman until only four months ago. She's the mother of your child. Going for a meal to discuss what's best for him doesn't have to be interpreted as a declaration of war or an attempt at reconciliation. Just take her for a meal, tell her how you feel about it and give her the time to tell you as well. Then talk about it and see what you both think."

Asking Elaine out for dinner was a novel approach. I couldn't imagine how I would suggest the idea and certainly had no inclination as to how she would react, let alone whether she would accept. But I'd jumped into this counselling thing with both feet and if the folded twenties I handed Brenda each time we met were to be worth anything, then I had decided early on that I would follow through on her advice. I still wasn't happy as I left but at least I had a plan. And that, to me, was progress.

Chapter Twenty-Two

I ONLY HAD to wait another twenty minutes before Duggan and Sheridan arrived, placing their pint glasses on the small round table alongside another bottle for me. I had to agree with Harry's assertion that it was going to get harder to resist growing pressure for the release of Simon Murrell's body for burial. His parents, from whom he had been estranged for more than five years, regarded a dignified Christian funeral as the one final responsibility they could discharge for their son in death. I wanted to resist a while longer, because despite the detail of Andy Cook's post-mortem report, something had convinced me that Simon Murrell's body could yield even more. It would be much easier for us to gather all the information we might need now, rather than have to cope with the whole emotional and legal wrangle that would accompany an exhumation further down the line. But I knew we couldn't hold out for long.

"The fact that one of the neighbours talked about a thick set, heavily tattooed man with close-cropped hair lurking around Simon's house puts Weaver squarely in the frame as far as I'm concerned."

Harry pulled three packets of peanuts and two bags of

crisps from his various pockets, spilling them across the tabletop.

"Well if you're so convinced Weaver's responsible, then maybe somewhere on the body there are traces of engine oil or grease that will tie him in?"

"Maybe, maybe not."

I swiped traces of beer away from my top lip with my tongue.

"No jury would convict on the presence of engine oil alone. It's not exactly DNA. In any case, our Dean may not be the biggest intellect on the planet, but he *has* been round the block a few times and even he would have been smart enough to wear gloves."

"That's true," reasoned Duggan. "But if there are traces of oil, you know he's got to be a line worth pushing. Even if there isn't it doesn't mean he didn't do it. It's got to be worth a shot."

"Maybe SOCO found evidence of him at the bedsit?"

I opened a second bag of salt and vinegar crisps, using the one crisp remaining from the previous packet between the index and forefinger of my right hand to emphasise my point.

"I didn't see anything in my report, but then again they wouldn't have specifically been looking for it. We could send the team back in. I just don't think it's him, but anything that puts him inside the bedsit turns him into a liar because he's adamant that he and Simon never met."

"What about the wife?" Duggan asked.

"She certainly needs to be hauled back in because I get the distinct feeling she's been playing us for arseholes. I've left a message for Lesley to go get her."

"What I don't get is why she came in to see us in the first

place if she was only going to feed us all that bollocks about not having seen him."

I shrugged my shoulders.

"You can ask her exactly that question. There's lots going on here that I just don't get at the moment. But when I do, I have a feeling that we won't be a million miles away from catching our killer. Why don't you talk to Andy Cook about engine oil on the body and get SOCO back to the bedsit again to check for traces of Weaver?"

"Now, another round of drinks and you call tell me all about Santuary Holdings."

I returned from the bar a few minutes later and distributed more drinks, by which time Sheridan had taken out his notebook. I placed the palm of my right hand on its cover and forced it shut.

"From memory, Mike, and instinct; not from notes. I want your gut feeling on this one."

Sheridan placed his hands around the rim of his pint glass as if warming them on a mid-winter cup of hot chocolate. He started by staring into the beer.

"At first nobody was available to talk to us but I wasn't having that, so we started getting a bit noisy, making a fuss, and suddenly the meeting that the finance director and financial controller were in came to an early finish. We were just grateful that they were able to break into their heavy schedule and give us a few minutes of their valuable time. Obviously. The finance director's a greasy, oily twat called Piers Crouch. Late forties, I'd guess, all old school tie and slicked back hair. He stared us up and down a few times before deciding it was okay to talk to us, like he had a choice. The long and short of it is that he confirmed the payments in

Simon's bank statements had come from them and that he had been on their payroll as a consultant."

"How long had he been working for them?"

"They couldn't be absolutely certain without checking the records but they think he came on board a few months after the crash."

"The crash?"

"The Lloyd's Crash," Sheridan advised. "Between '89 and '93 the Lloyd's insurance market suffered losses like it had never seen before, caused mainly by massive compensation payments that had to be made because of unprecedented claims for hurricane damage, oil tanker disasters, that kind of thing. Basically they all hit the market at roughly the same time."

"And?"

"And the bill came to literally billions, which had to be footed by the so-called Lloyd's Names. These are the minted individuals who invest in the market with the intention of taking a hefty wedge of its profits."

"But in this case they had to take on the losses?"

"Big time, and many of them simply couldn't cope with the size of the bill and they ended up losing everything. And guess what? Simon Murrell was a Lloyd's Name."

"And he lost everything?"

"I need to do a bit more work on that but I guess so."

"Well the dates fit. It would explain why he was so down on his luck and would also square with what Maria said about him having money troubles. So what did he consult with this lot on?"

"They weren't able to tell us. Apparently, he provided personal consultancy to their chairman."

"What the fuck does 'personal consultancy' mean? And who's their chairman?"

"That's where it starts to get a bit tasty. The chairman is one Crispin Monk who, surprise surprise, is also a Lloyd's Name."

"So it's an old boys' network after all. They're looking after their own. How touching. I think we need to know a bit more about Mr Monk and then I think it's time we paid him a visit."

"But that's not all," Sheridan interrupted. "Remember the snatch of newspaper that was found in Simon's hand?"

"It may not be significant, but I got the whole page from the archives. On one side was an article on drug misuse, the threats to society of different types of drug and the various counselling services available to young addicts, that kind of crap. I thought that was probably the relevant bit, so I was about to file in until the next team meeting until I read the other side of the page."

"Which was?"

"Which was a three-quarter page profile of Crispin Monk."

Chapter Twenty-Three

I HADN'T SEEN Keith Doughty for more than five years and, given that I was calling for a favour, I felt guilty getting in touch after so long.

"Jack Munday, you old bastard," was the opening line in his distinctive Australian drawl as he returned the message that I had left on his voicemail at The Times. "It must be, Christ knows, three or four years. I thought you were probably dead. Kept scanning the obits here but they don't seem to cover low life like you. Man, it was good to hear your voice. How are you doing and how's that drop dead gorgeous wife and kid of yours?"

"She's okay," I lied, "and Connor's fantastic. Growing up too fast, though. Listen, I'm sorry, I know I should have been in touch earlier. Best intentions and all that. I wanted to know if we could get together and catch up on old times, but I've got to be honest, the real reason for the call was for some help. I'm trying to do some research for a case I'm on and I figured you might be the kind of guy to set me right."

"Official research?"

"Semi-official," I fudged. "I need some background on some stuff and rather than just sit and wade my way through files without knowing properly what I'm looking at, it would be great if you could give me a top line on it. We could hit the curry and lager trail again. It would be just like before."

"Mate, I'm too old now to end the evening puking my guts up on the inside of a cab."

"Okay, so maybe not *exactly* like before."

"Christ, of course I'll meet you, whatever the reason. It would be great to catch up, and you know I'll help however I can. But you *do* know where you called me, don't you? I cover business for The Times, not crime. I haven't done crime since I left the locals."

"Your new stuff probably suits my needs better. I need some background on the Lloyd's Crash, as much as you can give me, and anything you know about Crispin Monk."

"The MP?"

"The same."

"Lloyd's is easy. What do you need to know about Monk?"

"Background stuff really: where he came from, what he stands for, who he mixes with and who he doesn't; that kind of thing. I want to know what the world you move in thinks of him."

"Monk's the coming man, the Tories' great white hope. If you're telling me he's in bother, it's one motherfucker of a story and I'm telling you now, I'm having it when you're ready."

"A profile that The Times ran on him a couple of months ago found its way into the closed fist of the body of a man who used to know him at university. It could well be nothing; it probably is nothing and it's certainly way too early to say more but, of course, if there *is* more, the old rules apply."

"Top man," bellowed Doughty down the phone line. "You're a gent. Give me a couple of days, I'll call you back and let you know what I've got. Then we can meet up for a ruby."

Chapter Twenty-Four

THE BREEZE FROM an open window in Interview Room One carried the scent of Lesley Hilton's perfume towards the door as I entered. Despite the humidity, she looked a model of composure, standing with her arms folded, her lower back resting against the cold radiator, her legs crossed just above the ankle. The sunlight caught the lighter blonde streaks in her hair. She looked up at the sound of the door and smiled in my direction. Her face carried just as much make-up as was needed to show she'd made an effort. She wore a well-cut, light blue man's-style shirt, tucked neatly into a navy blue pencil skirt; the hem rested just above the knee as her tanned, sculpted legs drifted away into navy court shoes. In the previous few weeks I had become more aware of her as a woman and less as just another colleague.

In the corner, a standing fan laboured hard on our behalf but merely recirculated the same stale, dry, hot air, and didn't provide the relief that its efforts deserved.

"I apologise that we can't make the environment any more comfortable than this."

I smiled at Maria Murrell, who sat on the other side of the

table with a look that implied she felt she was about to be unfairly chastised.

"I suppose the big banks that you and Simon were used to would have been all air conditioning, large atria, tropical fish tanks and chilled mineral water, but I'm afraid these old police stations were never really built with comfort in mind. What's the term they use for all that kind of stuff, Lesley?"

"Feng shui?"

Lesley was trying to be helpful but wasn't completely clear in her own mind as to the direction I was taking.

"I think you mean ergonomic," offered Maria, speaking for the first time since I came into the room. It was her only reaction to my small talk, but then again I hadn't expected too much.

"That's it, ergonomics. It's not feng shui, Lesley. It's ergonomics. You've been watching too many of those home improvement programmes."

I pulled a chair away from the table, lifted myself onto the wide radiator and turned the chair with my right leg to enable me to rest my feet on it. It also placed me higher than Maria Murrell and psychology is important in these situations. Another Ravenism.

"You see, Mrs Murrell – and by the way, thank you for coming back into see us again – I'm much more interested in cold, hard facts. Like why, when a person tells me that she hasn't seen her estranged husband for more than a year, we get a confirmed sighting of the same woman going at it with the same estranged husband only a couple of days before his body turns up. Now, you can tell me I'm splitting hairs if you want to, but my old mum used to call that a lie and maybe it's my years of training or my copper's intuition, but liars around a murder enquiry tend to arouse suspicion."

Maria remained still. Her head was slightly bowed in a mix of defiance and humiliation; her eyes were fixed resolutely down at the tabletop. Beside her sat her solicitor, a corpulent man with unkempt curly hair and a cheap, stained blue and white striped tie draped over the topography of his stomach. I made no attempt to catch his name.

"Shall we start from scratch? We can pretend our first conversation never happened, if you like. I mean, after all, we don't know how much of that was true and how much was a lie, do we?"

"Everything I told you was true, except for the fact that I had been to see Simon that afternoon."

"But that's fairly central to our enquiry, wouldn't you say?"

"Maybe I forgot. We didn't see each other for long. It wasn't as if we were planning to get back together."

"I'm sorry, Maria," pitched in Lesley, "I just don't buy it. You go to see your estranged husband, with whom you have enjoyed the most phenomenal lifestyle, with whom you had a particularly torrid relationship that you told us ended acrimoniously, whom you haven't seen for more than a year and then you expect us to believe you simply forgot to mention that you saw him at all?"

We sat in forced silence for what seemed like minutes but was almost certainly less.

Maria Murrell looked up. She had started to cry; not full-blown weeping, but the sort of tears that just appear no matter how hard you try to suppress them. She dabbed her eyes with a screwed-up paper tissue and nodded.

"So you did go to see Simon that Saturday?"

She nodded and I asked her to repeat her confirmation for the tape recording. She did so.

"I went to warn him."

It was the first new piece of information that she had actually offered.

"To warn him against what?"

"Gail called me. She told me that that animal of a husband of hers had found out she and Simon had been sleeping together. She was frightened of what was going to happen to him."

"So why did she call *you*?"

"I guess she didn't have anyone else to turn to. She was terrified. Dean had already started hitting her and I think she was really scared about what he might do to Simon if he got hold of him."

"That all makes sense but I still don't get why she called *you*?"

"Gail and I were still in contact. We're friends. Alright, so we hadn't seen or spoken to each other in a while but she thought I probably still cared enough about Simon to pass the warning on."

"And did you? Care enough, I mean?"

Maria asked for some water. I nodded to the WPC who had been waiting in the far corner of the room pending our arrival. She climbed out of her chair with exaggerated effort and left in a manner that suggested she begrudged having to fulfil such a menial task.

"I guess I must have done. Whether I cared about Simon or Gail more, I don't know, but she sounded pretty desperate, and whatever I thought about Simon, I didn't want to see Dean Weaver get his hands on him."

"So you kept in touch with Gail even though you knew she was sleeping with your husband?" Lesley asked.

Maria smiled.

"Yes, I did. But then, if I stopped talking to people simply because they'd had sex with Simon, believe me I'd have nobody to talk to."

"And Gail gave you Simon's address?"

Maria nodded.

"He didn't have a telephone any more. I suppose he couldn't afford it. I had to go and wait until I saw him come home."

"And when he did?"

"I watched him come down the street and waited for him to go inside. It upset me because even from a distance I could tell he wasn't the same man that I married. I mean, he was still only in his thirties but he seemed so much older, shuffling rather than walking. He somehow looked like he had been dragged down by it all. Simon was always a showman, the life and soul of every party. The Simon I married would never have allowed himself to be beaten like this."

We all looked towards the door as the handle turned and the WPC with the attitude problem returned with a jug of water and three tumblers balanced precariously on a small black tray. Without speaking, she placed the tray on the table top and returned to her seat in the corner. I made a mental note to have a word with her afterwards.

"So you watched him come home. And then?"

"I waited for him to shut the door behind him and got out of the car to walk across. My heart was in my stomach. I can't remember the last time I felt that nervous about anything. I rang the bell and waited for him to answer."

"And how did he respond?"

"He looked at me and I think, for a few seconds, a smile began to come across his face and then he just seemed to stifle it. I think he was ashamed of where he was living and *how* he was living. He wouldn't invite me inside, which is why your witness heard all that they did."

"You argued?"

"I asked him what he thought he was doing still playing around with Gail when Dean was out of prison. I told him Gail was terrified that Dean was going to come after him, and that Dean had already been hitting Gail. That she had asked me to warn him off. He lost it with me. He thought I was lying to him. He told me I was bitter about the way things worked out for us and said I was trying to drive a wedge between him and Gail because deep down I still wanted him for myself."

"Is that true?"

"No, not at all. I did still care about him, of course I did. I didn't want to see him beaten to a pulp by Dean Weaver. If that had happened and I hadn't tried to warn him, what kind of person would that have made me?"

I stood up and turned my back on her before speaking again.

"The alternative view is that you were the wronged wife. You felt excluded, spurned, thrown onto the scrapheap by him. You resented the fact that the lifestyle he promised you had been taken away as a result of his own extravagance. You wanted your own back; you were vengeful. You argued, not about Gail but about *you*. Perhaps you went inside, perhaps you got him drunk, and perhaps you strangled him. Perhaps."

Maria Murrell looked horrified. Her solicitor tried to

interrupt me but a combination of my glare and an extrava-
gant hand gesture to wave him away persuaded him back into
his seat.

"You can't seriously believe that. Look at the two of us.
Do you really think that, drunk or not, I'd have had the
strength to kill him, even if I wanted to?"

"Maybe not on your own," Lesley chipped in. "Maybe
you were angry with Simon for your reasons and Dean was
gunning for him for his own. It kind of makes sense for the
two of you to get together. A marriage of convenience. You
could have got Simon relaxed, drunk, drugged even. Catch up
on old times and then let Dean in to finish him off."

"That's just not true. It's ridiculous."

"Then, once you were pretty sure he was dead, the two of
you lifted him into the black bag and disposed of the body
together. Is that how it was, Maria?"

"Absolutely not. I came here to help, not to be accused of
murder."

She looked towards her ineffective solicitor for support,
but received none.

"No-one's accusing you of murder, Maria. But we already
have enough to start talking to you about withholding
evidence and attempting to pervert the course of justice. How
can we be sure you're not concealing anything else? For all I
know, it may only be a short hop, skip, and jump from lying
about seeing Simon to lying about killing him."

Maria sipped earnestly from the water in front of her. She
slumped back in the chair and breathed hard. I walked away
from the table and looked out of the window. I turned back to
face her again.

"Do you know what a Lloyd's Name is, Mrs Murrell?"

She looked directly at me and nodded.

"And did you know that Simon was a Lloyd's Name?"

A second nod.

"Do you remember how that came to be?"

She sipped more water and concentrated on how to respond to the question.

"He didn't tell me too much about it at the time. Other than, of course, it was going to make him even richer. I remember thinking that it was just another one of Simon's moneymaking ventures. He had seen how much others had made out of Lloyd's and he obviously wanted a piece of it. That's no bad thing. Simon was very driven by success and at that time, in our world, success and money were inextricably linked. But there was also something in the status of being a Lloyd's Name that got Simon excited; he was obsessed with status. I think it was something to do with his background and always wanting to be accepted by people he perceived as having come from better. I think he thought being a Lloyd's Name would give him the chance to mix in more exalted circles."

"Which would have been fine if everything had gone to plan and he made lots of money from the market?"

"I guess so."

"But when the market crashed?"

"Simon's lifestyle – our lifestyle – was unsustainable. I knew that at the time but I decided the ride was worth it. Simon thought he was invincible; that he would go on winning and earning and there would never be a downside. It's a classic gambler's mentality. So everything was bought on credit, which could be serviced because money was flowing freely. Then, it all caught up with him. The lifestyle that his job provided was eventually his downfall. He lost his job because of the drugs and with it the income that funded the lifestyle. And then when Lloyd's crashed and not only cut off the money supply but actually left him with massive debts, he was finished and he didn't know how to handle it."

"So he blamed you?"

"I think he blamed everyone but himself. He was very much the victim. Everyone and everything had conspired against him. He was the only one who had lost out."

"So the people he had trusted were to blame?"

"Very much so. We were all guilty of having led him to this point. That was rubbish, of course. He lashed out at the people closest to him and sank further and further."

"Do you know that to become a Lloyd's Name, an existing Lloyd's Name has to nominate you?"

She shook her head.

"Have you any idea who might have nominated Simon?"

"No, but I don't think I'd have liked to have been them when everything collapsed."

"You think he'd have taken out his frustration on the person who persuaded him to become a Name?"

"I don't think he'd have needed much persuasion, but he would certainly have been angry."

"Particularly if they escaped unscathed when he lost everything?"

"Well if that *was* the case then I can imagine Simon making it his life's work to destroy them."

Her words lingered in the air as Lesley checked to make sure the interview was still being recorded.

"Tell me about Dean Weaver."

"I can't say I know him well."

Maria repeatedly twisted a tissue tightly around her left index finger before releasing it.

"I've met him once or twice and what I've seen of him and heard of him from other people I think he's a very angry and very dangerous man."

"Why dangerous?"

"Because he revels in violence. It's his life. It excites him. Gail once told me he got turned on – actually turned on – by the sight and thought of violence."

"How can you be so sure? She might be lying to you. She's still with him after all."

"She's only still with him because she's terrified what would happen if she tried to leave. She thinks she'd just disappear without trace."

"Isn't she just frightened of Dean in the same way you were frightened of Simon?"

"There's no comparison. Simon and I fought, of course, but Simon loved people. It was the fact that he loved too many, too much, and too often that got him into trouble. Dean Weaver hates people. I've seen the scars on Gail over the years that prove it: the bruises and the cuts. He doesn't even care about trying to hide it. He's not remotely ashamed of it. He hits her even when he knows the scars are going to show. He wants people to see the type of thing he's capable of. It's like a badge of honour for him; his way of showing that he controls what his wife can and cannot do."

I interlocked my fingers and pushed my hands down together until you could hear my knuckles crack.

"So Dean Weaver's a violent man. Tell me something I don't know."

"He wasn't going to miss the opportunity to show Simon

and anyone else who was watching that you can't mess around with what he sees as his property."

"And he'd have made sure that everyone knew it?"

She nodded.

"So when you went to see Simon, you really thought that if Dean Weaver had got his hands on him, he'd have beaten Simon to a pulp, like he did with Gail?"

Maria nodded again.

"To teach him a lesson, to show him who's boss?"

Another nod.

"From what you've told me, if Dean had got his hands on Simon it would have been a frenzied, bloody, out of control attack. He wouldn't have been able to contain himself. He'd have made a real mess of Simon."

"I wouldn't have been surprised."

"Cuts, bruises, and a real battering?"

"I'd have expected so."

I folded my arms in front of me and smiled at her.

"But Maria, you identified Simon's body for us."

Again, she nodded, looking directly into my eyes.

"There wasn't a mark on him. No cuts on his face, no battered bruising, no part of him had been beaten to a pulp. It doesn't sound to me like a frenzied attack by an out of control madman. From the way you've described him, the way Simon died doesn't sound like Dean Weaver's way at all, does it?"

Chapter Twenty-Five

CALL IT PROFESSIONAL pride or just a reluctance to look completely unprepared in front of an old mate, but I had resolved to do a little research of my own about Crispin Monk before meeting up with Keith Doughty. If I was looking for Keith to fill in the details, I figured that I, at least, ought to get to grips with the basics for myself. So I found myself back in Mario's café, cappuccino froth spilling out of the top of a scratched, white ceramic mug, struggling to fold *The Times* clipping into a manageable size. A broadsheet profile of a high rising politician was something of a departure from my normal newspaper reading, which usually extended no further than scouring the Sunday red tops for the previous night's lottery numbers, the footie reports and who's shagging who.

I unfolded the cutting to its full size, taking care not to let the corners fall directly into the cappuccino, and flattened it out across the table with the outside of my right hand. Four faces beamed out from the carefully choreographed photograph that dominated the upper half of the page. Monk, who but for the fact that I knew his age would have struck me as at least five years older, was pictured with his family outside the front of their country house somewhere in the Cotswolds. He and his wife, Francine, stood behind a waist-high, moss-covered stone wall whilst their immaculately groomed children, Max and Tabitha, sat on top of it between their mother and father. Monk carried the casual air of a country squire, a tweed jacket covering a checked shirt, his hair cut short enough for National Service and his small, piercing eyes seeming to reach out from inside the page as if to try and read my mind. I found myself doing the same in return. His right hand was tucked firmly into his jacket pocket, his other rested gently on Max's shoulder. Despite the physical contact there seemed an absence of genuine affection in his manner. But it was only a newspaper photograph and I had to guard against reading too much into it. On the right hand side of the photograph stood Francine, a fraction taller than her husband. She also wore country tweeds, covering a white polo neck sweater, her hair flowing softly on her shoulders. Her affection for her daughter seemed to be more natural. She struck me as fastidious about her appearance and resolutely behind her husband's relentless ascendancy.

The article itself was instructive as to how and why Monk had become the poster boy of the Conservative right. Not only was he well-educated and, as illustrated by the photograph, a committed family man, he was not afraid to speak his mind on the issues that he perceived mattered to Middle England behind its twitching net curtains. He crusaded – his language intentionally carried a kind of missionary zeal – on behalf of the nuclear family unit as the only way for society to be organised. He deplored any way of living that fell outside of those narrow parameters and saw no reason for the state to support those groups, let alone promote what he referred to as "diversified alternative lifestyles". He had gained most recognition for his strident opposition to anything that he labelled as "going soft", whether that involved rehabilitation of offenders, recreational drug use, and particularly homosexuality. I read in disbelief his quote about "deviant lifestyles producing a deviant society" and wondered if I was the first person to read it and be genuinely horrified. He had advocated that students caught smoking cannabis lose their places at university and be subject to the full rigours of the law, and that those in employment doing likewise should lose their jobs. He referred to "undisciplined behaviour" as being a "blight on society", claiming it as one of the reasons why Britain would struggle to regain the kind of pre-eminence and influence in the world that he and those like him regarded as their birthright.

I read the profile three times to try and get under the skin of Crispin Monk. I wanted to know whether these were, as he claimed, legitimately held beliefs or whether they had been carefully nurtured on the fringes of extremism as a mechanism to get him noticed. It also made me wonder whether the Crispin Monk staring out at me from the broadsheet page was the same person that Simon Murrell would have known at Cambridge and, if so, how that friendship could have ever developed. Even after the third read I remained uncertain. But, for the first time, I felt I had an outline. I would look to Keith to add colour to the picture.

I folded *The Times* cutting into a neatly pre-formed square and returned it to the inside pocket of my leather jacket, lifting a small, buff-coloured folder onto the table from the seat beside me. Across the cardboard cover Sheridan had used a black marker pen to write "Lloyd's" in his unruly hand. The

227

ink from the marker had begun to bleed across the cardboard, giving the lettering a feathered edge. As with Monk, I didn't want to reveal too much of my ignorance of Lloyd's to Keith so I had asked Sheridan to put together an idiot's guide for me. I was about to order a second coffee and read on when the shrill tone of my mobile pierced the hubbub in the café. It was Duggan. Chloe Hailey and her Head Teacher were waiting for me back at the station. He suggested I return. I closed the Lloyd's folder, leaving the contents as unread as before, paid my dues and departed.

The timing of Chloe's arrival had not been pre-arranged but neither had it been completely unexpected. When I first telephoned the school in Folkestone I had asked for the Head Teacher's co-operation. She had introduced herself with the authoritative manner that only a Head Teacher could muster. She was Sylvia Blake, a teacher for more than 30 years, the last ten as Head. She would act in the best interests of her school and her pupils and, if necessary, I would just have to work around that. What I saw – or heard – was what I was going to get, but I liked that. At least we understood each other. I had told her the reason I wanted to speak to Chloe and she understood the sensitivity of the situation. She hadn't known Ben, as he attended a different school, but did know of the family situation and had seen first-hand the impact that Ben's disappearance had had on Chloe's demeanour, concentration and confidence. She told me that this once gregarious girl had retreated into a shell and any information or reassurance I may provide could make a significant difference to her present as well as her future. It was Sylvia's suggestion that she talk privately to Chloe and then bring her to see me, rather than arouse the interest of staff and other pupils by having the conversation in Chloe's school environment. She seemed so assured in her reasoning that I saw no merit in disagreeing.

As I entered the station, Tom Grayson nodded in the direction of a middle-aged woman and a young girl who sat uneasily in the corner, head bowed, nursing a plastic cup of water between her hands. Sylvia Blake was shorter and stockier than I had imagined. Her greying hair was cut close to her head but in a manner that remained feminine. Her make-up was subtle and didn't disguise a fine bone structure in her face that made her appearance more intriguing than conventionally attractive. She wore a black business suit with a mauve shirt beneath, her legs crossed at the knee, and a beaten black briefcase slumping as if exhausted by her side. I turned and walked with purpose in her direction.

"Mrs Blake?"

I tried to project a smile that said we were on the same side.

"I'm Jack Munday."

She stood and took my hand firmly in her own. Chloe remained seated.

"I'm sorry we have arrived unannounced, Mr Munday, but Chloe was understandably anxious to hear what you have to say and I didn't feel inclined to delay her."

Sylvia urged her young charge to stand. Chloe rose and, though almost the same height as her Head Teacher, remained in her shadow, using her as a shield against some unseen, hidden threat. She hadn't spoken a word.

"And this must be Chloe?"

I offered my hand. For the first time she lifted her face and trained her eyes on me. She blushed, smiled a weak smile of tainted innocence but wouldn't shake my hand.

"Come with me. I'm sure you could both use something to drink and eat. I know I could. Perhaps Sergeant Grayson here can rustle us up something good from the canteen, if that's not a contradiction in terms, and have it brought to Interview Room Five for us?"

"Interview Room Five?"

Tom knew no such room existed. I planned to take Chloe and Mrs Blake into the room that we used to question potential rape or abuse victims. It is a relatively recent addition, less stark and more welcoming than a standard interview room, softer around the edges, with sofas rather than desks and chairs, good natural light, carpet rather than vinyl flooring and walls painted in delicate pastel shades. But I could hardly announce out loud "let's go to the rape suite".

"Yep, Interview Room Five, Tom. The one with the sofas."

The penny dropped. He nodded vigorously and with just a hint of embarrassment.

I unlocked the door to the Rape Suite and ushered Chloe and Sylvia Blake inside. Sylvia escorted Chloe to a deep navy blue sofa with contrasting yellow and red scatter cushions that sat adjacent to a large picture window. The leaves on a variegated fig in a floor-standing blue ceramic pot needed shining. A low, light wood coffee table and framed IKEA posters of abstract art lent the room the artificial feel of a studio for a daytime television programme. Chloe, looking in some ways smaller than her fourteen years and in others a lot older, clutched one of the scatter cushions to her chest. She pulled her legs up onto the sofa beneath her and, for the first time, almost looked comfortable.

Tom arrived soon after we did, with tea, coffee, and soft

drinks and more chocolate biscuits than you would lay out for a child's party. Chloe waited for an invitation to take and then began to unwrap a two-finger Kit Kat. I gestured for Sylvia to join me back outside for a second.

"I know that you clearly rank as a responsible adult here but I'm in two minds as to whether to call in a social worker. She seems much more withdrawn than I was expecting."

"Are you surprised, Mr Munday? She hasn't heard from the brother she idolises for Heaven knows how long. She probably thinks you're going to tell her he's dead."

"WHAT! You haven't told her he's alive?"

"I told her that I had had a call from a policeman in London who wanted to talk to her about Ben. I don't want to raise her expectations artificially."

"I can't believe you let her go on thinking he might be dead. She's a minor, Mrs Blake. You do realise we shouldn't be doing this without her parents here; certainly not without their knowledge? I really should call social services at the very least."

"If you're getting cold feet, Mr Munday, it's a bit late to be telling me. That girl's confidence has taken enough of a dent without you raising her expectation levels and then cutting the floor away from under her feet."

She was feisty and she brooked no disagreement.

"I'm not getting cold feet. I'd just feel more comfortable with her parents' consent. I may need to go and make contact before I talk to Chloe."

"No need. Her parents know. Or at least her mother does. I spoke to her privately and, of course, she wanted to come with us. I managed to persuade her to let me bring Chloe alone on condition that I telephone her as soon as we leave. She's probably waiting, so can we please get on with it? I don't know what Ben may have told you but she's still his mother and she's worried sick about him. She's not about to upset any development that may give her the peace of mind she's been looking for."

"Okay, but I need to be careful what she's told. I'm doing this as a favour to Ben; as a friend, if you like, rather than as a copper. Ben really doesn't want to be seen to be giving in. He doesn't want them to think that he's about to come home with his tail between his legs. But then again, he's not exactly having a ball himself. He won't admit it but he needs to find a way out of the mess that he's landed himself in. You have no idea how difficult it was for me to persuade him to let me find Chloe. I've just about earned his trust; I'm not going to throw it away by involving his parents at this stage."

She smiled a motherly smile.

"I understand and, more importantly, so does his mum. Shall we get on with it?"

I stared in at Chloe through the nautical-style, metal-rimmed porthole that sat two-thirds of the way up the white painted door to the Rape Suite. She was licking the chocolate off the top of a second digestive. I opened the door and made for an armchair opposite where Chloe sat, back alongside Sylvia, on the sofa. I poured coffee for the two of us. Chloe already had an open can of 7-Up.

"Tell me about Ben."

Chloe looked directly at me.

"Do you know Ben?"

I nodded.

"Is he okay? Is he here?"

"He's okay. He knows I was going to try and find you. He

really wants you to know that he's okay. I'll tell you what he's been up to in a minute. You tell me about him first."

Chloe stared down at the biscuit in her hands; the chocolate was beginning to melt and coat the tips of the thumb and index finger on her right hand. She wiped them with a serviette and began to cry. Sylvia tenderly placed an arm around her shoulder. Chloe sipped from the can and swallowed hard.

"Ben's my big brother and I miss him very much."

"How long is it since you've seen him?"

For the first time, Chloe smiled. Ben was right; she was a pretty girl.

"I think it's 257 days but I may have miscounted."

"That's a long time not to be in touch."

She nodded.

"My mum just sits and cries all day long. I think she cries herself to sleep. She blames my Dad. He blames himself. None of us really talk about Ben. It's too upsetting."

"And you?"

"Soon after he left I collected as many photos as I could and put them all together in an album. I keep it under my bed. When I turn my light off at night I lie there and try to imagine where he is, what he's doing, that he's safe, that he's not lonely or afraid. I'd hate for him to be afraid."

She spoke with a composure and poise that belied her age.

"I say a prayer each night for God to keep him safe and to let me see him again. I don't know if it works but sometimes it makes me feel closer to him. I'm not sure I believe in God any more."

"That sounds tough."

"It is. It was my birthday a few weeks ago and the only present I wanted was to see Ben again. I prayed so hard for him to phone. I wanted to hear him sing me happy birthday as badly as he usually did. There was nothing else I wanted. People have told me it won't hurt this much as time goes on but I just want to have my brother back."

"Do you know why Ben left home?"

Chloe looked uneasy. She turned to Sylvia Blake for guidance. Sylvia smiled and gently nodded.

"Ben and Dad didn't get on. My Dad drinks a bit too much and Ben found that difficult to live with. He tried to reason with him but he always felt like he was banging his head against a brick wall. He was very frustrated and it all kind of got on top of him. He told me that going away was the only way he could deal with it. I begged him to take me along but he said no."

I poured more coffee and sat back in the chair.

"Chloe, I knew it was your birthday."

She looked at me confused.

"Ben told me."

Her confusion became more palpable. I reached behind me to a pile of papers I'd placed on a table when we first entered the room. I handed Chloe a pink envelope, its creases and bends reflecting the fact it had been roughly carried around for quite some time. She looked inquisitively at me at first, a smile breaking out across her face when she looked down at the envelope.

"It's Ben's handwriting."

She ripped the envelope apart and laughed out loud as she read the message inside.

"I'd recognise it anywhere. He had such girly handwriting.

I always tease him about it."

"Ben bought the card, wrote it and intended to post it so that you had it in time for your birthday, but at the last minute he just couldn't. I promised him I'd pass it on."

Chloe was so caught up in the card that I don't think she heard my last comment. She closed the card and placed it, together with the remains of the envelope, neatly on the coffee table in front of her. Confidence seemed to have flowed back into her within a matter of minutes. Her apologetic posture had been replaced by a new self-assured stance.

"When can I see him? Is he here? I need to see him."

"Ben knows I was going to try and contact you. I did that with his permission. But he's nervous about seeing you again. It's not that he doesn't want to, because he wants nothing more than to see you. But he's not sure how you will react to him and, just as important, he's not sure what your parents might think."

"You can't bring me all the way up here and not let me see him. You have to let me see him."

I sighed. I had started this process with the best of intentions but I could already see that it had the potential to become a huge diversion. I still had a murderer to find. Equally, though, there could be no going back.

"Here's the deal, Chloe. Why don't you and Mrs Blake use that telephone over there to call your mum and let her know what's been going on? Together you can decide what's best for you to do. The only thing I *will* say is that I think it's still best for your mum and dad to stay at home. If you do that for me, I'll try and find Ben this evening and see if he wants to meet you."

I reached inside my wallet and pulled out a business card.

"Here, on my card, is my mobile number. Why don't you call me later and let me know where you are and what you've decided, and we can take things from there? Do we have a deal?"

Chloe looked at me and realised that she had no option. Ben, through me, remained in control and her co-operation was the best chance she had of seeing the brother that twelve hours earlier she thought may be dead.

Chapter Twenty-Six

"I'M NOT GOING to pretend that I like you. In fact, I'm not even going to pretend that I wouldn't get enormous satisfaction from sending you straight back inside, because unlike you, I'm going to be completely honest. I think you're scum and I think we're better off without people like you on the streets. The problem I have, though, is that I don't think you murdered Simon Murrell. You're such a bully and such a coward that I don't think you've got the restraint to kill somebody the way Simon Murrell was killed. If it was *your* work, you would have needed everybody to know it; it would have had to look like something out of a Tarantino movie."

For the first time since our conversation started, Dean Weaver made eye contact with me. Our faces were inches apart. I could smell the sweat on his brow.

"So am I free to go?"

"Well, that depends. You may not have killed him but that doesn't mean I don't think you've be lying through your teeth to us. You told me quite categorically that you had never met Simon Murrell. You said that you had watched him, but never met him. They were your words, Dean, weren't they?

Remember?"

Weaver gave no acknowledgement.

"So imagine my surprise when one of Simon's neighbours told us that she had seen—" I opened my notebook to read the quote verbatim, "—a thick set, heavily tattooed man with close-cropped hair hanging around Mr Murrell's bedsit. Now does that sound like anyone you might recognise?"

"Like I said, I kept watch on them."

"So you did. But I got the impression from the neighbour that she had seen you talking to Simon rather than just keeping a watch on him. Hounding him as he walked down the street was the way I think she put it. So I'm left with the conclusion that somebody's telling lies and I'm trying to work out who. And let's face it, Dean, you haven't got the greatest track record in the world when it comes to truth-telling."

Weaver remained silent. I sat back down and faced him across the table.

"Look, I can't do you for murder because I know you didn't do it. But I could still do you for perverting the course of justice and I could have a bloody good go at having you for GBH on your wife. Both of those would secure you a return ticket to the Scrubs. So if you want me to be nice to you, and I strongly suggest that you should, you had better start telling me everything that happened between you and Simon Murrell. And you'd better hope that I believe you're telling me the lot."

Weaver coughed. He looked at his solicitor who confirmed without speaking that this was going to be the best offer on the table. He coughed again.

"I only spoke to him once. I kept watch on them like I told you, mostly from the car. I didn't want to confront them while they were together."

"Why not? Didn't you rate your chances against both of them?"

Weaver ignored the comment.

"But you saw Simon on his own and you took your chance then?"

"He was walking down the street towards the house. Carrying some shopping, I think. I was going to stay put, but for some reason, I got out of the car and started walking towards him. I wasn't going to hit him. I just wanted to frighten him."

"Did he know who you were?"

Weaver nodded.

"So how did you frighten him? What did you say?"

"I stood in front of him as he came towards me, kind of blocking his way on the pavement. He tried to get past me, said he didn't want any trouble, but I wasn't having any of that. I told him that he already had trouble. I told him I knew everything about him and Gail and I told him what would happen if it didn't come to an end."

"Which was?"

"I had a blade with me. I showed it to him. I told him I'd cut him."

"And did you?"

"You know I didn't."

"What did he say to that?"

"Not much. He told me that Gail didn't love me, that she probably didn't love him either, but that I must have expected that something like this would have happened while I was inside. So I told him I wasn't interested in how he was going to fucking justify it. I told him I was judging him by my rules; he'd taken something that was mine and so he'd have to pay for it."

"Was he scared?"

Weaver asked for some water. I poured from a chipped glass jug and handed him a glass. He swilled it around in his mouth and for a moment appeared to be looking for somewhere to spit it out, before swallowing it.

"He started to laugh; not loud, just quietly to himself. He said he understood what I was saying because he'd had people take things of his and they were also going to have to pay for it. So if I was going to cut him, I better just get on and do it."

"What do you think he meant by that; that other people were going to pay?"

"Haven't a clue and to be honest I couldn't be arsed. I just turned around and walked back to the car."

"Just like that? You just turned around and walked away?"

"Yep. It was the first and only time I ever spoke to the man. And that's the truth."

DANNY THORNE STARTED singing in a faux opera style as he pushed his way through the doors of the Incident Room, back bending under the strain of five large cardboard pizza boxes. Like maggots to a rotting corpse, the team jumped to their collective feet to try and grab lunch from him before he was more than six feet inside the room.

"Easy tigers. The pepperoni is on top and I expect to see some left for me. There's got to be some reward for being the one that drags himself out to get all this stuff."

"I told you to have it delivered," I called from across the room. "It's your own fault."

"Dodgy pizza delivery men with a questionable legal right to be in the country, driving almost certainly unroadworthy

Toyotas, for some reason don't jump at the opportunity to deliver pizzas to a nick."

By the time Lesley Hilton had handed out paper plates, the guys had already helped themselves straight from the boxes and were precariously guiding pizza slices towards their mouths before toppings fell off onto case papers.

"Heathens," was her only comment, as she delicately placed a thin and crispy piece of ham and pineapple onto the plate in front of her. I hadn't really thought it possible for anyone to eat pizza seductively until I saw her scooping a stray piece of pineapple into her mouth with her tongue. I needed to refocus.

The lunch had been my idea: a way of bringing the team together, comparing notes as a unit, and then getting them focused on what I hoped would be a final push. The interview with Dean Weaver had made things a little clearer in my mind and I was becoming increasingly convinced that Mr Monk and his friends probably had information that would be relevant and helpful. We just had to uncover it.

"Okay, listen up. I just want to try and draw some strings together and then agree where we're going from here. Dean Weaver, man monster," I said, pointing to a photograph of Dean on the wall. "He was where my initial money was. He had everything going for him, motive – Simon was shagging his missus – opportunity; he's a psycho with form. But he didn't do it. First, there's no physical evidence linking him to the body or the murder scene and second, for Dean, the ultimate accolade would have been to leave Simon's face so beaten up that it looked like a relief map of the Lake District. It's just not his MO."

I picked up a piece of garlic bread as Duggan took over.

"So we come to Simon's wife; the lovely Maria. She told us she hadn't seen him for more than a year but lied to us about going to warn him about Dean. She has motive because she's pissed off about the way their relationship ended and because he was cheating on her with one of her friends, Weaver's wife Gail."

"But I thought Simon was shagging everybody?" asked Sheridan.

"Lucky bastard," interjected Thorne.

"Not that lucky," I smiled, tapping the autopsy photograph with the crust of the garlic bread. "But you're right, Mike, so maybe the answer lies in one of his other liaisons."

"And then," continued Duggan, "we've got Simon's bank accounts. Mike and I have visited Sanctuary Holdings, an insurance company and a firm of underwriters in Docklands, who appears to have been making regular payments directly into Simon's account. But they don't seem to be able to explain why."

"And what's really interesting here," I butted in, much to Duggan's irritation, "is that Sanctuary is chaired by the MP Crispin Monk who, as we were told by Father Tom O'Neill, the Catholic priest seen by the homeless lad talking to Simon in the café, was an old university friend of both himself and Simon Murrell."

"There's other money too," added Duggan, regaining the initiative. "In addition to the thousand a month from Sanctuary, we also know he was getting a regular seven hundred and fifty a month from two additional sources, paid directly into his account, in cash. All of these payments stopped the moment he died."

"It could be drug money," offered Thorne. "Didn't the

wife say that one of the reasons the marriage broke up was because he was a user? Once he was down on his luck he'd have needed an alternative source of income to pay for the habit."

"That's why we need to know who from and what for."

"Was he dealing?" asked Thorne.

I shrugged my shoulders.

"No evidence to suggest he was."

"Blackmail?" asked Paul Price.

"It's a line worth pursuing."

"As for cause of death, there's no doubt it was strangulation, but we still don't know what with," I continued. "You've all got a copy of the post-mortem report. He'd had sex, taken drugs and eaten a Chinese just before he died."

"An ordinary Monday evening, then," Thorne chipped in.

"In your dreams, pretty boy," chided Hilton.

"This means that Simon was almost certainly killed at home. SOCO found the remains of the takeaway boxes that match the contents of his stomach and evidence of sexual activity on his sofa. Interestingly, though, they found evidence of two separate types of semen. So it was at least a threesome, which means the woman they were shagging and the other guy must be our prime suspects. There was no particular evidence of drugs in the flat, but they may have cleared up before they left. It's difficult to be sure, but it doesn't look like robbery was a motive. So let me fly a kite… He invites people into his bedsit, they share a meal, they decide to get jiggy and it either goes too far, or they had a proper motive. But whichever, Simon dies and then they, together, decide they have to get rid of him and so move him that night from the bedsit to the charity shop."

"Somebody that he knew?" contributed Sheridan.

"I reckon so. We'll need DNA samples from anyone even vaguely on our radar. Rob, Paul, I want you to go back over the CCTV footage from the area surrounding the charity shop. Frame by frame. Check out every car that appears in the area from about 9pm onwards."

They nodded as one.

"Danny, Simon's wife mentioned his lifestyle and friends at university. Take a trip up to Cambridge and see if you can find anybody who remembers them: old tutors, porters, that kind of thing. I want to build up a picture of this group of people. Maria also mentioned an old university friend, his best man, who emigrated to Canada. His name is Patrick Ramsden. Find him. I want to talk to him."

Thorne nodded, wiping stray melted cheese from the corner of his mouth with a paper napkin.

"We need to start talking to more people within that Cambridge group. Father Tom mentioned a guy called Seb Brown. He was the lawyer of the group. Mike, you go with DS Duggan and introduce yourself to him and find out what you can. When did he last see Simon? Lesley, please make an appointment for us to meet Mr Crispin Monk MP. I think he'll want to see us. In the meantime, I'm going to pay the priest another visit. Rattle his collection tin, if you know what I mean."

"CONNOR'S ASLEEP," SAID Elaine. "If you'd have called to say you were coming, I would have tried to keep him up, but he was dog-tired. He can't cope with football and swimming on the same day. I'm not sure he would have made it."

"I haven't come to see Connor. I wanted a quiet word

with you."

Although the evening was mild, nerves had sent a chill through my body. I felt an involuntary shiver run across my shoulders as I stood on the driveway of my own house, the eyes of my former neighbours burning into my back.

"Do you want to come in? I don't know if you've eaten, but I'm sure I can knock up some pasta."

There was a tenderness in her response that was as unexpected as it was welcome. In that moment, I felt good.

"No thanks. I don't want to take up too much of your time or ruin your evening. I just wanted to ask if we could talk."

"The text message about the Peak District?"

I nodded.

She sighed heavily and ran her hands through her hair. As she did so, she stretched herself up and exposed the contours of the breasts that I had fallen in love with so many years ago. She leant against the frame of the open door and smiled.

"I'm sorry about the text. It was a shitty thing to do. I shouldn't have sent it. It's just something I was considering, but it wasn't the most sensitive way to break it to you."

"Water under the bridge. But I would like to talk to about it."

"So let me make you that pasta and we'll talk?"

"Not tonight. I want a bit more time to think about how I feel about it. I just came round to ask if we could talk about it over dinner in a week or two, unless there's any particular rush? I'll book a table somewhere."

"There's no rush. And if you'd feel happier on neutral ground, that's fine."

"Nothing to do with neutral ground. I just want us to be

able to talk about our son over a quiet meal together. Who knows, we may even cut each other a bit more slack if we're out like grown-ups."

Elaine stood perfectly still for a minute. She fixed her gaze on me, standing emotionally exposed on the driveway, illuminated by the white light of the security lamp I had fitted to the garage door, like some sort of Sinatra walking on stage at the opening of show in Vegas. She looked me fully up and down, trying to uncover my hidden agenda. She didn't find one because, for once, I didn't have one.

"No," she replied. "It's not too much to ask."

Chapter Twenty-Seven

"WHY DO I have a knot in my stomach and feel so uptight about seeing my own little sister?" Ben asked, quietly shaking his head as we each nursed a mug of coffee at the table by the window at Mario's place.

For the first time I noticed the effects that living rough were having on him. His hair had lost any semblance of life; his eyes had become more sunken than I remembered and now resided within a sallow, almost translucent complexion. His breath was stale. He looked as if he were suddenly feeling the consequences of a wild night on the town, as most kids his age probably should once in a while. The collar on the checked shirt he wore had bobbled with the grime of street living; the third button from the top was absent and revealed an equally soiled tee-shirt underneath. Dirt lay apparently out of reach beneath the few fingernails that hadn't already been bitten to the quick.

"Actually, it makes perfect sense, if you think about it."

I wiped away cappuccino froth from my lip with my tongue.

"You've no idea what kind of reaction you're going to get

from her. Will she be so relieved to see you that she'll just throw her arms around you in sheer excitement or will she bear a grudge? Will she be angry? Will she feel like you deserted her? Has she come all this way to tell you that she never wants to see you again?"

Ben looked up from his coffee.

"That makes me feel so much better." A smile started in the corner of his mouth.

"For what it's worth, I don't think you've got too much to worry about."

The summer weather was threatening to break as we conducted the fifteen-minute drive from Mario's to the station in complete silence. Although an end to the humidity would be welcome, I hoped that the forecast storms were not a portent for either Ben or myself. He stared intently out of the passenger window, his eyes locked on some point or another in the threatening grey sky, his hopes and fears being fuelled by his racing imagination. Even my lurching handbrake stop in the station car park failed to bring him round. We sat for a few quiet seconds in the car, him alone with his thoughts and me contemplating mine, before I tapped him on the shoulder to let him know we had arrived. Momentarily, he looked through me with no recognition in his eyes. Then, as if suddenly galvanised, he nodded to confirm his readiness.

Ben's first steps were tentative ones. I placed the palm of my hand against the lower half of his back for reassurance. He kept his gaze straight ahead and said nothing. I could hear him breathing slowly and deeply, in through his nose and out through his mouth, drawing in as much oxygen as he could. As if what was about to happen next might deplete his reserves. We walked through the reception area. I punched my security code into the panel on the wall to release the door and we passed through and turned right towards the interview room where Sylvia Blake was waiting with Chloe. With each step we took, Ben seemed to get slower, his legs more leaden, his anxiety more apparent. By now I could feel the sweat through the back of his shirt and could see it catching the light like varnish on his forehead and his neck. He stopped suddenly.

"I feel sick."

"You're going to be fine. The first moment will be the worst and then everything will be fine. Trust me."

"No, I mean, I'm really going to be sick."

Five minutes passed and Ben and I sat in the adjacent interview room, sipping tepid water from white plastic cups. He hadn't been sick because there had been nothing of any substance in his stomach to bring up, but he had retched to the point that his throat felt scorched and the muscles in his side strained. He had leant forward in his chair, his head resting in his hands, his eyes fixed on the marked linoleum floor. He spoke without lifting his head.

"How do I go about saying sorry for something like this?"

I put my arm back around his shoulder and pulled him a little closer. As I held him, I wondered when the last time could have been that he had felt the warmth of human contact; probably as long ago as me.

"Is this about apologising or starting over?"

Ben shrugged his shoulders. I sought to reassure him.

"We had a whole conversation about this in Mario's weeks ago. This was never about apologising or going back. Don't you remember? This was about you re-establishing a relationship on your terms. It's about you saying 'look at me,

I'm not the same person I was six months ago, I've changed. I've got different priorities. I realise I want you to be part of my life and me yours but it has to be on my terms.' Isn't that what you wanted? Because if it isn't, you need to say so now and we should go."

Ben thought for a moment. He sat up and turned his body ninety degrees to face me.

"Have you ever felt that someone has taken a big paper cup and put it on top of you so that whichever way you turn, you still come up against a wall?"

Although I knew exactly how he felt, I shook my head.

"That's how it feels; completely trapped. The frustrating thing is I know I hold most of the cards. I know they want to see me again. I know they would probably do anything, agree to anything just to put a stop to all of this. Well, Mum and Chloe certainly would. But if it's going to work and, like you say, it's going to be on my terms, then I've got to find the energy to push that cup off of me and make them hear what I've got to say."

"And your point is?"

"I'm not sure I have the energy I need to do it."

"You know, energy, strength, determination, balls – call it what you want – it's a strange thing. It's like one of those bad science fiction films where the monster regenerates itself. The more strength and energy you show, the more you'll find you have. You only have to dig down for it once, just once, and you'll see that it'll just flow into you after that."

Ben wore a weak and uncertain smile but still, I sensed, the smile of somebody who had finally realised what needed to be done.

"Don't tell me that leaving home and living the way you

have been hasn't taken a certain type of strength and determination. Without that, you would have given up months ago. You've just got to put it out there, on show, for a while."

He sipped more of the tepid tap water before turning and opening his arms. We hugged. He sat back, smiled again, though with more confidence this time and, then, in a voice that was on the edge of breaking, he whispered, "I guess we'd better do it."

When she heard the door open Sylvia Blake looked up from her seat at the table. She had been attempting a word search in a cheap puzzle magazine. The slight figure of Chloe had been straining to get a view of the station car park out of a scratched but still frosted window. She turned, disbelief and anticipation meeting across her face. I ushered Ben in ahead of me and let the door close of its on accord behind us. In one glance all anxiety subsided, giving way to relief. Fear succumbed to pure elation. They locked in an embrace, Chloe's head nestled under Ben's neck, her body shaking as she sobbed, his arms around her as if he was protecting the most precious possession on earth. He turned to look at me, tears streaming down his face, leaving dirt trails in their wake. He mouthed "thank you".

I wiped my eyes and nodded in silent acknowledgement. Sylvia and I left them alone.

Chapter Twenty-Eight

"SLICK IS THE only way I can think of describing him; slick and smug."

"And conceited?" I offered.

"Yeah, definitely conceited; and patronising. A real patronising little shit."

"So he was slick, smug, conceited, and patronising."

"That's about the long and short of it," Duggan replied.

"It doesn't sound like the two of you particularly hit it off. I can only imagine what he must have thought of you."

"What's that supposed to mean?"

I shrugged my shoulders to reassure Harry that it meant nothing at all. I was just being playful.

"Those types of people just do my head in," he went on. "They always have done. They've got too much money, too much influence and they think they can dangle both in front of you like some sort of carrot. Well, it doesn't wash with me."

"I'm glad to hear it," I teased. "After all, he can dangle whatever he likes in front of you; you've still got the full authority of the law on your side."

Harry crossed my office and flicked the switch on the

illicit kettle.

"You're taking the piss, aren't you?"

He slapped the kettle hard on the side to try and make it boil faster.

"Well, you've not really told me anything other than the fact you're clearly not going on holiday with him. What did you actually find out? What conclusions did you reach about Mr Sebastian Brown?"

Harry dropped two tea bags into mugs and tipped sugar into both direct from the bag. He paced like an expectant father waiting for the kettle to boil.

"He's a smart, savvy corporate lawyer, all Saville Row suit and silver cufflinks. He probably, no certainly, earns more in a day than you or I earn in a month. The shag pile in his office is deeper than anything I've ever stepped on before. If he knows anything or, worse still, if he's involved, he's not going to be stupid enough to let anything to slip to us."

"He may not be stupid enough but sure as hell he'll be arrogant enough. If he's really the kind of bloke you're describing, he'll think he's untouchable. He may even feel so secure that he'll be comfortable enough to goad us. Did you get anything out of him?"

Duggan brought a mug of tea across to me and, freehand, slung a few digestive biscuits in my general direction. Two of them broke into almost even halves as they hit the computer keyboard, scattering crumbs across the desktop.

"He's clearly done very well for himself. The office is amazing. South side of Southwark Bridge, high up and virtually fully glazed. There's a roof garden outside his office door, properly tended as well, with this amazing view of the river and the London skyline. I'd get no work done at all if it was my office. I'd just be looking out of the window all day. Who said that when a bloke is tired of London, he is tired of life?"

"Buggered if I know," I shot back with a look to suggest that he may have been speaking a foreign language. "So aside from admiring his office, his view, his carpet, his suit and his cufflinks and taking an instant dislike to the man, did you actually *ask* him anything?"

"We talked about Simon and the whole Cambridge friendship circle thing. He was being very careful with what he said. He didn't offer anything we didn't ask for directly."

"He's not a lawyer for nothing, you know."

"He said he hadn't seen Simon for years. He said he *had* heard on the grapevine that he'd lost a ton of money, but he couldn't be sure it was through Lloyd's; he thought it could just as easily have been drink and drugs. He said that at Cambridge Simon was always the member of the group that didn't quite fit in. He came from a different background, had different experiences and he thought Simon had a bit of a chip on his shoulder about it."

"Well, there's your first odd point. Father Tom told us that of all the guys in the group, Seb was the one that Simon was tightest with. So, did he say when he first heard that Simon was dead?"

"I asked him that but he was very hesitant; as if he was trying a bit too hard to remember."

"You don't believe him?"

"For whatever reason, I'm not sure he wanted to tell us when he heard or, perhaps more importantly, how he heard; who he heard it from."

"Anything else about that university group?"

"He mentioned Monk, told me that he was sure we would know by now that he was part of their group. He also mentioned your Patrick Ramsden guy."

"Well, let's hope Danny's having some joy with the Canadians trying to find him. Did he say anything about Father Tom?"

"I mentioned we'd seen him. Not much of a response. He just smiled and called him 'God's representative on Earth'. He gave me the impression that the others all thought Tom turned out to be a bit of a disappointment. I can imagine Seb Brown's current life being something like an extension of his university life. He can do anything he pleases, buy anything he pleases, have anything or anyone he pleases. I'm sure there's not too much room in his day to day for faith. There was one other thing, though. When we first went to see the priest, I noticed he was wearing a really expensive watch. A Tag. I'm a geek about these things. It's far more expensive and showy than you would expect a man of the cloth to be wearing."

"It could have been a gift. What's your point?"

"It may have been a gift. It may well be nothing. But Seb Brown was wearing an identical watch."

I WATCHED FROM the end seat of the second to last pew in St Mary Immaculate as a small, elderly woman, her hat held securely in place by a pearl-edged hat pin and her winter coat buttoned up despite the late summer warmth, carefully closed the door of the confessional box behind her. She checked the gold clasp on her black leather handbag and, as she made her way out of the church, I rose and let myself into the confessional in her place. I sat with my head resting against the varnished mahogany panel, just able to make out Tom

O'Neill's form through the ornate, perforated brass plate that acted as a screen between us.

I listened as the young priest cleared his throat.

"In the name of the Father, and of the Son, and of the Holy Spirit," he began. "Amen."

He waited for me to speak.

"Forgive me Father for I have sinned. It has been twenty years, give or take a year or two, since my last confession."

"And do you have sins to confess?"

"The usual ones, of course, of being proud and lazy and stubborn but I also feel the need to repent for not giving you a harder time when we last met."

There was no response. I waited for a few seconds, then spoke again.

"There is one question I'd like to ask you, Father."

"Go on."

"I'd really like to know if *you* have sins to confess."

Tom O'Neill stood on the other side of the brass plate and exited the confessional. We met outside, a glint of anger and frustration in his eye.

"Aren't you going to grant me absolution, Father?"

Conscious of the fact that at any moment one of his parishioners might enter the Church to assuage their own guilt, Tom O'Neill kept his evident fury in check. But evident it remained nonetheless.

"I have no problem you coming here to talk to me, Mr Munday. But I *do* have a problem with you doing so in a way that shows such flagrant disrespect for the sacrament of the Church."

"I apologise if you find me disrespectful, but I try not to let respect get in the way of finding a murderer."

"So, do you have questions you want to ask or can I get on with my work?"

He knew I wasn't going to let him get away that easily or that quickly.

"I want to talk to you about Simon, Seb, Crispin, and Patrick Ramsden again."

I sat back down in the pew from which I had originally risen. He sighed and did likewise.

"As I told you the first time, it's all a very long time ago. But if you must, then you should ask your questions."

"Oh I must. When we first met you told us that you had first seen Simon Murrell again at a church-run soup kitchen, that he had recognised you and that you then saw him on a number of occasions in the ensuing weeks, culminating in that final meeting in the café in Tottenham."

"Your recollection is correct."

"The last time you saw Simon, in the café, what did you talk about?"

"I don't recall; probably no more than pleasantries."

"The café owner remembers you being there that morning."

"Mr Munday, even *I* know I don't exactly blend into the background. There aren't too many young, red-headed, pony-tailed priests around."

"He – the café owner – says you looked as if meeting Simon that morning had taken you by surprise. Is that true?"

"Only in the sense that I hadn't arranged to meet him, if that's what you're saying."

I paused for a moment and glanced around the church. I returned my gaze to the priest and smiled broadly, the way my mother used to tell me to in the school photographs of my childhood.

"The last time I spoke to you, you told me that Simon had mentioned that things had been picking up for him. You said he told you he now had money coming in."

The priest nodded.

"Where do you think that money might have been coming from?"

"I have no idea."

"You didn't ask? I find that a little strange. One of your flock and somebody you have known personally for more than twenty years, who you know has been down on his luck, tells you that he's now got money coming in and you don't ask why? How come? You don't ask him if he's got a job? You don't make the same polite enquiries that any of us would make just to seem interested, even if we're not?"

"Maybe we work in different ways, Inspector."

"Maybe we do. Now, about your university friends. You told me you have no contact with them."

"That's correct."

"Yet, you told us that Seb Brown was always the closest to Simon."

He nodded.

"But you've not seen Seb Brown since 1986?"

"Sounds about right."

"So how do you know that Simon and Seb Brown were close?"

"I was talking Cambridge days."

"Oh," I smiled. "My misunderstanding. So you definitely don't see any of them any more? Crispin Monk? Patrick Ramsden?"

"Well, that's a name from the past, but no, I haven't seen any of them."

"Do you know what happened to Mr Ramsden?"

He shook his head.

"By all accounts, though, the life you all led at Cambridge was a pretty hedonistic one. You said as much yourself."

"I kept myself away from all that."

"I'm sure you did, but university is one of those really intense periods in your life. Friendships that are made in a matter of months last a lifetime. What I'm struggling to get my head around is the notion that this group of friends, who lived together, laughed together, got drunk, stoned and slept together for three years, suddenly went their separate ways on leaving university and never met up again. Not even for old time's sake."

"If you put it like that then, yes, it does sound strange. But that's how it was, unless they've been having reunions behind my back and just not inviting me."

"Well, look," I smiled, cracking my finger joints rather dramatically, "that'll do for now. Obviously if we think of anything else, we'll come back again."

Looking relieved and a little surprised at the seemingly abrupt end to the questioning, Tom O'Neill nodded, stood and offered me his hand.

"Just one last thing," I said, suddenly.

"Anything."

"Do you have the time?"

He clearly thought it a strange request but Tom O'Neill pulled back the cuff on his black jacket and checked the Tag watch to which Harry had referred.

"It's coming up for three-thirty."

"Thank you," I smiled. "That's a beautiful watch."

"No problem."

"Tell me, it's my Dad's birthday soon. A big one. Where would I get a watch like that?"

"It was a gift."

"A grateful parishioner? Left to you in a will?"

"No, just a friend."

"Well, it is beautiful and very distinctive. I shall have to look out for another one. Thanks again for your time."

HARRY AND I sat in the car across the road from the church.

"He's not telling us anything. Nobody's telling us anything. It's like there's some kind of conspiracy of silence: a very polite, very helpful, very smiley conspiracy of silence. I'd bet my last fiver they all, or at least most of them, still keep in touch and until we get those relationships sussed, we're going to be going down dead ends. Brown swore blind to you that it was Simon who was the one who didn't fit in, true?"

"True."

"And you believed him?"

"As much as I believe any of them."

"So, assume he's telling the truth. How could Tom have fitted in as part of a close-knit group of friends if he wasn't drinking and shagging and smoking like the rest of them? The answer is he couldn't possibly have done. So why then does Brown say Simon was the odd one out, not Tom? We know from Simon's wife that he drank like a fish and shagged anything with a pulse. If we crack the dynamics of that group, we'll be on our way to working out what's going on here. Danny's supposed to be going to Cambridge. Call him. I want him to find people that knew them, old tutors, porters, anyone. I want to know who slept with who in that group, who drank with who, who got stoned with who and, more importantly, who doesn't want anybody to know about it now."

Chapter Twenty-Nine

I F YOU DIDN'T know that The Spice of India existed or
had a particular reason for finding it, chances are you'd
walk right past, oblivious to the fact. Tucked apologetically in the middle of a row of shops, between a bicycle store
and an off-licence, The Spice of India has the least inviting
facade of them all; darkened windows, stuck-on golden
illustrations of traditional Indian dancers, many of which have
long since started to peel away, and a grubby dog-eared menu
stuck to the glass with multiple layers of worn sticky tape.
Once inside you'd probably classify the decor as retro-Punjabi
kitsch if it weren't for the fact that the decor hadn't changed
at all since Keith Doughty and I had first started going there.
This is authentic Punjabi kitsch – there is nothing retro about
it. The flock wallpaper didn't seem as heavy as I had
remembered it, though the red table lights still lent it the air of
a sub-continental gambling den and brothel. The dropped
trelliswork ceiling from which plastic ivy trailed across the
whole restaurant was reassuringly familiar. In some areas,
particularly close to the kitchen doors, the saffron, cumin, and
turmeric used liberally in the kitchen had stained the ivy an
unnatural ochre colour. Behind the bar, pride of place had

been given to an autographed but yellowing photograph of the great Indian fast bowler, Kapil Dev, though I had never believed the owner's assertion that he had ever eaten there. A framed letter from the local Environmental Health office commending the restaurant on its adherence to stringent hygiene regulations hung on the wall near the entrance. It didn't seem appropriate to ask about those parts of the letter that had been masked by another piece of paper, which almost certainly included recommendations for even more rigorous adherence. It hardly seemed important. For me, professionally at least, this was still home turf; for Doughty it represented an outing back into yesteryear.

"Fuck me," he yelled in his Australian burr as I walked through the door, "I swear these stains on the table cloths are the same ones that were here the last time *we* were. In fact, I'd swear blind we caused most of them."

Doughty hadn't changed. I don't know why I thought he would have. He rose and came out from behind the table and greeted me with a bear hug. Seeing him again felt even better than I had expected. He was a bit thicker set around the middle and though some grey was sneaking through, he had retained the bleached blond hair he'd regularly used to convince girls he was a former champion surfer 'back home'. I was pretty convinced the hair had got him into more beds down the years than it ever had waves. He certainly did all he could to give him that impression. In jeans, a denim shirt and a brown leather jacket, which he now tossed aside, Keith Doughty looked on top form.

"Let me look at ya," he bellowed, taking a step backwards. "Yep, same scrawny little runt I left behind. Come, sit down. Let's get a beer inside ya and talk." He put one arm across my shoulder as if I needed guidance to the table and ordered a bottle of Kingfisher from the waiter with the other. The beer came and as the waiter poured it expertly into a straight pint glass, Doughty caught me eyeing him up.

"What?"

"Nothing. I just can't quite believe we're sitting here again after all these years. How the hell are you?"

"Large as life and twice as beautiful." He cracked the top papadum on a pile of six; each one balanced more unevenly on the next than the one below it, and scooped a heap of mango chutney onto it from the three-bowl stainless steel condiment dish that the waiter had brought with the beer. Some of the chutney fell like a slow motion orange waterfall from the edge of the papadum before Doughty could shovel it into his mouth. It landed on the worn, pale blue table cloth, held taut on the table top by large metal clips at each end.

"Heck, another stain for old time's sake." He tried to erase traces of the chutney with his napkin but, in reality, only made the stain even more evident.

I sipped the beer and helped myself from the papadum pile.

"Thanks for seeing me," I started, lifting my beer to clink glasses with his. "I appreciate it."

"Whatever. A man should never let his work come between him and his food. So, we order and then we talk?"

It seemed like a plan. We spent a few seconds browsing the leather-backed menu, though I suspected that we would order the same as we always had in the past. I was right, and when the waiter returned, pen poised expectantly above his notebook, Doughty took charge.

"Mate, we haven't seen each other for, like, a thousand

years," Doughty explained to the waiter, "so I think we need to pig out to celebrate. You don't have a problem with that, do you?" As if the waiter was ever likely to object.

Doughty ordered multiple portions of onion and cauli-flower bhaji, meat samosas and chicken tikka and another two bottles of Kingfisher to start. To me, this already seemed like enough to be getting on with but Doughty pressed on and added a lamb pasanda, a prawn bhuna and a meat madras, several portions of pilau rice, a Bombay potato and a couple each of stuffed and peshwari naan.

"Should I remind you there's only you and me here?"

"Don't go all lightweight on me. We've got a lot of catching up to do. Besides, if you're paying, sure as hell I'm eating."

"SO, HOW'S LIFE at *The Times*?" I asked, before placing a second piece of papadum, this time laden with minted, chopped onion, into my mouth.

"It's cool. Proper grown-up. I get to write about companies that people have actually heard of rather than the type of scum that you spend your whole life chasing. No offence, mate. It kind of opens doors as well. I get some cracking invites and, before you say anything, not just to annual general meetings. You'd be surprised how many CEOs have some very appreciative PAs, if you know what I mean." He winked a sleazy wink, cutting an onion bhaji in half and pushing a lemon wedge and a sprig of wilted parsley towards the edge of the plate. "When you tell them you're writing for *The Times*, whether they're happy about it or not, they certainly treat you different."

"Five years ago I could never work out how much of what you said was true and how much of it was just pure

Aussie bravado. I still can't."

"Believe me, it's all true." He winked again.

Doughty lifted an empty bottle of Kingfisher as a hint to the waiter to bring two more. His gesture was recognised with a courteous smile and a nod.

"How's Elaine?"

I took a mouthful of beer while I played out in my mind how to respond. There are some people you can bluff in this world and some you can't. Keith Doughty can see through me like an open window.

"She's okay, but we're not together any more."

He put his pint glass down, screwed his napkin tightly into a ball and rested his fork to the right of the one remaining piece of chicken tikka.

"Since when?"

"Getting on for five months now."

"I'm sorry," he said, with uncharacteristic sensitivity. "I had no idea."

"There's no reason why you should."

"What happened? Did you just grow apart?"

"It would be much easier for me to tell you that we did."

"So?"

"Do you want the long story or the short?"

"Well, the hors d'oeuvres are still on the table, the mains haven't arrived yet, and you look like you could use a talk."

He topped up my glass with the third of beer that remained in the bottle.

"I hit her."

"You did what?"

"I hit her. God knows, Keith, I'm not proud of it. You're the first person, aside from my counsellor, I've ever told.

Everyone else thinks I'm hard done by and I admit I've done nothing to put them right. That, in itself, doesn't make me feel great. And before you say anything, yes, it was the first and only time."

"You shouldn't hit a woman, mate. Not cool at all."

I turned my beer glass in a slow circular motion, pressing down hard as if to try and drill a hole through the table with it.

"Don't you think I know that? Anyhow, it wasn't a full-on punching session. I didn't land her in hospital or anything like that. But we were arguing. I was pissed. I was tired. I was tired of arguing. I guess I was also tired of being pissed. But she just kept on prodding and poking and having a go. I snapped. I don't remember what came over me. I slapped her round the face. Just the once. That was the end of it."

"Or rather it wasn't."

"Or rather it wasn't," I repeated slowly.

"And now?"

"And now, I live in a nasty little bedsit off of the Seven Sisters Road and she's in the house with Connor. And we speak when we have to. We try and be civil. Civil, note; that's not always the same as friendly. Sometimes it works, sometimes it doesn't."

"That's a bastard, mate," Doughty offered with masterly understatement. "But what are you doing about it?"

"She doesn't want me back if that's what you're getting at."

"It wasn't necessarily. But the two of you are still married – at least, I presume you are. I mean fuck all else moves that fast in this country, so I doubt *that* does either. You've got a kid together. That gives you responsibilities. So what are you doing about it?"

I was starting to lose my appetite and we hadn't even got on to the main reason for our meeting.

"When you say it like that it all sounds so simple; just as simple as 'you shouldn't have hit her in the first place'. I've lost count of the number of times I've told myself that."

Doughty shrugged his shoulders.

"She's agreed to have dinner with me."

Doughty shook his head.

"Don't knock it," I protested. "It's a start. For the first few weeks we were at each other's throats all the time. It became easier not to communicate at all. But then you realise that's not a solution either. So we spoke, albeit through gritted teeth, tried not to let on to Connor just how bad things were between us, which was ridiculous, because he's not an idiot and had worked it out for himself."

"And now?"

"And now, at least we're talking. We've managed a couple of conversations that haven't ended up in a slanging match and she's agreed to have dinner with me so we can talk things through like adults on neutral ground."

"What do you want to happen?"

"I want us to get back together. I've said sorry so many times and in so many ways, I'm not sure that's even a possibility. I think if she was serious about us getting back together, she would have said yes by now. I think the fight was probably the straw that broke the camel's back but things were bad even before. This just provided the opportunity. One thing I know now is that it's not something to bring up when we meet. Slowly slowly catchy monkey and all that. I need to prove to her that what happened that night was a one off. I need to prove I'm reliable, stable, and all the other concerns she had, a lot of which I admit I still don't know. If I can do that and she wants to try again, then that's great. If not – and I think it's more likely not – then at least I can feel like I responded the right way. I can't undo what I did but I *can* control how I react now."

"Sounds like you have it pretty well thought out."

"Under instruction from my counsellor."

Doughty smiled and made way for the arrival of more food.

"At least you're talking to somebody. That's good. And presumably that's why sorting this case is so important?"

"Sorting this case is important primarily because a man's dead and somebody did it. But, yes, work's also the one thing I've got going in my favour at the moment, so I'm not going to sit here and deny that putting this one to bed wouldn't be good for other reasons as well."

"Then let's see what I can do to help."

A team of waiters encircled the table and laid a coterie of stainless steel dishes around our elbows, leaving almost no available space on the table top. Before they'd finished, Doughty had ripped a piece of naan bread and wiped it enthusiastically through the lamb pasanda.

"You didn't give me much to work on when we spoke," he garbled, his mouth still full. "But I did what I could."

I spooned some pilau rice and a portion from each of the oval dishes onto my plate. I had always loved Indian food. It was my comfort food; the one thing I turned to in times of despair. The scent of the spices rose from the plate and I could feel the saliva welling into my mouth.

"I have a corpse," I started, wiping away a stray piece of rice that had become lodged in the corner of my mouth. "He

270

is a guy who, it appears, made a shed load of cash working in the markets and enjoying all the baubles that come with that, if you get what I mean. Then it seems that he was attracted by the prospect of becoming a Lloyd's Name, probably around 1990. By 1993 the Lloyd's Crash appears to have taken him for everything he had, and by all accounts he had plenty. I need to know what attracted him to Lloyd's, and more importantly, what he did after he'd lost the lot."

"And Crispin Monk, how does he fit into the equation?"

"Monk and my corpse were in the same circle at university; a very tight-knit group, by all accounts. They've all gone on to achieve great things in their respective fields, though we're finding it hard to really pin down how many of them are still in contact with each other. I think we're being spun some misinformation."

"Being given the run around?"

"Beginning to think so. But in addition to all of his political stuff, Mr Monk is also chairman of a pretty niche insurance company called Santuary Holdings. We discovered that since late-1994 Santuary Holdings has been paying our corpse a not insubstantial fee for – their words not mine – personal consultancy to the chairman."

"That's not necessarily illegal."

"Not at all. But since the end of 1994 our corpse has been living almost as a down and out, hanging around local cafes, and visiting soup kitchens. It doesn't sound like the kind of scenario in which you would also be providing personal consultancy to the chairman of an insurance company."

Doughty nodded, picking at his gums with a wooden toothpick before spooning more food onto his plate.

"Still doesn't mean anything illegal's been going on," he

offered. "But you're thinking blackmail?"

"It's a possibility but I don't know – or I haven't found about – what. Yet. The other theory is that Monk was the one that lured my man into becoming a Lloyd's Name. He didn't have old wealth to fall back on in the same way that Mr Monk did and so the Santuary money was all part of a guilt trip put on him when my man lost everything."

"You can't become a Name unless you're nominated by another, that much I do know. But the Crispin Monk I know isn't such a soft touch as to fund another man's debt out of the goodness of his heart. Plus, none of what you've said actually points to murder."

"I know; it's just one line of enquiry. It may well lead to nothing. But I *do* need to know how my corpse first got involved with Lloyd's, what kind of consultancy he was providing to our blue-eyed Tory boy and why Mr Monk was so keen to pay him so handsomely, if he *was* keen to pay him. And before I put those questions to the man himself I need to at least look like I know what I'm talking about."

Doughty laughed.

"So what can I tell you?" He opened a buff wallet folder. "Feel free to stop me if I'm teaching my grandmother to suck eggs."

I nodded.

"First up, you need to understand what Lloyd's is. It's not a single organisation, but rather a big market of companies and individuals competing against each other for business. The whole premise of it is about spreading risk. Every risk is underwritten by a number of syndicates, each of which is backed financially by individuals – your Names – as well as by corporates. The underwriters will take the risks from brokers on behalf of the members of each syndicate that they represent. If they get their sums right, then the cost of settling claims and giving the Names a financial return can be done from the premiums that companies pay."

"But it doesn't always work?"

"Like they say in the ads, the value of your investment can go down as well as up." Doughty took more naan and wiped it once more around the remnants of the lamb pasanda. Thankfully he swallowed before continuing.

"Here's where we get to the Crash. Very occasionally a combination of events means that the value of claims outstrips the premiums that you receive and you get major, humungous, fuck off losses. Between '89 and '93 they had claims for everything from asbestosis, hurricane damage, and even the cleaning up after Exxon Valdez splashed its oil everywhere. Mate, the bill came to fucking eight billion. That's what screwed the Names over."

"And they lost everything?"

"Well, don't be too sympathetic, mate. This may be a game of chance but it's served them pretty well over the years. Chances are you're going to make big, big money out of Lloyd's, but you have to accept that sometimes the losses are going to be big as well. That's the judgement, I guess, will the profits in the good years cover the losses in the bad ones? It's the old story; you shouldn't play with fire if you can't afford to get your fingers burnt."

"And my corpse couldn't?"

"I don't know enough about him to be able to tell you that. All I know is that there are ample opportunities to make money if you're a Name, but there's a catch. One day, claims will exceed premiums. It's kind of like the law of the jungle.

And when you become a Lloyd's Name, you take on unlimited liability for the risk that you underwrite. That's how one fucking huge claim can take you for everything you've got. 'Right down to your last cufflink' was how it used to be put to them when they first signed up. It's amazing how people manage to ignore what they don't want to hear."

"Just how wealthy do you have to be?"

Doughty smiled.

"You only have to prove private wealth to the value of £350,000 which, when you think about it, ain't that much. But if that's basically the extent of your wealth and it all goes tits up, you can see how bad the impact could be."

"So why do it?"

"Why do you think? Because if it doesn't go tits up, you win big. Loads of them also got seduced by the whole status thing. It's like slapping your dick on a card table to show you've got the biggest. These guys can be pretty shallow."

The waiter arrived to clear the table. Doughty ordered more beer, which was already bloating my stomach and distracting my mind. I ordered strong black coffee to nullify the effects.

"How many of these guys are we talking about?"

"Probably not as many as you think. It had always been only a few thousand people but then someone seems to have gone on a recruiting drive. At the start of the Eighties there were 6000 of them but by the end of the Eighties, there were over 30,000 of the bastards. Now there's only 3000 or so of them. But these new guys were like your corpse; self-made professionals lured by a safe investment that paid a good return. Now even I know that's about as believable as 'the cheque's in the post' and 'I won't come in your mouth'."

Doughty bellowed at his own joke to the point where he turned heads on other tables. The coffee arrived and, as I sipped, I felt it begin to revive my mind and then my body.

"So if my corpse lost everything in Lloyd's, why didn't Crispin Monk? Is it all down to old money?"

"Difficult to be certain without a bit more digging, but most of the losses were concentrated on about a third of the syndicates. These were the ones the contained most of the passive investors – 'outsiders' as they were called – and most of them appear to have been exposed to the biggest asbestos and pollution claims. Literally thousands of them were bankrupted. But, and this might be key for you, while these syndicates were racking up the losses, other syndicates, largely funded by Lloyd's insiders, were making enormous profits."

"So my corpse is lured into becoming a Lloyd's Name by Monk, loses everything he has in one syndicate while watching Monk getting richer in another. That would piss you off, wouldn't it?"

"Big time."

"Enough to want some of those profits to help you back on your feet?"

"I'd say so."

Doughty's information had given me food for thought and certainly enough to feel confident about holding a conversation with Crispin Monk. He passed across the wallet folder.

"Tell me a bit about Monk."

"Well, this comes third hand," he began. "I got one of our political hacks pissed on a bottle of Syrah. It's a fairly conventional upbringing: public school, university, working in his vacations as a paid gopher for an MP. I think they're called researchers these days. Anyhow, he got a taste for it in the late Eighties at the height of the Thatcher period working for her mentor Keith Joseph. That gave him access to people that counted and made him quite visible where it paid to be seen. He served on every think tank that was going, helped formulate policy for the '92 election. So, by the time '97 came around he was already pretty well connected when safe seats were being given out."

"And his extremist views?"

"One man's extremist is another man's freedom fighter, isn't that what they say? Monk won his seat in '97 up in Norfolk somewhere but arrived in Westminster as part of a Tory party that had basically been wiped off the face of the Earth. Whilst Blair was being cheered and waved at by bussed-in crowds, the Tories were looking for someone to blame. There was recrimination, soul-searching. They couldn't talk about new directions because the country had just chosen one. But they *could* talk about reinventing themselves."

"So he lurched to the right?"

"I don't know how far he lurched or how far over he already was, but Monk's an opportunist. He has an eye for the main chance. In a party that was tired, defeated, and robbed of any personalities, he knew there was an opportunity to become the main man. It almost didn't matter what he was saying as long as he was saying something different and it stopped short of being dangerous."

"Are you telling me he's not dangerous?"

"I never said that. He's one very clever cookie, mate. If you read what he's said, it all sounds perfectly innocuous. It's all about the strength of the family, good moral values, a Christian Britain. A lot of it is hard to take exception to."

"But all that stuff in your paper's interview with him about gay people being deviants?"

"Think of the constituency he has to win over. First he has to win over his own party, make it his own. It was full of those old women, retired soldiers and quasi-fascist students with pinstripe suits, greasy hair and bad acne. He's playing a long game because he knows they're not going to win the next election and probably not even the one after that. That gives him a few years yet to claim what they always claim; that he's moderated his views. Striking out against drugs or homosexuals is going to get him headlines and give him the national exposure he needs and, providing he manages how, when, and where he says it, he probably feels confident dealing with any shit he might pick up along the way. I'm telling you it's a very carefully thought-through plan. A risky one, sure, but he's calculated the risk and he thinks it's worth it. Who am I to say he's wrong?"

"And the perfect family?"

"The perfect family indeed. A beautiful wife. She's a bright cookie too, but she put her legal career on hold to mastermind his political one. Word on the street is that she just might be more ambitious for him than he is for himself. And they have two perfect children, who go to a perfect prep school, play the violin perfectly etcetera, etcetera, etcetera."

With effected deference, the waiter left a small porcelain saucer holding the bill and two mint imperials. Doughty took both while I searched through my wallet for my Visa card.

"I guess the wife and kids are central to the image he's trying to cultivate?"

"Sure. Old Tory women love an attractive young family. It takes them back to how great they think Britain was fifty years ago. All bollocks of course but he's a crowd pleaser. He knows what his punters want and he uses his family to give it to them. That's why any whiff of scandal, particularly of the sexual kind, would undermine his whole basic values thing."

"Probably enough that he'd pay somebody lots of money to keep quiet?"

"Or worse if they refused?" Doughty drained the dregs of the Kingfisher and then fuelled the speculation. "You don't seriously think he's shagging around, though, do you?"

"I don't seriously think anything at the moment," I smiled, rising from the table to leave. "But I'll tell you for sure once I've met him."

Chapter Thirty

DUGGAN HADN'T SPECIFICALLY said anything that told me I wasn't in his good books; it was more what he *hadn't* said. He sat in the driver's seat, his head pointing forward, clicking his tongue against the roof of his mouth and occasionally drumming his finger tips on the top of the steering wheel; anything rather than talk. The atmosphere was as stifling as the late summer heat. I turned the air conditioning up a notch; he immediately turned it back down. I lowered the volume of the radio; he restored it to where it had been. A half hour of this was more than I was able to stand.

"If you've something to say, just say it."

No response.

"Come on, save us both the aggravation and just say it. Whatever it is, get it off your chest."

I turned in the passenger seat the way you do if you're trying to get comfortable on a sofa, only obviously with less room in which to manoeuvre, so that I was halfway facing him in the driver's seat.

"You're pissed off with me, I know you are. I can read you like a book."

He fixed his stare out of the driver's window.

"No need for me to say anything then."

"The childish bullshit doesn't suit you. Do I have to start guessing?"

"I thought you could read me like a book."

We drove for a minute or two more before Harry pulled over to the side of the road without warning. He wrenched the handbrake up before the car came to a standstill. We both jerked forward, the palms of my hands coming to rest flat down on the Mondeo's glove compartment. We faced each other across the handbrake; a red rash of suppressed anger progressing across Harry's face and neck, sweat bubbling up across his forehead.

"You know I could report you?"

"It wouldn't be the first time."

"You turn everything into a joke. Well, I'm telling you, not everything is a joke. Some things are bloody, fucking serious Jack. You never stop to think about the consequences."

"What consequences?"

"Yesterday. You were out of contact for three hours. Nobody knew what you were doing, who you were with or why, or how to find you. You could have been in the bottom of a ditch with a knife in your back, in a hotel with a hooker, or visiting your granny in an old people's home and we'd have been none the wiser. Your mobile was off all afternoon and then, when you finally do roll in, you're pissed. I could smell it on your breath."

"And?"

"Well, if you need me to spell it out for you-"

"So I had a few beers with an old contact over a curry. It helped grease the wheels and get me – no, get *us* – the kind of steer we're going to need when we sit down with Monk in, what, an hour?"

I glanced at my watch to confirm the accuracy of my estimate.

"It isn't the first time I've had a drink on duty. It won't be the last either, if that's where you're going with this. So if you or any of the guys have a problem with that, you'd better tell them to get over it."

"But why not tell us where you were? We're a team, Jack, you and me. That's what you always say. Well, it's bollocks isn't it? We're not a team. We're just your lackeys. We ferret around and gather information and then get nothing back from you at all. It's a joke. You don't even know the meaning of the word team. The job may be the only thing you've got to cling onto in your train wreck of a life, but you're losing your grip and you sure as hell ain't going to solve this one without us."

A traffic warden tapped on the driver's window. Before Harry had the chance to engage in conversation, I reached across him, pressing my warrant card against the glass with my right hand and giving him a one-fingered salute with my left. Affronted, he turned and walked away.

"How's Connor?"

"He's good."

"Are you seeing enough of him?"

"Not as much as I'd like but it's better than it was. Look, I'm touched by your interest but where is this going?"

"You picked him up from school yesterday afternoon,

didn't you?"

"You know I did. I told you I did. I picked him up and dropped him home before I came back to the nick. I had to sort out dinner arrangements with Elaine. But you know all this. What's the problem? Angry that I didn't record it on my timesheet?"

"You were pissed, that's the fucking problem. You left the restaurant pissed, you got in the car pissed, you drove to the school pissed – you drove your son home when you were unfit to do so. Now do you get it?"

"I took a cab-"

"The *fuck* you did! Keep on lying to yourself if you want to but don't you dare lie to me. You drove him and you weren't fit to. You know it and I know it. And everybody you saw at the school and back at the nick knows it. They could smell it on you before you even got out of the car. And you know what, Elaine probably knows it too. Christ only knows what she's thinking. Don't you get what the consequences could have been? What they could still be?"

I took out the nicotine gum in my mouth and screwed it up in a tissue. I lit a cigarette in its place.

"So are you going to report me?"

"What do you think?"

I exhaled.

"Thanks."

"I don't want your thanks. I want you to start treating us, treating me, the way we deserve to be treated. I don't give a shit if you want to ride around pretending you're the Lone Ranger, but I'm not going to let you endanger your own kid's life again and I'm sure as hell not going to play Tonto.

Understood?"

"Understood."

"Not such a great judge of character after all, are you?" Harry commented.

He pulled his seat belt back across him and started the car. We didn't speak again for the rest of the journey.

Chapter Thirty-One

L EAVE BEHIND THE tourist queues that encircle the
Palace of Westminster, cross the manicured lawns of
College Green, avoiding the television news crews
extracting sound-bites from hired politicians trying to make a
name for themselves, cut through Great Peter Street and past
the red brick buildings of Little College Street, and you'll
arrive at the unassuming entrance to Lord North Street. It is a
narrow but immaculately presented road, kept under the
watchful eye of the Church of St John's Smith Square, which
sits imperiously at the far end like a stern grandfather at the
head of a Victorian dinner table.

On both sides of the street stand uniform terraces of
Georgian houses; a roll call of black, gloss painted front
doors, brass numbers and matching doorknockers shining
brightly in the sun. Sash windows stand guard over painted
window boxes brimming with bright, crimson geraniums.
Railings, painted the same black as the doors, stand a metre
out from each threshold, creating just enough space for light
to fall through the windows of basement rooms. An orderly
line-up of Victorian street lamps lends the impression that this
could be the one street in London that time has left un-

touched.

Lord North Street, though, is anything but unassuming. A stone's throw from Conservative Party Central Office, it is home to political kingmakers, the influential politicians who ply their trade in the shadows behind the public personas of prime ministers and cabinet members. They are the 'unnamed sources'. Over the years the black gloss doors of Lord North Street have concealed greater intrigue and plot than anything seen in Westminster since Guy Fawkes laid down his gunpowder. It was here ten years previously that the kingmakers and would-be kings had gathered in secret, fevered convocation – like boys in the corner of a play-ground – to discuss the imminent fall of Margaret Thatcher and the consequent succession. That had been a seminal moment in the political upbringing of Crispin Monk.

Duggan and I sat on the steps of St John's, drinking water together, but still barely speaking.

"Hope you boys have slapped on the Factor 20. The sun's strong."

Lesley Hilton walked around the white stone steps of the church and sat down alongside me. I had asked her to meet us, ostensibly for her feminine intuition, but in reality because I just wanted to see her. And she knew it. She pushed her sunglasses up onto her forehead, shaking her hair back as she did so. Her lean arms, tanned from the sun, looked soft and gentle against the crisp whiteness of her sleeveless cotton shirt. Two buttons undone gave a hint of her cleavage and a glimpse of the white lacy top of the cups of her bra. The white shirt was tucked into tight belted chinos. A gentle breeze carried the scent of her perfume across my face. I don't know whether I was feeling genuine sexual attraction or whether I just missed any intimacy in my life completely and felt attracted by the possibility, however remote, that she may be interested in me.

"So how hard are we going in?"

I thought that the wording of her question was intentionally provocative. I swallowed hard.

"He's going to be slick. You don't get where he's got without being something of a performer. Let's just treat it as a chat. I want him to reminisce, take us through the old times at Cambridge. Let's catch up on some of those old names and then find out what he knows about Simon."

"Good cop, bad cop?" asked Harry.

"No. Bright cop, dumb cop. Throw in a few questions that are going to irritate him. I want to see how much it takes to get him frustrated. I want to see him fray around the edges. And while we're doing that, Lesley can look at him and pick up on the stuff she always says we're bound to miss. I want to know whether this whole perfect family thing stacks up."

As we were shown into the drawing room at the front of the house, Crispin Monk closed the book he had been reading and rose from a high-backed brown leather chair to greet us. He looked younger in the flesh than I had imagined from his pictures; offering a pale, slender, almost feminine hand, before inviting the three of us to sit on a matching leather sofa large enough only for two. Duggan remained standing. The room was small and decorated to a much older style than the contemporary taste for his age. On a side table stood a bottle of 15-year old Macallan whisky, four crystal tumblers and an empty ice bucket, whose silver tongs hung half in and half out. A glass cabinet to the right of an ornate white fireplace displayed matching china cups and saucers, each meticulously positioned to show it off. The colours were muted, mostly greens and creams, whilst thick, green paisley curtains swagged and tailed to each side of the window. An ornate pelmet framed the view onto the street. The cornices were deep and clean and the centre lights hung from intricate ceiling roses. Family photographs in silver frames occupied most available areas. To the left of the fireplace were floor-to-ceiling bookshelves bearing largely political works. I noticed biographies of Butler, Maudling, Moseley and Powell as well as volumes on Gaitskell, Bevan and Crosland, as if reading about the great Labour figures as well as the Tories was Monk's way of keeping an eye on the enemy.

His appearance was immaculate. The politician wore a deep blue Thomas Pink shirt, a navy and white polka dot tie, fastened in a Windsor knot, and held to his shirt by a monogrammed tie pin that matched his cufflinks. He leant back casually into his seat, lifting his left navy pin-striped trouser leg on top of his right knee to reveal similarly-monogrammed socks sliding into highly polished black brogues. He clasped his hands in front of his knee. His manicured nails bore not a scrap of dirt. He kept his jacket on, a white handkerchief folded in his breast pocket. His hair was short and brushed back to reveal a maximum amount of forehead. He was cleanly shaven, save for a small cut just below the sideburn on the left hand side of his face. He smiled, saying nothing for a matter of minutes, though scrutinising each of us in turn through narrow blue eyes.

"It's good of you to find the time to see us."

He acknowledged my thanks with a slight nod of the head.

"You and your colleagues do a fine and important job

protecting our citizens. I have gone on record many times saying so, so it would be a little hypocritical for me not to offer whatever help I can. Though I have to say, I fear I shall be of precious little value."

His words tailed off as his attention was drawn to the door opening. Francine Monk walked halfway into the room. She looked harassed, though still faultlessly made-up, her light brown hair cascading over the shoulders of a faux denim shirt with three-quarter length sleeves, which she wore outside of her black linen trousers. Her look was infinitely more current than her husband's. A delicate silver bracelet looked incongruous against her bandaged right hand.

"Just thought I would check to see if any of you wanted tea?"

We each accepted the offer.

"Earl Grey, Darjeeling, or English Breakfast? Do you have a preference?"

Given that I had made my one remaining supermarket own-brand tea bag last for three days, it seemed inappropriate for a beggar like me to be a chooser. Francine smiled and made for the door. Lesley, wanting to get Francine's take on what had happened to their old university circle, rose and offered to help in a manner which challenged refusal.

"We wanted to have a chat with you about the death of somebody with whom we believe you were acquainted."

Monk nodded.

"Simon Murrell?"

A second nod.

"And you believe his death to be suspicious?"

"Unless he strangled himself, tied himself up in a bin bag and then dumped himself outside a charity shop, I'd say that was suspicious, wouldn't you?" Harry had made the first stab at being a thorn in Crispin's side.

"I'd say it was."

Unflustered.

"Simon Murrell was someone you knew from university?"

"He was."

"A friend of yours?"

"At that time."

"But not recently?"

"Not a friend, as such, but somebody with whom I was still in contact, to a degree. Politics is such an unpleasant profession, gentlemen, that I find it pays not to have friends unless you know every skeleton in every cupboard. A sad state of affairs, one might say, but necessary nonetheless."

"From a self-preservation point of view?"

"Let's just say necessary."

"Did you like him?"

"At university?"

"At university, and more recently?"

"At university, yes, though we had little in common, we enjoyed good conversation. He had strong views on a wide range of subjects, much like myself, and this made for healthy and enjoyable debate. He was mainly friends with other friends of mine. More recently I can't say I knew him well enough to make a judgement."

Duggan stretched his left leg out and swung it across his right to mirror Monk's posture, but rather less immaculately. His trousers were too short, revealing three or four inches of white, fleshy, hairy leg disappearing into a laddered beige sock. His shoes were brown, shapeless and scuffed.

"So Simon had bones in his closet, did he?"

"I'm sorry?"

"You said you couldn't maintain your friendship because of skeletons in his cupboard. That's what you said, isn't it? So what were they, these skeletons?"

"It's a figure of speech. I have no idea whether he did or he didn't, I just use that as a precaution in all of my relationships."

Duggan considered for a moment, chewing the end of a blue plastic pen as he did so.

"But he obviously didn't have so many skeletons in his cupboard that you had a problem paying him a grand a month from your insurance company? Obviously not too much of a risk for that. How does that work, then?"

Monk shifted uneasily from his right leg to his left, evidently to relieve the pain in the arse that Duggan was becoming. I interrupted, apologising to him and reminding Duggan with false admonishment that nobody was being accused of anything. Monk thanked me.

"Tell me more about your circle of friends at university."

"What's to tell?"

"Well, who would you include in the group?"

He considered the question as if money was riding on his answer.

"There were essentially seven of us, I suppose, though I'm sure you know all this already. Myself, reading PPE; Francine, who read English; Seb Brown, who read Law; Tom O'Neill, who was studying theology; Richard Osborne, who was reading Economics, I think; Simon Murrell, who was also reading Economics and his friend, Patrick Ramsden. He was very much on the fringes and I regret I have no recollection of what, if anything, he was reading."

"Francine, your wife?"

"The same."

"I wasn't aware that you met at university."

"We met at university. We didn't really become close until afterwards. Francine was originally Seb's friend."

"This is also the first time I have heard the name Richard Osborne. Tell me about him."

"I wasn't aware he was part of your enquiry, Inspector."

"We don't know from one moment to the next what is and what isn't part of our enquiry."

Duggan's interjection produced another sideways glance.

"It's just good for background."

"Very well, but again I fear I can't provide you with too much detail. Richard Osborne, as I recall, was a highly strung individual, talented but prone to fantasy."

"Talented but prone to fantasy?"

"Talented in the sense that he graduated with a first from Cambridge and went on to become a successful property developer, I believe. He was also a very accomplished musician at Cambridge. Clarinet. He was a little like Simon: from a middle class background, probably the first from his family ever to get to Cambridge. He had a sense of fun. Work hard, play hard, I think they call it these days. The fantasy side largely related to him believing he was invincible, some inherent protection against anything going wrong. He was into extreme sports before extreme sports were really popular. Perhaps it was just the invincibility of youth that I remember. I suppose we all felt like that."

"Did you?"

"I suppose I did, though I'm far too long in the tooth to feel like that now. Anyhow, I lost contact with Richard soon after we all left Cambridge, so much of that information is second or even third hand. I am aware, though, that Richard was not as invincible as he would have liked to believe. I did hear that he had passed away three or four years ago; apparently he took his own life. A very sad business."

"Do you know the circumstances of his death?"

"I'm afraid I do not. I think I learned of it some time after the event. I couldn't even tell you who from."

Duggan sat forward and began chewing his pen again, periodically taking shards of plastic from between his teeth.

"You hear of something traumatic, like the untimely death of somebody that was supposedly in your close circle of friends at university, and you don't even recall who told you. I'm sorry if I'm speaking out of turn, but that's odd. I bet you remember where you were when you heard that Princess Diana had died but not an old, close friend?"

"I have no defence, Sergeant, although he was hardly still a close friend. In my line of work, I get so much information coming to me from so many different sources that unless it's vital that I actually note and recall the supplier of that information, I tend to forget. At that time, the sadness was that Richard had met with an untimely demise. How I found out about it hardly seemed important."

I observed Monk throughout Duggan's questioning. I was in no doubt that he felt uncomfortable, but his professionalism was carrying him through. I pulled myself forward to the front edge of the sofa.

"So how many of those university friends are you still in regular contact with?"

"Francine, of course," he smiled, "as I am fortunate to wake up alongside her each morning. I occasionally see Seb at

293

public speaking engagements but I have lost contact with the rest. I think, for many, my straight talking is something of an anathema. It is little inducement for them to maintain a friendship and, as I have already explained, it is not something I go out of my way to encourage."

The tea arrived. Lesley entered the room holding a tray of china cups and saucers, milk jug and sugar pot, matching floral teapot and a small metal strainer. She laid the tray down on the table at the back of the room and began to pour. Francine Monk followed her into the room with a plate of biscuits. Whatever conversation Lesley had had with her outside had made her seem noticeably less comfortable.

"I hope that's everything you'll need. There's nothing very inspired about the biscuits, I'm afraid, but you are more than welcome to them."

I thanked her as she left the room. I poured and handed each of us a cup in turn. I looked back at Monk, who was laying a silver teaspoon in the saucer beside his cup. He took a sip of Earl Grey.

"What do you know of them?"

"Well, Seb is a lawyer; not difficult to find, he's quite celebrated these days. My wife still sees him from time to time in connection with her charitable commitments. Tom O'Neill, I assume, became a priest, though I can't confirm that for you, and Patrick Ramsden I have absolutely no idea about. As I said, he was always Simon's friend rather than ours."

"And Simon?"

"Simon was a likeable rogue. He came from a fairly modest background, certainly more modest than the rest of us, though if that was ever a problem for him, I don't recall him showing it. He had an eye for the main chance. In some respects it was something of a surprise that he graduated at all, as he was always happier partying and in the company of ladies than in the company of textbooks."

"But he did?"

"He did and he built himself a successful career by all accounts."

"But you had no contact with him?"

"We were not in regular contact, no."

"So how did he come to be working for you at Santuary Holdings?"

"It was just a bit of consultancy work."

"For which you paid him £1000 a month?"

"He had a very informed view of the City and, despite everything, remained well-connected. Some of those relationships could have been quite useful to a moderate-sized company like ours."

"But if you had no contact with him, how did the relationship come about?"

Monk pulled back the pinstriped sleeve on his left arm and checked a gold analogue watch.

"He approached me. He wrote to me at the House of Commons and then called me to arrange to meet. He said he had an offer to put to me."

"And you met him?"

"Why not?"

"You weren't worried about the skeletons in his cupboard?" Harry interjected. Monk ignored him.

"And what was the offer?"

"It was more of a plea than an offer. His career had taken a turn for the worse. His job had gone and he was trying to earn money to support himself. I respected that. I wish more people would do that rather than rely on the state to support them in times of strife. And of course, what he was selling, Santuary was interested in buying. So it made sense."

"And at no time were you concerned about people prying into the circumstances of his career downturn?"

"Gentlemen, we can all kick a man when he's down. It's difficult to accuse somebody who's trying to support an old university friend through a troubling time in his life of anything other than compassion."

"Do you still have a copy of Simon's original letter?"

"I would have to ask my secretary to look through my correspondence files."

"I would be grateful."

Monk nodded again.

"So what exactly did Simon's work for you entail? How often did you meet him?"

"It was more of a retainer so that we could call on his services as and when we needed. He didn't have an office on our premises. He wasn't required to be in every day or even at all. That wasn't the way it worked."

"So how did it work? How many days in total did he attend your offices, because none of your colleagues down there seemed able to shed a great deal of light on his activities?"

"I have no idea."

"So it could have been once, twice, fifty times, or never."

"Possibly."

"And can you give me a specific example of some work that he did for you, a relationship he forged for you? Not hearsay but documentary evidence; perhaps emails, faxes, or phone logs."

"I cannot."

"Because there were none?"

"As I said previously, I retained Simon Murrell to use him as and when I needed to. I hadn't had the need to by that point."

"I just want to be completely clear on this. I want to be sure I understand correctly. You – or your company – paid Simon Murrell a grand a month for several months to provide you with consultancy. And for that money, not once did he attend your offices, meet with your colleagues, or provide you with anything that can pin down as tangible consultancy."

"If that's how you choose to characterise it."

I was becoming frustrated.

"Mr Monk, with respect, I don't give a stuff about your reputation. All I want to know is why you had Simon Murrell on your payroll because it sure as hell wasn't out of the goodness of your heart. And I'm damn sure I'm going to find out."

"I think you may be seeing intrigue where there is none to be seen, Inspector."

I sat back down.

"Tell me, how damaging would it be for you personally and politically to be publicly linked to Simon Murrell's death?"

"But I am not linked to Simon Murrell's death."

"But if it were to come out in the papers tomorrow that you were linked, however tenuously, to this high profile murder case, that surely wouldn't be good news for you?"

"Are you threatening me, Inspector?"

I shook my head.

"In which case, neither good nor bad. I am not linked, even tenuously, to this murder case and I'd be grateful if you would refrain from intimating that I am. I am linked to the victim, I accept that. And of course I was greatly saddened by the loss of an old friend and colleague. I, for one, have great faith in the police to catch Simon's killer and will provide whatever assistance I may be able to offer to help them in that endeavour."

"The sounds like a prepared statement."

"An occupational hazard, I'm afraid."

I lifted myself from the sofa and replaced by cup and saucer on the tray.

"Can I ask you about Lloyd's?"

Another nod.

"You are a Lloyd's Name?"

"You know I am."

"Has that been profitable for you over the years?"

"Is that an appropriate line of questioning?"

"I apologise. Were you aware that Simon Murrell had been a Lloyd's Name?"

"I was."

"He suffered very badly after the Crash."

"As did many."

"Were you one of the many?"

"Thankfully I was relatively well insulated. But for many it was ruinous."

"It certainly ruined Simon Murrell."

"I believe it did."

The conversation had become like a game of chess. Each move was countered by a defensive manoeuvre by the opposing player.

"I understand that you can't become a Lloyd's Name unless you are nominated by an existing Name."

"You've done your homework, Inspector. That is true."

"Did Simon Murrell ever discuss with you how to become a Lloyd's Name?"

"You know that he did, Inspector. You also know that I was the person who nominated him."

First unforced error, as they say in tennis.

"Actually, sir, I didn't," I lied.

Another nod.

"That would have been back in 1993?" I pressed.

"Around then."

"But I thought you were no longer in contact with Simon Murrell."

"He contacted me to ask for my advice."

Duggan laughed out loud.

"He seems to have made a habit of this, writing to you with offers, requests, pleas. If you did all this for somebody you didn't keep in touch with, I can only imagine what you'd be prepared to do for a friend."

By now, Monk was paying Harry no attention. He checked his watch again, more impatiently this time, and focused solely on me.

"So he asked for your advice and you nominated him?"

"It wasn't quite as simple as that. We had two or three conversations, by the end of which he was very keen on signing up. My nomination was merely the enabler that got him what he wanted."

"And then he lost everything?"

"Lloyd's is a game of chance, Inspector. It's like playing poker. To play, you have to have enough to lose as well as win."

"And Simon Murrell didn't?"

"If you say so, I believe you."

"And doesn't that make you feel just a little bit guilty?"

"Absolutely not. It was simply one man's free will colliding head on with a powerful dose of bad luck."

We were in the conversational equivalent of a cul-de-sac. Every point we made was being played back to us with a dead straight bat. I rose, brushing biscuit crumbs from off my lap and offered him my hand to shake.

"Just a couple of final questions, Mr Monk. Where were you over the Bank Holiday weekend?"

He looked coldly, but directly into my eyes.

"I can check my diary if you wish but I'm certain that I was in my house in the Cotswolds on the Friday and Saturday, and then drove across to my constituency on the Sunday. I stayed there until the Wednesday morning, when I drove back to London."

"And do you mind me asking you what you drive?"

"I have a Land Rover Discovery and a Jaguar."

"And which did you use that weekend?"

"I had the Jag with me. The Land Rover stayed in London."

I LEFT WESTMINSTER believing we had something important. The difficulty was I didn't know what. But that there was more to uncover about the relationship between Crispin Monk and Simon Murrell, I was in no doubt at all. That was now the task in hand.

Chapter Thirty-Two

O NCE I HAD found a copy of his death certificate, finding Richard Osborne's grave didn't require extensive detective work. I was intrigued about the story behind the other death from within this supposedly close group of friends.

The grave had obviously been lovingly and regularly tended. The surrounding grass was neatly clipped against the pathway, the way a barber trims and shapes a beard. The headstone seemed cleaner than those that neighboured it, despite shadows from the branches of nearby trees casting patterns across its porcelain appearance. Fresh white roses stood tall in a vase placed directly at his feet. It mattered – he mattered – to somebody.

To a soul which had passed from this world to the next in such apparently tortured circumstances, this cemetery must have felt like coming home. The torment was over; the long and longed-for rest could begin. I sensed myself being wrapped in a consoling peace disturbed only by birdsong and the occasional whisper of others in muted conversation with those who had gone before. A warming breeze played tag through the leaves on surrounding trees. I found myself in a reflective mood.

The headstone told the bare facts of his story. Richard Matthew Osborne was a much loved son and brother who had left this world on October 17th 1997 at the premature age of just thirty-four. He was sorely missed but remembered always in the hearts of those who loved him. Beneath the inscription, at the foot of the headstone and in a smaller type, was recorded a quotation from the book of Micah, Chapter Seven, Verse Five. "Do not trust in a friend; do not put your confidence in a companion."

"I don't think we've met."

The voice made me start. I turned on one foot to find a portly, balding man whom I instinctively placed in his early sixties, sitting at one end of a varnished bench some ten feet away across a tarmac path. The sleeve of his navy blue jacket rested on the arm of the bench, his hands clasped, his white unkempt hair, almost yellow in its hue, framing a deep, ruddy complexion. Even at a distance, I could make out a roadmap of veins in his cheeks. As he leant back into the bench, he folded his right leg over his left knee. It took no little effort.

"Were you one of Richard's friends?"

I completed my turn and walked the five or six yards towards him, shaking earth from my shoes as I reached the pathway. He stood and proffered his hand, which I took into my own. He held on to my hand longer than the greeting required, giving me a matter of seconds to view him up close. There was a sorrow in his eyes that made him appear older, perhaps wearier, than I initially thought he was.

"My name's Jack Munday," I offered. "And no, I wasn't one of Richard's friends."

"So can I ask you what brings you to my son's grave?"

"I'm a policeman," I smiled, gesturing for him to sit back down on the bench. I lowered myself next to him. His eyes studied me.

"So you're a policeman. That still doesn't explain what brings you to my son's grave."

"I'm investigating a murder and I believe there may be a connection between your son and the victim in the case that I'm investigating."

He moved his bulky frame in a three-quarter turn so that he sat face-on towards me rather than side by side, his jacket falling away to reveal a sizeable stomach encased inside a checked cotton shirt, open at the neck, a few wisps of white chest hair catching the light breeze.

"But my son took his own life, Mr Munday," he said in an undertone. "That is something which has never been in doubt."

"Tell me about Richard," I said after a while. "I want to know what he was like."

The man let out a deep sigh, as if he'd been waiting all these years for somebody, anybody, to give him the opportunity to talk about his son, and yet now that the opportunity had presented itself, it was almost too painful to contemplate.

"Richard was our eldest son. We have another, Anthony. There were four years between them. I don't know whether it's because he's no longer with us, but with hindsight, there always seemed something special about Richard. Not that we don't love Anthony. We do. God knows, we do. Especially since, well, you can imagine. It's just that Richard was one of those people who could light up a room simply by walking in. He had a knack of making you feel good about yourself; always a smile, always a hug, always a joke; the ordinary stuff.

303

It's the ordinary stuff we miss the most. It's been seven years and yet I still expect him to come in and drag me down to the pub for a pint before dinner."

"People tell me he was successful, a good musician, that he had so much going for him?"

"Perhaps."

"So how comes he ended up taking his own life?"

"Well you're right, Richard was all of those things. He went to Cambridge; the first in our family to do so. My wife was particularly proud. We still have his graduation photograph on the wall at home."

"Did he enjoy university?"

"He never said anything to make me believe that he didn't. Richard worked hard but Cambridge also allowed him to indulge his love of sport, skiing in particular. He would do that as often as he could. He even tried bungee jumping. I'd never heard of anything so ridiculous and then, when he showed us the pictures, I told him he was mad. I told him he'd never catch me doing something as insane as that. Richard also played clarinet in an orchestra that toured. I remember one year he played in a carol concert in Prague. He found that quite magical."

"Did you ever visit him at university?"

"Not really. We took him up there when he first started like everybody else, but for the rest of his time there, he tended to come and go by train or coach. He preferred it that way. Nobody wants their mum and dad trailing behind their every move, I suppose."

"Did you know any of his university friends?"

"We didn't know them but he talked about them. He wouldn't say much but he gave us the impression that he was slightly in awe of them. Most of them came from much more affluent backgrounds and I think he found it eye-opening some of the things they got up to. My son was no angel, of course, and I'm sure he sampled a lot of what was on offer to him but he still was in shock. The only one we know now, of course, is that hideous Crispin Monk. Richard used to like him very much, but he would be appalled to hear some of the things Monk is saying these days."

"How so?"

"Just that Richard was a friend to everyone and he wouldn't be comfortable with all of this anti-this one, anti-that one talk."

"And after Cambridge?"

"After Cambridge, he tried a number of different careers, mainly finance. His dream was always to own his own property portfolio, so he worked for a few of the large estates in London and for a couple of developers before beginning to put together his own properties. He was starting to be quite successful when…"

"When he passed away?"

"…when he passed away. Well, before that, actually. We don't know very much but after his death we found out that he had lost a lot of money in the Lloyd's Crash. Unbeknown to us he had been seduced to become a Name by one of his contacts, but the losses robbed him of literally everything, including his reason for living."

"Do you mind me asking what happened?"

"It was a weekend; Saturday morning to be precise. We'd been expecting Richard to come for the weekend. He was due for dinner on the Friday evening but, to be honest, we weren't that concerned when he didn't arrive. It wasn't that out of the ordinary. We assumed that either he had been held up through work and would be here the following day or that it had been our misunderstanding in the first place and that he always intended to come on the Saturday. But when he didn't arrive on Saturday morning either, we began to get quite worried. He wouldn't answer his phone so, to reassure us, Anthony drove over to his place in Belsize Park and let himself in. He found Richard dead in bed. He told us he looked just as if he was sleeping. Apparently, he'd consumed a quite considerable number of painkillers and sleeping tablets and nearly a litre of whiskey. It was no accidental overdose. The doctors told us he'd been dead for more than twelve hours when Anthony found him."

"That must have shaken you both."

"Nothing prepares you, Mr Munday. Richard may have been in his thirties, apparently successful in his own right, but he was still our child. Nothing can ever prepare you for the loss of a child. It's not the natural order."

"Did you find out what prompted his suicide?"

"Not really. He left a note that didn't give much away. It talked about feeling let down, about friendship being a heap of bullshit, his phrase not mine, and how he hoped one day people would reflect on what they had done. He was a religious, sensitive young man. I can't imagine what pressure he must have been under to plan to take his life and to not feel able to talk to anybody before he did so."

"And you have no idea?"

"Nothing for sure. Anthony told us some months after Richard's death that he also believed – and had for some time – that Richard was gay, even though he had never come out to us. He felt that Richard had been conflicted by his sexuality and his Christian beliefs and that maybe it would have been a disappointment to us. The truth, of course, is that he was our son and our love was unconditional. His sexuality would have made no difference. I think it had more to do with money."

"You know, I wondered for a moment what my own headstone would say and who would come and place fresh flowers by my feet."

"I hope that's not something you have to consider for a very long time."

I smiled. "The quotation on Richard's headstone."

"From the book of Micah?"

"Who chose that?"

"Richard did. He had included it in the letter that Anthony found. We don't know what he meant by it but clearly it was important."

"Do you have a copy of that letter still?"

"I do. We have it in the box with all of Richard's other stuff. His photographs, some of the poems he used to write. It's our way of keeping Richard alive in one small place."

"Would he have photographs in there from university?"

"I expect so. Even after seven years, we haven't summoned up the courage to go through it. We found it in his flat."

"Would you show it to me?"

"If you think it could help you with your murder case, I guess you can see it. As long as you promise to give it back to me intact."

"I guarantee that with my life."

IT WAS LATER that same day that Richard Osborne's brother,

Anthony, delivered the box to the police station. I met him in person at the front desk and thanked him as sincerely as I could for letting me have access to something so precious. He was taller and of slighter frame than his father but there remained the same haunted look behind his eyes. I carried the box carefully to my office, wondering about the secrets it might yield.

The small wooden box was rosewood in colour, varnished to a high gloss and with a frosted glass panel across the middle of the lid. I examined it from all angles for fifteen minutes without being sure what I expected to find. For a while I denied myself the right to open the lid; when I picked the box up and held it close to my face I felt like a child sneaking downstairs on Christmas Eve to rattle a present or two from under the tree.

I lifted the lid and pushed it back on its squeaky brass hinges and, using my gloved right hand, lifted folded pieces of paper, delicately and one at a time, out of the box and onto the desk top in front of me. There were three bills, two utility and one from a credit card company. There was also an old receipt from Links of London for silver cufflinks, but no indication of who the recipient might have been.

The fourth item I removed was a white piece of A4 paper, folded twice to a DL size. I unfolded it to find a print out of an email from Simon Murrell to Richard and Patrick Ramsden sent at 10.52am on September 5th 1997, just one month before Richard's suicide. In the text, Murrell informed them that "everything is working exactly as I planned. They're all just freaked by the whole fucking thing, especially Crispin. It's wiped the smug grin off his pretty little face. One day soon, I'll have to tell you both all about it over a nice cold beer.

Keep smiling, Richard. They're going to get what they all deserve."

I made a mental note – we needed to get into Simon's email. But why would Richard print out and keep this particular email, and what others would I find if I got into Simon's inbox?

I dug deeper. There was his security pass from one of the property companies with which Richard worked, a membership card to the Soho House club and a season ticket from the 1995/96 season to Chelsea Football Club. Right at the bottom of the box was a buff coloured envelope, creased from years of handling and wearing away at the corners and down the folds. I lifted out the batch of photographs that sat inside and began to spread them out in front of me. I looked closely and began to recognise the faces that stared back.

In one, a young Simon Murrell, with collar-length hair, his arm round Tom O'Neill's shoulder and a cigarette drooping at a 45 degree angle from the left corner of his mouth, seemed to be toasting whoever was holding the camera with a half empty pint of bitter. Father Tom appeared to be equally at ease. The image was clearly old and I suspected the venue was a student bar at Cambridge. I moved on, through countless similar group shots. The young Francine Monk sitting on Seb Brown's lap, his hand cupping her breast in seaside-postcard style; to the right of them sat Crispin Monk, outwardly ill-at-ease. A further group shot revealed two new faces, who I presumed to be Patrick Ramsden and Richard Osborne.

The next images were more startling. The first showed a young and not unattractive Francine Monk, naked, lying on her back, her legs spread graphically apart, her head propped up on some pillows so that her identity was clearly visible. The image showed a man, unidentifiable by the angle, also naked, astride her right leg, buttocks towards the camera lens, with his head latched onto her right breast. At the same time, in her left hand, she was gripping the erection of a second naked man, who stood substantially out of frame.

There was a second shot, this time with Francine facing the camera, a close-up look of pleasure on her face. This time a man's naked body was visible behind her, penetrating her from behind.

A third shot. It was Francine again, though this time her back was towards the camera as she straddled a man who lay naked and flat on a bed. The image was poor quality but there was no mistaking the identity of the man whose face peered out to one side of her unclothed body. It was Tom O'Neill. A second man sat naked on the edge of the bed, watching as he smoked a joint.

A fourth shot showed Seb Brown naked, with an erection, kissing a naked Richard Osborne, his hand reaching down towards Richard's crotch.

I placed the four images alongside each other on the desk, and sat back. There were other prints still inside the envelope, but I wanted first to consider the implications of what lay in front of me. Francine was obviously more than just a friend of Seb, and what of Tom O'Neill? And why, in any of these photographs, was there no presence of Crispin Monk? And why did Richard have them? Had he taken them? How was he using them? The pictures might be embarrassing, but they were university shots from a previous time of life. Surely they would just be laughed off as the indiscretions of a hedonistic youth, wouldn't they? Unless, of course, it was still going on and Richard and Simon both knew it.

I fetched myself a coffee and removed the remainder of

the photographs. In the first, it took me a while to distinguish between the collage of flesh that looked back at me. The most immediate realisation about this image was that they were all men; all naked men. Simon, the guy I assumed to be Richard Osborne, and Tom O'Neill laid out in a triangular pattern on a bed, each with their faces in the groin of the next man.

The next photograph was similar; though in this one the three had been joined on the bed by Francine, with the hand of one of the men – I couldn't be certain which one – resting between her legs, a look of mischief playing across her face.

And then the fourth: a scene with three naked men; one in the middle, pale and skeletal, being penetrated from the rear by Simon Murrell, whilst himself performing oral sex on another man who stood in front of him. The man in the middle was clearly and unquestionably Crispin Monk.

I had never been trained in how to handle dynamite, but even I knew that caution would be the order of the day. There were now so many more questions and thoughts running around my head. Had Richard kept these for posterity? I doubted that. Had he shown them to anyone? Were there others? What damage could they do to the reputation of Crispin Monk? Were they to be the subject of a blackmail attempt? Had they already been so? Whatever the answers, the existence of the images simply couldn't become public knowledge.

I placed everything back in the box in exactly the order that I had found it and then put the box itself in the bottom right hand drawer of my desk and locked it in. I called Harry and asked him to meet me in an hour; I was convinced that what I had seen had changed everything and now I needed a council of war on how to direct the enquiry from here.

Chapter Thirty-Three

"SO HERE'S THE deal," I told the team, dipping buttered toast into a mug of tea, "I'm more convinced than ever that blackmail is behind all of this. I'm just not sure yet who was blackmailing who, and why they were doing so. If we can nail that, we'll know who murdered Simon Murrell. I am circulating the photographs that we found in Richard Osborne's box. They don't leave much to the imagination and I need hardly have to tell you the damage they could do if they get out. So, if any of these leak, I will know how it has happened and I will have each of you strung up by your testicles until I know which one of you did it."

"And what about those of us with no testicles?" asked Lesley.

"You don't even want to think about what I might have planned for you."

There were a few crude remarks from Danny Thorne's direction as the first of the photographs began to reach him.

"Guys, the answers we are looking for lie in these photographs somewhere. We still need to find out who was in Simon's flat on the night he died, who he shared the Chinese meal with and who he had sex with. We are now at the point where I think we need to start collecting DNA samples. So we're going to start asking our suspect list for swabs and let's see what gets thrown up. Lesley, will you visit Francine Monk; Danny, will you take Father Tom; Harry, visit your old friend Crispin Monk – but be polite, okay – and Paul and Rob, will you visit Seb Brown. Mike, I want you to visit Mrs Murrell and Gail Weaver. I'm not ready to rule them out just yet."

The team nodded as one.

"Stay in contact and if anything comes up while you're out and about, let me know. I think we're closing in, I'm just not certain on who. But if *I* think that then *they* probably think it too and that may mean they start taking risks. And don't forget. I still want a report from all of those CCTV cameras in the area."

Paul Price held his hand up in acknowledgement.

"I'm still working through it so if it's okay with you, Rob will take Mr Brown and I'll carry on going through the footage."

"Fine. Now all of you, go."

AFTER BRIEFING THE Chief Superintendent and agreeing to a 6pm press conference to provide an update on the progress of the investigation for the media, I returned to my desk. Twice I tried to call Elaine and twice hung up before she had the chance to answer. I was still in a state of shock that she had agreed to have dinner with me and whilst I really wanted to hear her voice again, I didn't want to take the chance that she may have changed her mind. I was psyching myself up to try once more when my mobile rang. It was Lesley.

"I've just bumped into Rob."

"That's nice for you. I'm glad you felt the need to call and tell me but shouldn't you be on your way to Mrs Monk?"

"I was. I reached their house as she was leaving so I decided to follow her for a while to see what she might be up to. That's when I bumped into Rob. He was doing the same to Mr Brown."

"Are you suggesting that Mrs Monk and Mr Brown are together?"

"Mrs Monk and Mr Brown have just taken a table for lunch at L'Escargot. Or I'm guessing they have. They arrived separately, but I'm thinking it would be a big coincidence if they have both chosen the same restaurant on the same day to have lunch with other people."

"Interesting. I'm coming up. Keep an eye and if they leave, follow them. Otherwise, I think we'll join them for coffee."

I still get amazed by how quickly a flashing light and a siren can cut your way through Central London traffic and so, it was within forty minutes that my driver brought our unmarked car to a quiet stop in Greek Street, one of the narrow thoroughfares that connect Soho Square at one end with Old Compton Street at the other. Soho is one of London's cultural melting pots, an area which, now rid of many of the sex stores and strip joints that created its reputation, retains the sense of being London's deviant side. It is, though, also home to theatres and restaurants and the streets are thronged each day by media types, the avant-garde, tourists and show-goers of all kinds, including those seeking performances of the flesh. L'Escargot has long been one of the area's landmark restaurants. The tables behind its discreet, almost anonymous entrance are much coveted by businessmen, American tourists, and the occasional celebrity. Lesley and Rob stood across the street from the front entrance drinking coffee from polystyrene cups.

"Still in there?"

They nodded. It was 2.30pm.

We crossed the road and entered the restaurant, walking down the narrow passageway to the reception desk at the end. A besuited elfin-like woman, with a hint of Audrey Hepburn about her, was retrieving coats for diners from wardrobes off to her left. She smiled, laughed at whatever they had said to her and bade them farewell. She turned towards us and asked if she could help in heavily French-accented English.

Her reluctance to give us details about where particular diners were sitting lasted as long as it took me to produce my warrant card. She escorted us inside, turning right past the bar and two courteous waiters and upstairs past tables of diners, so wrapped up in their own conversations they wouldn't have noticed our presence. In contrast, Francine Monk noticed us immediately and gave an uneasy smile as we approached. Brown sat with his back to us. Francine could do little to pre-warn him until I placed my left hand on his back and offered him my right hand to shake. He took it almost as some kind of default reaction and looked up at me in confusion.

"Mr Brown, we've not been introduced. I'm Detective Inspector Jack Munday. I think you had the pleasure of meeting my sergeant, Harry Duggan."

"Indeed, Inspector. He made quite an impression on me."

"And you on him. Good afternoon, Mrs Monk. Has your lunch been nice? The tuna carpaccio here is meant to be particularly good."

Francine Monk smiled nervously and watched as the three

of us sat at the next table. I ordered a double espresso for me and a cappuccino each for Lesley and Rob, which duly arrived in understated white crockery, accompanied by small macaroons and a bowl full of brown and white boulder-like sugar lumps.

"So I hope we've not interrupted anything important," I started. "But I was a bit surprised when my colleagues here told me that you were lunching together."

"Why should that surprise you?" said Brown. "We're two old friends."

"Of course, your husband told me that you and Mr Brown meet occasionally. I think he called it your 'shared charitable commitments.'"

"Exactly that," Francine smiled. "Seb and I are big patrons of the opera. We are discussing what help we might be able to give to get a plan for an opera festival in Hyde Park underway."

"And do your charitable endeavours extend to friends who have fallen on hard times?"

"I told your sergeant all that I knew about Simon," Seb replied impatiently.

I dropped one sugar lump into my espresso and stirred.

"I have a problem. We know that at least two people were with Simon Murrell in his flat on the night that he died. One of them was a man and at one of them was a woman. I shall leave it to your own powers of deduction to work out how we are sure of that. So I will ask you again, Mr Brown, was one of them you?"

"And I shall tell you again, Mr Munday, that it was not."

"And you, Mrs Monk, did you stay in contact with Mr Murrell?"

She shook her head, clutching nervously at her bandaged hand.

"How did you hurt your hand?"

"I caught it in the car door."

"Ouch, that must have been painful. Did you see your doctor about it?"

"Good grief, no. I bought some Witchhazel and a bandage from Boots, bathed it and wrapped it up myself."

"Still painful, though?"

"It was my own stupid fault."

The waiters were hovering, like overly attentive insects waiting to strip a plate of food, as they sought to clear the tables and prepare for the evening sitting.

"I think our friends here would like us to leave," I volunteered.

Seb Brown raised one finger to the waiter as a request for the bill. And when the chip and pin machine was brought he made an elaborate gesture of including our coffees.

"So if neither of you met Mr Murrell, then presumably neither of you would have a problem coming back to the station with us to have a chat and give us a DNA sample so we can properly eliminate you from our enquiries?"

"This afternoon?"

"This afternoon would be good. Alternatively we can storm into your office tomorrow morning, making lots of noise and arrest you on suspicion of perverting the course of justice?"

"But I haven't perverted the course of justice."

"That's why it's called suspicion."

"Seb, let's just do it. Get it over and done with."

"I'll have to make calls and rearrange meetings. It's most

inconvenient, you know."

"You can call from the car. Rob will take you with him; Lesley will escort Mrs Monk and I will see you both back at the station."

"Okay. As long as we don't make it look like an arrest as we leave."

"Scout's honour. We will make it look just like old friends leaving after having lunch together."

SEB BROWN TOOK a sip of water from the plastic cup on the table in front of him in Interview Room Three. He was stocky, with wiry auburn hair that I thought had probably been coloured. The five o'clock shadow was becoming more evident and, from the look of his spade-like hands, he bit his nails. He asked to remove his jacket, revealing a white double-cuffed shirt, removing the cufflinks and winding the sleeves up to reveal hairy, tanned forearms. He loosened his navy blue tie and undid the top button of his shirt.

"Tell me again, Mr Brown, why were you having lunch today with Mrs Monk?"

Seb Brown sounded weary in his reply.

"She is an old friend of mine and we share many cultural and charitable interests. Today we were discussing a plan to hold an opera festival in Hyde Park. It's part of our shared ambition to make opera more accessible to ordinary people."

"And how do you characterise ordinary people?"

"You know as well as I do that opera is perceived to be an art form favoured by the upper classes. The reality of course is that most operas were written for the masses though few these days can afford – or think they can afford – the prices at places like Covent Garden. Take it into Hyde Park and make the tickets cheaper, make it more of an event and I think that we could attract many more people. Nice though it is to chat, Mr Munday, I do hope you haven't taken me away from my day to discuss opera?"

"Of course not. Tell me about your friendship with Mr and Mrs Monk."

"Francine and I met in our first year at Cambridge and Crispin became a friend of ours. We became close friends and I am pleased to say we have remained so."

"You and Francine or you and both of them?"

"Both of them, I would hope."

"It's just that Mr Monk gave us the impression that he saw you very rarely."

"Crispin's a very busy man as you can imagine. Me too. Usually."

I smiled.

"And you and Mrs Monk dated whilst at university?"

"Dated is such a funny term. If you mean were we sleeping together then the answer is yes."

"And then she ditched you for Mr Monk?"

"I'm not sure if ditched is quite right. After a while she just seemed to gravitate towards Crispin. He's a very charismatic guy."

"And did that annoy you, upset you?"

"Maybe a bit at the time. But it's a long way behind us."

"Your university days seem to have been very heady."

"Aren't everybody's? What is it they say; if you remember it, you weren't really there?"

"Lucky then that Richard Osborne and, I guess, Simon Murrell kept photographs like these to remind you all."

I laid a selection of the images from Richard Osborne's

box on the table in front of him. His posture became immediately more defensive, his agitation more apparent as I pointed to one of him, Simon, and Francine naked together.

"Let me ask you again. Have you seen Simon Murrell recently?"

"No."

"Have you had any contact from him?"

Hesitation.

"Mr Brown, if you have something to say, I strongly suggest that you start saying it. We will find out what happened and it's so much better for you if your side of the story comes from you."

He nodded.

"Now had you had any contact from Simon Murrell?"

He swallowed hard.

"About a year ago, initially by email and then once by telephone."

"And what was it about?"

"He had worked out by following us that Francine and I were still seeing each other."

"You and Mrs Monk have been having an affair?"

He nodded again.

"For how long?"

"On and off for four years. He had photographs of us arriving and leaving hotels together. He emailed me some of those images together with some of the old university ones. He wanted money."

"Or he would send the images to Mr Monk?"

"It was more the media I was concerned about. Crispin knows about Francine and I and he always has done. He turns a blind eye as long as she plays the dutiful political wife. And actually, she wants to be the wife of the Prime Minister, so that was another reason to keep Simon quiet."

"So you paid him?"

"It was strange. Given how much some of these images would have fetched from the tabloid press, he only asked me for a thousand a month."

"Why didn't you report it?"

"And risk it all coming out? Plus, last year I earned just shy of one million pounds. To fork out a thousand a month for peace and quiet didn't seem a lot to me."

"And you never met?"

"Never. The instructions came by email with details of his bank account. As long as I paid the money in by cash on the dates that we agreed, he would leave me alone. And I have to say he did."

"Until?"

"No until. He left me alone."

"But it must have irritated you, being held to ransom like this?"

"I could have done without it, if that's what you mean."

"Surely you must have been tempted to a put a stop it?"

"Maybe early on."

"So you didn't visit his house on the night he died?"

"Absolutely not. As I told your sergeant, that night I was hosting a dinner party at my place in Chelsea Harbour. I am more than happy to give you the names of my guests."

I PUSHED OPEN the door to the interview room where Francine Monk sat with Lesley Hilton.

"I don't mind doing whatever I can to help, Inspector, but leaving me in here for the best part of an hour is really not on. I've had to call our nanny back on her day off to collect the children."

"I'm sorry Mrs Monk, that must be most inconvenient. Tell me, does she not fill in for you when you're banging Mr Brown in a hotel of your choice?"

Lesley turned sharply to look at me. I smiled broadly.

"Mr Brown has been telling me about your cosy little arrangement and how he'd been paying Simon Murrell to keep it quiet. Mr Monk can't be too happy."

"Not that this is any of your business, but my husband and I stopped sleeping together five years ago. Some of us get off on sex, others on power. He has known about Seb and me since the beginning and as long as we do nothing to spoil the perfect family image that we present to the public he is happy to go along with anything."

"Anything?"

"Well, not murder, if that's what you're suggesting?"

"I'm not suggesting anything, Mrs Monk. So he was blackmailing Mr Brown and your husband?"

"He wanted revenge on Crispin for the whole Lloyd's thing. It was his own fault. He should never have become a Name. He harangued Crispin for ages to nominate him and when he lost everything, suddenly he became very threatening. He had those images from Cambridge and the information on Seb and I, either of which would have blown Crispin's career out of the water."

"Mrs Monk, are you familiar with the name Richard Osborne?"

"Of course I am. Richard went to university with us. He took his own life a few years ago, I believe."

"And were you aware that Richard Osborne was also a

Lloyd's Name? And that he also lost everything he had in the Lloyd's Crash and that his father believes that this could have been the reason for his suicide?"

She shook her head. As she looked up at me, she seemed to have shrunk inward. Her eyes were reddening and her hands were noticeably shaking. She made every effort to prevent them from doing so.

"Was Richard Osborne also nominated as a Name by your husband?"

She sighed heavily.

"I don't know. You will have to ask him."

A short knock on the door was followed swiftly by Paul Price's head coming round the door. He beckoned for me to follow him out of the room. We stood side by side in the corridor as uniformed officers passed us by.

"A couple of things. I've been through Christ knows how many hours of CCTV footage from I don't know how many cameras and I think I may finally have something. The same car appears in the roads around Simon's flat early evening, driving away from the same area after ten and then is picked up on another set of cameras less than half a mile from the charity shop and travelling in that direction."

"And the car is?"

"It's a Land Rover Discovery. I've run the plate through the database and the car is registered to one Crispin Monk."

"Something else?"

"Yep, we've made contact with Patrick Ramsden in Canada. He has confirmed that both Richard Osborne and Simon Murrell were nominated to be Lloyd's Names by Crispin Monk. They wanted him to join them but he said he always had a bad feeling about it so passed it up. He also reckons the losses were the reason for Richard Osborne's suicide. He says that the suicide as much as the losses were the driving force behind Simon Murrell's determination to get even with the others."

"You're a star. I do believe we're making progress."

I waited a moment to consider how best to raise this new piece of information before returning to an increasingly anxious Francine Monk. I re-entered the room and noticed how she suddenly seemed smaller, more vulnerable than she had been when I had left.

"Mrs Monk, I think it's time we levelled with each other. Why were you at Simon Murrell's on the night that he died?"

"I wasn't."

I leant close into her face and struggled to contain my anger.

"YOU WERE. *I* KNOW YOU WERE. *YOU* KNOW YOU WERE AND SOON I'M GOING TO BE ABLE TO PROVE IT."

Lesley put her arm across my chest and urged me away. I raised my hand in apology.

"Mrs Monk, where were you over the Bank Holiday weekend?"

"I was in the Cotswolds with my husband. He then went to the constituency and I returned to London on the Sunday."

"Isn't it customary for you to accompany your husband to the constituency?"

"Usually, yes, but I had a charity event on the Sunday evening and the children had friends' parties in London."

"And you stayed in your home in Westminster?"

"Yes."

"And you stayed within Central London?"

She nodded.

"Your husband told us that he had his Jaguar with him that weekend."

"I believe so."

"So can you explain to me why on the Monday evening your Land Rover Discovery was picked up on CCTV cameras within a mile or two of where Simon Murrell lived and where his body was found?"

Her head fell forward into her hands and, almost inaudibly, she began to cry.

"Shall we start again?"

She breathed in deeply. She nodded.

"Did you visit Simon Murrell on the night that he died?"

"Yes."

"Why?"

"I was angry with him. I was angry that he was blackmailing my husband and I was angry that he was blackmailing Seb. I was unhappy that he was using those photographs from when we were students to threaten us now. I always got on well with Simon. I wanted to talk to him."

"And what did you say?"

"Well exactly that, really, but he wasn't having any of it. When I arrived, he was drunk and he'd already been injecting something and also doing some coke."

"You argued?"

"We argued. He was irrational, angry. I ordered us some food. I just wanted to talk to him."

"So at what point did you decide to have sex with him?"

Humiliation occupied her face.

"We were drinking, we were talking about the university photographs. He kept on asking why I was attracted to Seb and to Crispin but not to him. I told him that I did find him attractive but that university was a long time ago. But he kept on and on at me. At one point, he leant forward, pushed me onto my back and started kissing me. He unbuttoned my blouse and started clutching at my breasts."

"And at what point did you take the decision to kill him?"

"I didn't kill him. I promise you I didn't kill him. When I left him, he was fine. He probably died of an overdose."

"Mrs Monk, we know he died from strangulation. Drugs won't do that to you. What time did you leave him?"

"I don't recall. Maybe half past nine."

"So how come your car appears on CCTV close to the charity shop where Simon's body was found around half past ten?"

She stayed silent.

"One final question for now."

She looked up.

"Who was the other man with you that night?"

"I was alone."

"Mrs Monk, you were not alone. There was another man who had sex with you and Mr Murrell and I will find out who it was."

"Somebody could have come in after I left him."

I shrugged my shoulders. I turned to Lesley.

"Please read Mrs Monk her rights. We are charging with her on suspicion of the murder of Simon Murrell. We can talk some more tomorrow."

I left the room to the sound of Francine Monk in tears.

Chapter Thirty-Four

"YOU'RE IN MY church now and this is my confessional, so you had better start talking, Father."

Tom O'Neill appeared as if all confidence had been sapped from his body. He sat, broken, in the Interview Room, visibly trembling and stifling his tears, the way cowards do. I, in contrast, could feel energy levels rising.

"Forgive me Inspector for I have sinned. Shall we start with that?" I said. "I'm going to ask you a series of very simple questions. I suggest we start with some very simple answers."

Still he wouldn't make eye contact.

"Were you at Simon Murrell's house on the night that he died?"

He nodded.

"Aloud please, for the tape."

"Yes."

"Were you there alone or with another person?"

"I went with Francine."

"Francine Monk?"

Confirmation received.

"Why did you go?"

"Simon Murrell had been blackmailing me."

"You as well?"

"Yes. I only found out a few days earlier that he had been blackmailing the others too. When he first came to the area and saw me, he sent me copies of the photographs he had and told me he'd send them to the Bishop and the media unless I paid him to keep quiet."

"So you did?"

"I had to. Those kinds of images, even from so long ago, are not compatible with a life in clergy. I don't earn much but I had to pay him five hundred pounds every month. It has almost crippled me."

"How did you come into contact with Francine Monk again?"

"When Simon started blackmailing me I thought that he would probably try the others too. I decided to warn them. Francine was the easiest person for me to reach, so we met and kept in touch after that."

"So when Simon saw you in Mario's cafe that day?"

"We had an angry exchange. I told him that what he was doing was unfair, dragging up things from many years ago to hold us all to ransom now. He told me he didn't give a shit and to just carry on paying the money."

"So you hatched a plan with Francine to get revenge?"

"No, nothing like that. Francine just felt that if we went and confronted him together; appealed to him as old friends, maybe see if there was another way that we could help him, then perhaps he would drop the blackmail stuff and destroy the pictures. I was never sure it would work, because you could never be sure how many copies of the pictures he had.

Besides, he was desperate."

"So you went to see him?"

"Yes."

"Pre-arranged."

"No. We thought that if we pre-arranged it, he would not turn up. Crispin was away in his constituency so Francine called me to see if I would go with her. I was really unsure about it but what else did I have to lose? At first he didn't want to let us in. The place was a mess. He had been drinking and Francine thought he'd been doing heroin or something. He was borderline out of it."

"Then what?"

"We brought takeaway with us. Chinese. We really just wanted to try and sort things out. We ate. We drank but he wouldn't talk about the blackmail at all."

"And the sex?"

He looked at me inquisitively.

"We know Father that Francine had sex with Simon Murrell that night. And now, thanks to a DNA match, we know you did too."

Tom O'Neill ran his hands roughly through his tied-back hair and screamed out in frustration.

"To be honest, Father, breaching your vow of celibacy seems like one of your lesser problems at the moment."

"Simon started getting it on with Francine. He was being a bit rough with her, but she seemed happy to go along with it. What can I say; I joined in. I'm not proud of it. Hell, I'm not proud of any of it. It got more and more rough and I became more and more uneasy. She was scratching him down his back just to try and force him to get off her. He even bit her on her hand and drew blood. He was all over her, pushing

331

her back and holding her down. He didn't know what he was doing and I was getting scared that it was all getting really out of hand. I did it to save her, to get him to let her go."

"Did what?"

"I pulled him back. I only meant to put a stop to it all, but suddenly his whole body just went limp and landed on her."

"What did you strangle him with?"

"I reached out to find anything and picked up Francine's bra. He was laying down on top of her, his head was buried in her breasts. She was egging me on to do it. I just looped the bra around his neck, tied it in a knot and squeezed as tightly as I could. I didn't want to stop until I knew that she was safe, but by then Simon was just lifeless. When we rolled him off of Francine, she could tell immediately that he was gone."

"What did you do next?"

"I don't remember too much of what happened next. I was a bit of a wreck to be honest. Francine took control. She got black bags from underneath the sink in Simon's kitchen and we doubled them up and rolled him inside. We cleared up as much as we could but she said the important thing was to get rid of the body."

"The charity shop?"

"She wanted to take him into the forest and just dump the body there. I wasn't happy with that. I wanted him to be found. I wanted him to have a proper Christian burial. I know that might sound ridiculous given what had just happened but it's the truth. The charity shop just happened to be the first convenient place we came to. There was nobody around, so we lifted him out of the back of Francine's car and left him with the other bags."

"And then she took you home?"

"And then she took me home. We vowed not to speak about it again. And we didn't until after you visited me for the first time and I called her. That's when she said we need to meet to discuss how to handle things."

"What a mess, Father. Aren't greed and envy two of the seven cardinal sins?"

"His or ours?"

"You know we have to charge you?"

He nodded.

"You need to start thinking about a solicitor. You've got a long journey ahead."

"For what it's worth, Inspector, I'm sorry."

"For what it's worth, Father, me too."

And with that, I left Harry to do the formalities so I could brief the Chief Superintendent that the case was coming to a close.

Chapter Thirty-Five

"CONNOR'S BEEN TELLING all his friends that his Dad is a celebrity."

"Really, why?"

Elaine and I were sat at a corner table in Al Fresco, a family-run Italian restaurant close to the house, almost out of sight of the other diners who were coming in after us. Red linen tablecloths crossed over white ones, and candles held in old Chianti bottles gave it the homely, rustic feel that we had always liked. We had been there so many times that the owner's son, Luca, an impossibly handsome young man in his late twenties, with swept back ebony hair and movie star eyes, knew instinctively what each of us would order. He greeted us like the old friends we had become, hugging Elaine and kissing her on each cheek, clasping my hand in his and slapping me firmly on the back. In spite of this, he read us the list of specials in any case.

"Mamma's got some beautiful whitebait this evening and some special calves' liver, pan-fried in a little sage and butter. 'Tis very good."

"I think we'll stick with the usual, Luca, if that's okay?"

"The usual is beautiful too. I'll bring some wine, some

335

water, and some bread."

I looked across the table at Elaine. She looked beautiful. The candle positioned between us cast a glow across her face that caught the sparkle in her eyes.

"So why am I a celebrity?"

"He saw you on Sky News talking about the arrests. He's very proud."

"Are you?"

"I guess so. These are some big fish that you've caught. Crispin Monk, he's a *seriously* big fish."

"Only on perverting the course of justice. It's the other two on murder that will do the long time."

"Yes, but you've done enough to spare the country from that horrible, vindictive man becoming Prime Minister."

"I guess so, though that wasn't really what I set out to do."

"Connor says you're the most celebrated detective since Sherlock Holmes."

"Hardly."

"Just accept it. Enjoy the fact that your son is revelling in your success."

I poured us both some wine and some water. We clinked glasses.

"How are you?" I asked.

"I'm okay," she replied, cutting a piece of Parma Ham and scooping it onto her fork with a slab of juicy green melon. "Jason and I are not seeing each other any more."

"Should I say I'm sorry?"

"You don't have to."

"Good, because I'm not. What on Earth possessed you?"

"It was a reaction. Don't judge me."

She gave me a smile that reminded me of our earliest days together.

"So you've put away the nasty criminals and now you're being promoted. Should I call you Detective Chief Inspector?"

"Not yet. There's no DCI job down here for now. The Chief wants me to go for one that's available in Manchester."

"And you?"

"You know, I thought about it. I don't know how important all that is to me. If I've learnt anything over the last year or so, it's that I love my job, but I love my family more. I could be a DCI in Manchester and see nothing of you and Connor or I could stay here and still be close. At the moment, this is where my home is, my friends are, and more importantly this is where you and Connor are. I'm happy to wait. But if you and Connor are going to the Peak District, maybe Manchester would make more sense."

"Ah, yes, the Peak District. I'm sorry about that."

Luca had removed the completed starters and brought our main courses in their place. Elaine had her customary linguini with clams, tomato, and plenty of garlic. I feigned amazement, as I always did, at the size of my Escalope Milanese, which fell off the edges of my plate, a man-sized heap of Spaghetti Bolognese resting to one side. I pushed my fork hard into the lemon wedge, twisted once and then again and watched as the juice dripped all over the veal's golden breadcrumbed coat.

"No need to be sorry," I replied in this new spirit of reconciliation.

"I think I was looking for an escape. You know, looking to just draw a line under what happened and go somewhere

337

new to start afresh."

"I can understand that. So?"

"So I began to think whether that would draw a line under it or whether what happened would follow me wherever I went. I also wondered about taking Connor out of school, away from his friends. That hardly seemed fair."

"He'd adapt."

I couldn't believe I heard myself saying that. This was not how I had anticipated the evening going on. I didn't believe we would be arguing; one of the reasons I chose the restaurant was to guard against the risk of voices becoming raised. But neither did I believe that such honesty and understanding would break out on either side.

"He might adapt," Elaine said, swirling Chianti around in her glass, "but he might resent being taken away from you. I also wasn't sure how well *I'd* adapt."

"So what now?"

"What now, indeed?"

"I think we have a lot more in common than we have that's different. We have so much history. We have Connor, a beautiful, amazing son that we made. We both want what's best for him. He wants us both to be there for him. He's demanding it. I think we should probably listen."

"That's why the Peak District is not happening."

Those words buoyed me.

"What do *you* want to happen, Elaine? Not Connor. You. This is your life too."

"I wanted us to be like we always used to be. That's all I ever wanted. It wasn't me that changed the goalposts."

"I get that. But what happened, happened. I can't turn back time. The question now is what we do about the future.

338

And I can only start that by knowing what *you* really want."

"I want to be happy. Nothing more, nothing less. I want to be happy, to feel safe, to feel looked after. To feel loved."

"And do you think I can make you feel that way again?"

Elaine looked at me, her lip giving way to a tremble, a tear in her eye. She shrugged her shoulders and mouthed "I don't know" as she began to cry.

"I think I can make you happy. I think we can be a family again. I just need you to give me the chance to prove it."

She looked down into her coffee, playing across the surface of the black liquid with the back of her teaspoon.

"Can we try?"

She breathed in deeply and heavily. She looked up, wiped her eyes with her napkin and reached across to hold my hands across the table.

"No," she said simply, "Not yet."